JAPANESE GOTHIC TALES

Izumi Kyōka

Translated by

Charles Shirō Inouye

University of Hawaiʻi Press
Honolulu

Printed in the United States of America
05 06 07 08 09 10 8 7 6 5 4 3

Library of Congress Cataloging-in-Publication Data
Izumi, Kyōka, 1873–1939.
[Short stories. English. Selections]
Japanese gothic tales / Izumi Kyōka ;
translated by Charles Shirō Inouye.
p. cm.
Contents: The surgery room — The holy man of
Mount Kōya — One day in spring — Osen and Sōkichi.
ISBN-13: 978-0-8248-1737-4 (cloth : alk. paper). —
ISBN-13: 978-0-8248-1789-3 (paper : alk. paper)
ISBN-10: 0-8248-1737-0 (cloth : alk. paper). —
ISBN-10: 0-8248-1789-3 (paper : alk. paper)
1. Izumi, Kyōka, 1873–1939—Translations into English.
I. Inouye, Charles Shirō, 1954– . II. Title.
PL809.Z9A25 1996
895.6'342—dc20
95-45935
CIP

University of Hawai'i Press books are printed on acid-free paper
and meet the guidelines for permanence and durability
of the Council on Library Resources.

Book design by Paula Newcomb
Printed by The Maple-Vail Book Manufacturing Group

www.uhpress.hawaii.edu

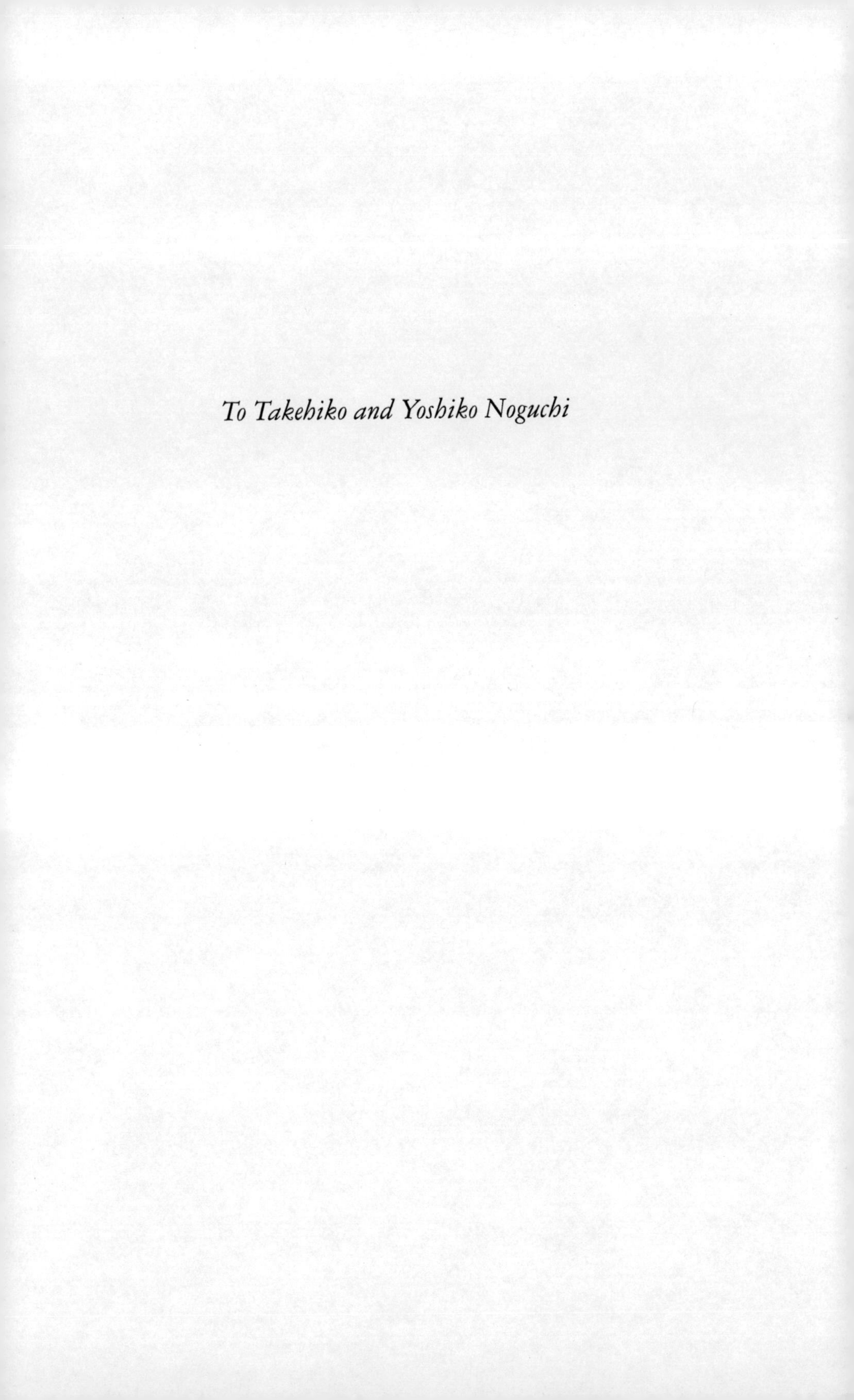

To Takehiko and Yoshiko Noguchi

CONTENTS

Introduction

THE FAMILIARITY OF STRANGE PLACES

The comparison can be misleading, but it is a useful one to make for those who are unfamiliar with the general contours of Japanese literature: in the way that American scholars have had to ponder the stature of Edgar Allan Poe, readers of Japanese literature have had to wonder about how best to understand the accomplishments of Izumi Kyōka (1873–1939), another writer whose influence seems out of proportion with the category he has been customarily allotted by literary history. Kyōka's writing flows from assumptions very different from those that provide the bedrock for Poe's dank and desolate creations, but to the extent that the term *gothic* can hold meaning in a cross-cultural dimension, it is worth applying to both writers, if only to bring attention to the dissonance the category creates. If anything, Kyōka's writing is a frontal attack on the barbarous and uncouth values to which European gothic supposedly owes its genealogy. Yet Kyōka does share with Poe a decadent romanticism, and this point of sameness leads us to consider how it is possible that writers of the uncanny and the macabre can be highly regarded at all.

The dissonance created by the possibility of "great gothic writers" can be understood on a number of levels. On the plane of literary history, major achievements within minor categories implicate the validity of the framework itself, as is made clear by the recent accomplishments of feminist criticism. In this case, the challenge is not to the assumption of female inferiority but to a hierarchy of the imagination. Despite the limitations of Poe's work, for instance, he remains one of the most influential American writers. Consider his importance to Charles Baudelaire and the French symbolists, his pioneering efforts with the short-story form, his place as the originator of ratiocinative narrative, and, by extension, the presently burgeoning world of the mystery novel. Whatever our opinions regarding the quality of such contributions, there is simply too much symbolism, short fiction, and mystery writing still around to allow us to ignore the creator of William Wilson.

Although his impact on subsequent generations is harder to determine, a similar sketch might be drawn of Kyōka. (The Japanese custom is to list surnames before given names and to refer to a writer by the given pen name, if it exists, as it does here.) No one can deny the narrow and obsessive quality of Kyōka's vision. He had clear ideas about what he wanted to write; and once he had developed a formula that allowed him to make imaginatively present that which he desired, he was largely content to repeat himself. Yet this continuity of focus was also one reason he was able to accomplish so much as an artist: though we might wish for more breadth of subject matter, we hardly question the intensity of his desire or his sincerity. Suffering, like Poe, from the untimely death of his mother, Kyōka sought to memorialize her youthful beauty and maternal gentleness through hundreds of literary excursions into the world of the dead. In a word, this trespass or passing "through reality to gain access to a much greater power," (28:696) is the essence of Kyōka's long and productive career.[1] This concern determines its fundamental structure, the shape of its moonlit shadows.

The force that powers this trespass is fear, in the dual senses of horror and awe. Had Kyōka been driven only by the former, he would be much closer to Poe in sentiment. As it stands, the latter emotion, a profound reverence for the "two great supernatural forces in this world . . . the Power of Kannon *(Kannon ryoku)* and the Power of the Evil Gods *(Kishin ryoku)* . . . before which human beings are utterly helpless" (28:677) provides the crucial difference. Poe confronted death with the insistency of his own will, waging a self-aggrandizing battle of supposedly absolute and equal powers; he ended in despair. Kyōka, writing within a more polytheistic and animistic cultural context, maintained a more passive acceptance of his surroundings and managed to live to the age of sixty-six despite physical and emotional frailty. Although he nearly threw himself into the blackness of the Kanazawa Castle moat, and though he suffered greatly from depression and disorientation, he was able to survive by acting out his fears through his art and by depending on a small group of those who cared most deeply for him: his father, Izumi Seiji; his mentor, Ozaki Kōyō; his grandmother, Meboso Kite; his wife, Itō Suzu; and a few loyal friends, especially Sasakawa Rinpū, educator and editor, and the artists Kaburaki Kiyokata and Komura Settai.

In his writings, Kyōka found hope through the careful and insistent deployment of salutary figures. Most frequently they are women, archetypal heroines of beauty, wit, and grace. Reflective of his longing for his young mother, his heroines both seduce and save, tempt and chasten Kyōka's male characters as they wander in mountainous and watery territories of mystery and awe. By projecting the image of his mother onto these gallant though often unfortunate women, he was able to visit and revisit deprivation in a way that allowed him to find a measure of relief from dread and to vent his disdain for the crass, unfeeling world of *risshin shusse,* the Meiji-period (1868–1912) ethic of "success at all costs." Never doubting the miracle of a pure heart or the power of language and literature, he delivered himself from his many anxieties by establishing a fictive purgatory that is often precious and bizarre, though always genuine despite its melodramatic formality. This is a small and idiosyncratic world. However, Kyōka went deep enough in his search to find that place which is connected with all others, and the world of his imagining provides us with vistas of emotional territories that expand in every direction.

Akutagawa Ryūnosuke (1892–1927), the brilliant novelist of the generation that followed, coined the term "Kyōka's world" *(Kyōka no sekai)* for this eccentric place. As the coinage suggests, Kyōka's position within the modern tradition is not easy to describe. His originality is a synthesis of unexpected components, made both possible and suspect by the prevailing expectations of the era in which he worked. His rhythms and themes, his images and structures owe much to oral and performative traditions—folktales and legends, professional storytellers, traveling theatrical troupes, and kabuki and nō—as well as to the written texts of *gesaku* or "frivolous scribblings" that prevailed during the latter half of the Edo period (1600–1868) and into the first two decades of the Meiji period. *Gesaku's* supernatural and melodramatic elements were all the more relevant for Kyōka because of their clash with the positivism of the day. Given his own desire to commune with the dead, it is understandable that he should resist the agenda of those who called for methods that would preclude all but the most rational and realistic approaches to the world about him. Kyōka wanted to believe in and write about metamorphosis at a time when the antifigural force of modern language reform precluded the reality of ghosts and monsters. To dismiss this interest in the supernatural as simply retrogressive or anachronistic is, however, to misunderstand the significance of Kyōka's choices as a modern Japanese artist and to ignore the variety of narrative that was being produced in this age of the realistic novel.

The tendency to disregard nonrealistic forms of narrative follows from a still prevalent model of modernity. Contrary to the orthodox view, the birth of modern consciousness in Japan goes back at least as far as the character studies of Ihara Saikaku (1642–1692) and Ejima Kiseki (1667?–1736) and owes little in its earliest stages to Western paradigms. The "progressiveness" of Meiji Japan came, then, as a second flowering of bourgeois culture, at a stage when the dynamism and brilliance of Edo-period writing was already winding down. The Restoration of 1868 occurred at a point when the emergence of the individual had already begun, and the foundations of capitalism had already been laid.

This view is not articulated often enough by the critical literature on modernity, which tends to be poorly informed about life under the Tokugawa regime. Whereas the visual and theatrical accomplishments of Edo merchant culture are well known, the study and translation of its literary works have progressed more slowly, largely for the same reasons that marginalized Kyōka during his own day. Seeing itself as an improvement over what preceded, modernity tends to erase the past or reconfigure it as a traditional (and inferior) Other. That the present emergence of Kyōka's work in English translation should coincide so closely with an increased interest in late-Edo *gesaku* is not an accident. For it is, in part, the dissatisfaction with and unraveling of modern hegemonic systems that has led to an increased appreciation of what has up to now been dismissed as fractured, frivolous, and superficial. Indeed, the general effect of the poststructuralist critique has been to reconsider old categories and to usher in an age of Japanese literary criticism that resonates with the wider attempt to understand artifacts of culture on their own terms.

Perhaps Kyōka's greatest contribution will be to force his readers to consider what those terms might be. A sympathetic critique of his "traditionalism" tends to cast doubt upon critical methods that have prevailed throughout the colonialist era. Ultimately, his concerns are highly personal, embedded in a life of deprivation and emotional trauma. Yet because of the manner in which he sought to express the drama in his heart, borrowing openly and shamelessly from outmoded methods in order to articulate a very modern self-absorption, his work becomes a controversial site that provides, for one side of the debate, an important link between early-modern and postmodern Japan. Depending on how much importance we give to Kyōka's work, the "Western," late-modern phase of Japan's cultural development, from about 1880 to 1970, comes to look more and more like a curiously prominent bend in a surprisingly straight river. The meander formed when Western influence was at its greatest and came about because the traditional symbiosis of word and picture that had long supported the Japanese literary tradition deteriorated. It was at this time that the visual impulse of Japanese narrative yielded to the logocentric and phonocentric concerns of representational discourse as modern novelists tried to accommodate the new episteme of psychological realism. That Japan did not yield enough is the position of the historian Maruyama Masao who, being trained in the European tradition, held that modern Japan, upon abandoning democratic institutions and disintegrating into an absolutist state, never successfully established the primacy of individual rights or the subjectivity of a thinking, historically conscious people.[2] Today, it might be argued, Japan suffers less from absolutism than from affluence and the insatiable contentments of consumer culture (though it is hard, in the end, to set the one against the other). It can also be said that Japan's phenomenal economic success is a precondition for the vitality of, especially, technologically driven visual display and its undeniable link to the present reevaluation of Kyōka's work.

The so-called Kyōka boom began in the 1970s, with the staging of those of his plays that were simply too "far out" to have been performed a moment earlier. As before, the author's wider reputation still depends on performances of his work, most of them based on stage and screen adaptations written by others. Were it not for the quality of the original texts, though, Kyōka would not be so frequently mediated by performance and translation. And were it not for the seductive power of the original language, our need to revise literary history in order to explain his disquieting synthesis of early- and late-modern elements would not be as strongly felt, despite growing critical interest in, for instance, the dominance of *kusazōshi* (popular illustrated fiction) on the front end of the late-modern period and the explosion of *manga* (comic books) on the other.

Ultimately, the strength of Kyōka's work remains its own attraction. His encoded seduction of red and white is still powerful enough to lead us to places where we might not have otherwise chosen to venture. And his "marvelous but largely untranslatable gift of language"[3] was no doubt the reason for Edward Seidensticker's excellent translation of "A Tale of Three Who Were Blind," a brief but involving piece of writing that has, over the years, captivated many.[4] Despite the obvious difficulties, the virtuosity of Kyōka's prose has more recently drawn others to the task of rendering "Kyōka's world" into the stubborn abstraction and visual poverty of an alphabetic language such as English.

The lasting vividness of this eccentric place also explains why numerous Japanese writers who followed in Kyōka's wake have not only acknowledged his achievement but have felt compelled to offer their interpretation of its historical significance. Consider, for example, Mishima Yukio's (1925–1970) appraisal of Kyōka, whom he held to be perhaps the only true genius among modern Japanese writers.

> Kyōka was a genius. He rose above his time to deify his own individuality. With a dangerously playful style of Japanese, he cultivated a garden of peonies that steadily blossomed amidst the anemic desert of modern Japanese literature. His accomplishment did not arise from a sense of intellectual superiority nor from any sort of aristocratic pretense; neither did it derive from a contempt for the masses nor from any theory of aestheticism. Bound always to the ordinary

sentiment of the people, Kyōka was a pioneer of language, one who raised the Japanese idiom to its most extravagant level, to its highest potential. Using the narrative methods of popular historical stories [*kōdan*] and human-nature stories [*ninjō banashi*], he drew from a vocabulary as rich as the sea to craft sentences of lasting stone and to plunge into the deep forest of Japanese mysticism and symbolism.

> His style, which revived the *renga*-like leaps of association and the imagistic splendor of the Japanese language that modern Japanese literature had forgotten, was not the result of an intellectually contrived anachronism. He himself became a mirror of the artist's timeless spirit. Fervently believing both in words and in spirits, he ranks with E. T. A. Hoffmann in the pureness of his romanticism.[5]

Mishima, who felt that a novel was not properly a novel unless it connected the reader with the supernatural, had obvious reasons to sympathize with Kyōka. Here, he accurately locates the source of Kyōka's power in his regard for language while going on to attribute to him even national significance. "Kyōka . . . raised the Japanese idiom to its most extravagant level, to its highest potential." Characterized in this way, as a mystic and a symbolist, Kyōka was exceptional because he was able to revive the leaps of association essential to *renga*, or linked verse, and the "imagistic splendor of the Japanese language that modern Japanese literature had forgotten."

We are left to wonder what the "highest potential" of the Japanese language might be. Given Shimazaki Tōson's (1872–1948) more balanced characterization of the same tradition ("Japanese writers are essentially impressionists. This is both our strength and our weakness.")[6] we cannot easily say that the leaps of association and the imagistic potential admired by Mishima were uniformly appreciated. Indeed, Mishima's sense of modern Japanese literature having "forgotten" these aspects of the language is misleading. The writings of Tsubouchi Shōyō (1859–1935), Tayama Katai (1871–1930), and many others tell us that the abandonment of the "*renga*-like" was not a passive forgetfulness but an active attempt to reform the Japanese language so it would be sufficiently transparent to express a more positivistic worldview based on observation and on the ability to describe accurately.

To the extent that realism actually came to dominate Japan's literary culture, Kyōka, though recognized as a gifted writer even during his own time, eventually became marginalized and, in the estimation of Tanizaki Jun'ichirō (1886–1965), even neglected.

> Quite frankly, I believe that during the final years of his life, Izumi Kyōka was largely left behind and forgotten. But I also think that because he had accomplished so much as an artist he was not particularly bothered by this neglect. To me, it doesn't seem as though he suffered from loneliness, although we cannot deny that the aging Kyōka was excluded from the mainstream of the *bundan.* Now that he has passed away, however, a new historical significance and classical luster should accrue to his writings. We should read Kyōka in the way we read Chikamatsu or Saikaku, exploring the unique world of this great writer whose life spanned the Meiji, Taishō, and Shōwa periods.
>
> I use the word "unique" for a purpose. Truly, few other authors have spent their lives within a world so strikingly different from any other. Great artists resemble each other in their extreme individuality. . . . Sōseki, Ōgai, and Kōyō—each of these authors lived in his own world. But the difference among these men is less than that which separates Kyōka from them all. . . .
>
> Often mystical, bizarre, and obscure, his writing is essentially bright, florid, elegant, even artless. Its most laudable quality is its pure "Japaneseness." Though Kyōka lived during the high tide of Western influence, his work is purely Japanese. All the values that appear in it—the beautiful, the ugly, the moral, the immoral, the chivalrous, the elegant—are native-born, borrowed neither from the West nor from China. . . . He is at once the most outstanding and the most local writer that our homeland has produced. Shouldn't we, then, boast of this writer who couldn't possibly have come from any other country?[7]

The chauvinistic tone of Tanizaki's encomium, written in 1940, the first anniversary of Kyōka's death, is perhaps understandable in the context of Japan's increasing commitment to national aggression: the announcement by Premier Konoe of the New National Order *(Shintaisei),* the formulation of the Tripartite Alliance with Germany and Italy, and the inauguration of the Imperial Rule Assistance Association. Whatever the depth of Tanizaki's patriotism, its force here clearly weakens the argument he seems to be making. If it is true that great writers are extreme in their individuality, why place upon Kyōka's shoulders the mantle of Japan's identity? Indeed, to return to my original point and to reformulate a second, more immediate level of reading "great gothic writers," authors such as Poe and Kyōka are understandable across differences of time and space because, though they might speak eloquently of their particular cultures, their concerns transcend national circumstance.

To the extent that these two levels of reading, historical and personal, influence each other, it is not clear whether history requires greatness or whether greatness requires history. Perhaps this is why literary history gravitates toward measured rhythms and well-defined categories even when attempting to give order to the agitation caused by a beam of light upon a sleeping eye, or to the erotic pull of pale skin against a crimson lining. There is ultimately something both familiar and familial about gothic writers. Our appreciation of them springs from a bothersome genealogy, a closeness not always easy to admit. They are affected uncles and conceited cousins, more easily admired from a distance than invited regularly to the dinner table, even when we know they have given us something of themselves that is also something of value. In the end, it is as difficult to fault the giver of a perfect gift as it is to deny the familiarity of strange places.

NOTES

1. Numbers in parentheses indicate volume and page numbers of the collected works, *Kyōka zenshū* (Tokyo: Iwanami Shoten, 1973–1976).

2. Maruyama Masao, "From Carnal Literature to Carnal Politics," trans. Barbara Ruch, in *Thought and Behaviour in Modern Japanese Politics*, ed. Ivan Morris (London: Oxford University Press, 1963), pp. 245–267.

3. Donald Keene, "Izumi Kyōka," in *Dawn to the West: Japanese Literature in the Modern Era* (New York: Holt, Rinehart, and Winston, 1984), p. 217.

4. The story can be found in Donald Keene, ed., *Modern Japanese Literature* (New York: Grove Press, 1956).

5. "Kaisetsu, *Nihon no bungaku 4: Ozaki Kōyō, Izumi Kyōka*," vol. 33 of *Mishima Yukio zenshū* (Tokyo: Shinchōsha, 1976), pp. 553–555.

6. Shimazaki Tōson, *Shimazaki Tōson zenshū*, vol. 14 (Tokyo: Shinchōsha, 1949), p. 317.

7. Tanizaki Jun'ichirō, "Junsui ni 'Nihonteki' na 'Kyōka sekai,' " vol. 22 of *Tanizaki Jun'ichirō zenshū* (Tokyo: Chūō Kōron Sha, 1968), pp. 336–338.

The Surgery Room

(*Gekashitsu,* 1895)

Part 1

The surgery was to take place at a certain hospital in the Tokyo suburbs, and the Countess Kifune was the patient on whom my dear friend Doctor Takamine was to perform the operation. Driven by curiosity, I imposed upon Takamine to allow me to attend. In order to present my case as strongly as possible, I concocted an argument about my being an artist and why seeing the surgery would be useful to me. In the end, I prevailed.

I left my house at a little after nine that morning and rushed by rickshaw to the hospital. Once inside the building, I proceeded down a long corridor and toward the surgery room as a small entourage of women, presumably servants of some family of the nobility, emerged from the door at the opposite end. We met halfway down the hallway.

These women were escorting a girl of about seven or eight who was wearing a long jacket over her kimono. I watched them as they continued down the corridor and disappeared from view. As I covered the remaining distance from the infirmary's entrance to the surgery area and then down the long hallway that led to the recovery rooms,

I encountered numerous members of the aristocracy. Some were dressed in frock coats, others in formal kimono; there were officers in military uniform, and various women of the nobility—all of them distinguished in appearance. They seemed to weave within the corridor, intersecting here, converging there, now stopping, now walking. Remembering the many carriages I had seen parked by the hospital gate outside, I now realized whom they had brought. Some of those present looked grave, others appeared pensive, still others seemed flustered. All of them, though, shared a look of distress. The hurried scuffle of their shoes echoed against the high, lonely hospital ceiling, clattering in the rooms and down the long hallway; and the strange sound of echoing footsteps made the occasion seem all the more dismal.

Eventually, I found my way to the surgery room. Takamine was sitting restfully in a chair with his arms folded. He glanced over and greeted me with a smile. Though about to take on an awesome responsibility, one that seemed to concern the entire upper echelon of society, my friend Takamine, a rare example of composure, appeared perfectly collected, as if he were sitting down to dinner. Accompanying him were three assistants, one attending physician, and three nurses from the Red Cross. Some of these nurses wore medals on their uniforms, no doubt bestowed upon them for acts of distinguished service. Otherwise, no women were present in the operating room. There were a number of men, however, all of them relatives of various noble rank. One stood out among them—despondent, an ineffable expression on his countenance. He would be the patient's husband, Count Kifune.

The surgery room itself was bathed in a luminescence so radiant that I could count the particles of dust in the air. It stood somehow apart, stark and inviolate. And there in the center of the room lay the Countess Kifune, focus of concern for both those outside the room and those inside, who were closely observing her. Wrapped in a spotless white hospital gown, she lay on the operating table as if a corpse—face drained of color, nose pointing upward, chin narrow and frail, and her arms and legs seeming too fragile to bear even the weight of fine silk. Her teeth were slightly visible between pale lips. Her eyes were tightly closed, and her eyebrows drawn with worry. Loosely bound, her hair fell lightly across her pillow and spilled down on the operating table.

At the sight of this noble, elegant, and beautiful woman, now ailing and feeble, I felt a chill spread through my body. When I glanced over at Takamine, he appeared unaffected, showing no signs of apprehension or worry. He was the only one seated. His composure was reassuring, yet I could feel only dread as I looked at the countess in her weakened state.

At that juncture the door opened slowly and a young woman quietly entered. I recognized her as one of the servants I had passed in the corridor earlier, the most striking of the three. She approached the countess and whispered, "My Lady, the princess has stopped crying. She's sitting quietly in the next room."

The countess acknowledged her with a nod. One of the nurses went over to Doctor Takamine. "We're ready to proceed."

"Very well."

I detected a slight quaver in Takamine's voice. Scanning his face, I thought I could see a subtle change of expression. Any man, no matter how great, would certainly feel some apprehension when placed in a situation such as this. My sympathies went out to him.

Acknowledging the doctor's intent, the nurse turned to the servant. "Then we're ready. If you could be so kind as to—"

At this cue the woman approached the operating table and, placing both hands on her knees, bowed to the countess. "Madame, the medication. If you please, all we need you to do is count to ten, or spell out a word."

The countess didn't answer.

"Madame?" The servant repeated herself. "Can you hear me, madame?"

The countess responded. "Yes. I hear you."

"Then shall we go ahead?"

"With the anesthetic?"

"Yes, madame. For a short while until the operation is over. They say you must be anesthetized."

The countess did not answer immediately.

"I don't need it," she finally replied in a clear voice.

Everyone in the room exchanged glances.

"But the doctors can't do the surgery without it."

"Then I won't have the surgery."

The servant fell silent and turned to the count.

The count stepped forward. "My dear, don't be unreasonable. How can you do without anesthesia? Please now, cooperate."

At this point the baron intervened. "If you insist on this unreasonable behavior, I shall ask to have the princess brought in. Do you know what will happen to her if you don't get better?"

"I know what will happen."

"Then you'll take the medicine?" the servant inquired.

The countess slowly shook her head.

One of the nurses interceded. "But why not?" she asked in a gentle voice. "It's not at all unpleasant. You will feel a little drowsy and then it will be over."

At this the countess' eyebrows arched and her lips twisted as if she were racked with pain. She half-opened her eyes. "If you must persist, then I'll have to tell you why. I've been keeping a secret in my heart. And now I'm afraid the medication will make me reveal it. If I can't be treated without an anesthetic, then I refuse to have the operation. Please, leave me alone!"

If my ears did not betray me, the countess, fearing she might divulge some secret while in a state of unconsciousness, was actually willing to face death in order to protect what was in her heart. What, I wondered, was her husband feeling as he heard her say such things? Ordinarily, if a man's wife were to say something of this sort it would be cause for a scandal. And yet the people treating her were hardly in a position to ignore her wishes, especially as she was so adamant about not wanting anyone to know what she was thinking.

The count approached her bed and asked gently, "You can't tell even me?"

"I can tell no one," the countess replied firmly.

"But you don't know the medication will make you talk—"

"I do. It's something that's always on my mind. I know I'll say something."

"Now you're being unreasonable again."

"Then I'm *sorry*!" The countess seemed to fling the words down. With this she turned on her side, away from everyone. Her body was racked with illness. I could hear her teeth chattering.

Only one person in the room appeared unshaken, and that was Doctor Takamine. I had glanced over in his direction earlier. For a moment he seemed to have lost his composure, but presently his confidence returned.

Frowning, the baron turned to the count. "Kifune, bring the princess in. She'll change the countess' mind."

The count nodded and called to the servant. "Aya!"

"Sir?" She looked back at him.

"Bring the princess."

But then the countess interrupted. "Don't do it, Aya. Why do I have to be asleep for the operation?"

The nurse forced a smile. "The physician is going to make an incision in your chest. It would be dangerous if you moved even a little."

"Then I won't. I won't move. Go ahead. Just do it."

I shuddered to hear such a childish notion. I doubted whether even medical observers would have the strength to watch.

The nurse spoke again. "But madame, even if you don't move it will still hurt. It's not like clipping a nail."

At this the countess' eyes opened widely. She regained her composure and asked in a clear voice, "Doctor Takamine is doing the operation, isn't he?"

"Yes. The chief of surgery. But even Doctor Takamine can't perform the operation painlessly."

"Go ahead. It won't hurt."

For the first time, the attending physician interceded. "Madame, your illness is not trivial. We will have to cut through muscle and shave the bone. If you could only bear with us for a short while."

The operation was clearly beyond the endurance of any normal human being, yet the countess appeared unshaken. "I'm well aware of that. But I don't care, not in the least."

"Her illness has affected her mind," the count observed painfully.

"Perhaps we ought to consider putting this off to another day," the baron suggested. "In time we might be able to persuade her."

The count immediately agreed, as did everyone in the room—everyone, that is, except Takamine. "The operation can't wait! The problem here is that you all take this illness too lightly. All this talk about emotion is simply an excuse. Nurses! Hold her down!"

At his stern command, the five nurses quickly surrounded the countess and pinned down her arms and legs. Their duty was only to obey, to follow the doctor's orders without questioning, to allow no emotions to interfere.

"Aya! Help me!" The countess cried out in a thin gasp.

Her servant rushed forward to stop the nurses. But then she turned to the countess and spoke in a gentle, trembling voice. "Please. Just for a moment. Madame, can't you please be patient?"

The countess' face turned ashen. "You, too! All right, then go ahead. Even if I get better I'm going to die eventually. Operate on me! Just like this."

With her thin white hand, the countess weakly opened her kimono and revealed her bosom.

"Even if I die, it won't hurt! I won't move an inch. Go ahead. Cut me."

It was clear from her expression that nothing could persuade her now. Her dignity weighed heavily upon those in the room. No one spoke. Not even a stifled cough was heard.

At that sober moment, Doctor Takamine, who had remained as still as cold ash, nimbly rose from his chair.

"Nurse, the scalpel."

"What?" The nurse hesitated, her eyes widening.

As we all watched with astonishment, the nurse stared at Takamine's face as another assistant picked up the sterile scalpel with an unsteady hand and passed it to Takamine. He took it from her and, with a few brisk steps, moved to the operating table.

"Doctor, are you sure?" asked one nurse nervously.

"Yes."

"Then we'll do our best to hold her down."

Takamine raised his hand to stop her. "That won't be necessary." With this he quickly opened the patient's gown.

The countess crossed her arms and grasped her shoulders. Takamine, now transformed into a sacred, all-powerful being, spoke to her in a solemn voice, as if taking an oath. "Madame, I take all responsibility. Allow me to proceed with the surgery."

"Yes," she answered with a single word, her ashen cheeks suddenly flushing crimson. The countess gazed directly at Takamine, oblivious to the knife now poised over her naked breast.

A red winter plum fallen to the snow, the smooth trickle of blood flowed down her chest and soaked into her white gown. The countess' cheeks returned to their pallid hue, but her composure seemed complete.

It had come to this. Takamine worked with superhuman speed, not wasting a single movement. None of us in the room, from the servant to the attending physician, had a moment to utter a word. While her chest was being cut open, some trembled, some covered their eyes, some turned away, some stared at the floor. I was gripped by a cold chill.

In the space of a few seconds Takamine brought the surgery to its critical juncture as the scalpel found the bone. At this point the countess, who had been unable to turn over in bed for these past twenty days, released a deep "Ah" from her throat. Suddenly she sat up and firmly grasped the doctor's right arm with both hands.

"Are you in pain?" he asked.

"No. Because it's you. You!"

The countess slumped back. Her eyes stared upward and fixed themselves upon the famous surgeon's face in one last ghastly, cold gaze. "But you couldn't have known."

At this instant, she grabbed the scalpel from Takamine's hand and plunged it into her body, just below her breast. Takamine, his face ashen, stammered, "I haven't forgotten!"

His voice, his breath, his handsome figure.

A smile of innocent joy came to the countess' face. She released Takamine's hand and fell back on her pillow as the color faded from her lips. At that moment the two of them were absolutely alone, oblivious to earth and heaven and the existence of another soul.

Part 2

Nine Years Earlier

The date is May fifth, and the azaleas are in full bloom. Takamine, a medical school student, and I are walking through the Koishikawa Botanical Garden. We wander arm in arm, in and among the fragrant grasses, viewing the wisteria that grows around the pond.

As we turn to climb a small hill covered with azaleas, a group of sightseers emerges from the opposite direction. In the lead is a man with a mustache, wearing a Western suit and a stovepipe hat. He is a coachman for a noble family. Three women follow, each carrying a parasol, and then comes a second coachman, dressed like the first. We can hear the smooth, crisp rustle of silk as they approach. Takamine's head turns and follows them as they pass by.

"Did you see that?" I ask.

"I did." Takamine nods.

We climb the hill to get a view of the azaleas. The flowers are beautiful and brilliant, but they are not so exquisite as the women we have just seen.

Two young men, probably merchants, are sitting on a nearby bench. We overhear their conversation.

"Kichi," one says to the other. "What a day we've had!"

"Every once in a while I'm glad I listen to you. We're lucky we didn't go to Asakusa."

"All three were so beautiful. Which was the plum blossom, and which the cherry?"

"The one has to be married, though, with her hair done like that."

"Who cares how they wear their hair? They're beyond us anyway."

"What about the young one? You'd think she'd wear something a little nicer."

"Maybe she doesn't want to attract attention. Did you see the one in the middle? She was the most beautiful of all."

"Do you remember what she was wearing?"

"Something lavender."

"That's all you can say? 'Something lavender'? You need to read more or something. It's unlike you not to notice."

"But I was dazed. I couldn't look up the entire time."

"So you just saw her from the waist down. Is that it?"

"Cleanse your filthy mind, you idiot! I had such a quick glance I couldn't see anything."

"Not even the way they moved? It was as if their feet didn't touch the ground. They drifted along in a mist. Now I know what's so special about the way a woman walks in a kimono. Those three were a breed apart. They were completely at home in elegant society. How could common trash ever try to imitate them?"

"Harsh words."

"Harsh but true. Remember how I made that pledge at the Konpira Shrine? I said I wasn't going to see any prostitutes for three years. Well, I've broken my promise. I still keep the charm to protect me, but I slip over to the brothels at night. Luckily, I haven't been punished yet. But now I see the light. What's the point of hanging out with those whores? They tempt you with their pretty red colors, but what are they really? Just trash! Squirming maggots!"

"Oh, come on."

"No. I'm serious. Think about it! They have hands. They stand on two legs. They dress in fine silk. They even carry parasols. Judging from that, you'd think they'd be real women, maybe even ladies. But compared to those three we saw today, what are they really? They're dirty, unspeakably filthy! It makes me sick to think you can still call them women."

"That's an awful thing to say, but maybe you have a point. I'm a fool for a pretty face myself. But after today I'm purged. I'm starting over. Never mind about just any woman."

"You'll spend your whole life looking. You think one of them would ever be interested in you? 'Oh, Genkichi, please.' "

"Cut it out."

"Suppose one of them called you 'Darling'? What would you do?"

"Probably run away."

"You, too?"

"You mean you'd—"

"I'd run, definitely."

Takamine and I look at each other for a while, neither of us speaking. "Shall we walk some more?" I finally suggest.

We both get up. When we have left the two young men behind, Takamine can no longer contain his emotions. "Did you see how those two men were moved by true beauty? Now that's a subject for your art. That's what you ought to study!"

Because I'm a painter, I am indeed moved. I see, far across the park, gliding through the shade of a large camphor tree, a flutter of lavender silk. Outside the park gates stands a large carriage, fitted with frosted glass windows and being drawn by two fine horses. Three coachmen are resting beside it.

For the next nine years, until the incident at the hospital, Takamine never said a word about her, not even to me. Given his age and position in society, he could have married well. Yet he never did. If anything, he became even more strict in matters of personal conduct than he had been in his student days. But I have already said enough. Although their graves are in different places—one in the hills of Aoyama, one downtown in Yanaka—the countess and Doctor Takamine died together, one after the other, on the same day.

Religious thinkers of the world, I pose this question to you. Should these two lovers be found guilty and denied entrance into heaven?

The Holy Man of Mount Kōya

(*Kōya hijiri,* 1900)

1

"I knew it wouldn't do much good to take another look. But because the road had become unimaginably difficult, I lifted the sleeves of my kimono, made hot to the touch by the sun's rays, and reached in for the ordinance survey map that I had brought with me.

"There I was on an isolated byway, making my way through the deep mountains between Hida and Shinshū. Not a single tree offered the comfort of its shade; and on both sides were nothing but mountains, rising so close and so steeply that it seemed as though I could reach out and touch them with my hand. Despite the towering heights of these mountains there rode still others beyond them, each raising its crest above the next, blocking both bird and cloud from sight.

"Between earth and sky, I stood alone, the crystalline rays of the blistering midday sun falling white around me as I surveyed the map from beneath the brim of my sedge hat."

Saying this, the itinerant monk clenched both fists, placed them on his pillow, bent forward, then pressed his forehead against his hands.

We had become traveling companions in Nagoya. And now, as we were about to retire for the night in Tsuruga, it occurred to me that he had maintained this humility with perfect consistency, and that he had shown none of the airs of the self-righteous.

I remembered how we met on the train. I was traveling west on the main line that connects the cities of the Pacific Coast, when he got on at Kakegawa. He sat at the end of the car with his head bowed, and because he showed no more life than cold ashes, I paid him little attention. But then the train reached Nagoya, and everyone else got off at once, as if by previous arrangement, leaving only the monk and myself to share the coach.

The train had departed from Tokyo at nine-thirty the night before and was scheduled to arrive in Tsuruga that evening. As it was noon when we reached Nagoya, I purchased from the station vendor a small box lunch of sushi, which happened to be what the monk also bought. When I eagerly removed the lid, however, I was disappointed to find only bits of seaweed scattered on top of the vinegar-flavored rice and knew immediately that my lunch was sushi of the cheapest kind.

"Nothing but carrots and gourd shavings," I blurted out. The monk, seeing the look on my face, couldn't help but chuckle.

Since we were the only two passengers in the car, we naturally began a conversation. Although he belonged to a different sect, he told me that he was on his way to visit someone at Eiheiji, the great Zen monastery in Echizen, and planned to spend the night in Tsuruga. I was returning home to Wakasa; and because I also had to stop over in the same town, we decided to become traveling partners.

He told me he was affiliated with Mount Kōya, headquarters of the Shingon sect. My guess was that he was about forty-five or -six. He seemed a gentle, ordinary, likeable sort. Modestly dressed, he wore a woollen traveling cloak with ample sleeves, a white flannel scarf, a pillbox hat, and knitted gloves. On his feet he had white socks and low, wooden clogs. Though a man of the cloth, he looked more like a poetry master or perhaps someone of even more worldly interests.

"So where will you spend the night?" His question prompted a deep sigh from my lips as I contemplated the drearier aspects of staying alone in a strange place: the maids who doze off with their serving trays still in hand; the hollow flattery of desk clerks; the way everyone stares at you whenever you leave your room and walk the halls; and, worst of all, how they snuff out the candles as soon as dinner is over and order you to bed in the dim shadows of lantern light. I'm the sort who doesn't fall asleep easily, and I can't begin to describe the loneliness of being abandoned like that in my room. And now that the nights had gotten longer, ever since leaving Tokyo I had been preoccupied with how I was going to make it through that night in Tsuruga. I suggested to the monk that, if it was no bother, we might spend the night together.

He nodded cheerfully and added that whenever he traveled through the North Country he always rested his walking staff at a place called the Katoriya. Apparently the Katoriya had been a travelers' inn until the proprietor's only daughter, well liked by all who knew her, suddenly died. After that, the family took down their shingle and, though no longer in business, were always willing to accommodate old friends. For such people, the elderly couple still provided familylike hospitality. The monk suggested that if such a situation were agreeable to me, we would be welcome there. "But," he started to say, then paused for dramatic effect, "the only thing you might get for dinner is carrots and gourd shavings." With that, he burst into laughter. Despite his modest appearance, the monk had quite a sense of humor.

2

In Gifu, the sky was still clear and blue, but once we entered the North Country, famous for its inclement weather, things began changing. Maibara and Nagahama were slightly overcast—the sun's rays penetrated the clouds only weakly and a chill seeped into my bones. But by the time we reached Yanagase it started to rain. As my window grew steadily darker, the rain mixed with something white.

"It's snowing."

"So it is," the monk said, not even bothering to look up at the sky. If he found the snow uninteresting, neither was he concerned with the ancient battleground at Shizugatake or the scenery at Lake Biwa. As I pointed them out, he only nodded.

We neared Tsuruga, and I prepared myself for the annoying, or should I say frightening, tenacity of the solicitors who lie in wait at the station for potential customers. As I expected, they were there in droves, waiting for us to step off the train. They lined the road that led away from the station, forming an impenetrable wall around the travelers. As they closed in on us with their lanterns and umbrellas, all emblazoned with the names of the inns they represented, they called out and demanded we stay the night with them. The more brazen ones even snatched up people's luggage and shouted out, "Thanks! This way, please!" No doubt, those suffering headaches would have found their heads pounding because of this intolerable behavior. But, as always, the monk kept his head bowed and calmly slipped unnoticed through the crowd. No one bothered to stop him, and, luckily, I followed right behind, emitting a sigh of relief once the station was behind us.

The snow showed no signs of letting up. No longer sleet, its dry, light flakes brushed my face as they fell. Though it was still early in the evening, the people of Tsuruga had already bolted their doors for the night, leaving the streets deserted and quiet. We cut across two or three wide intersections, then walked for another eight blocks through the accumulating snow until we stopped beneath the eaves of an inn. We had arrived at the Katoriya.

The alcove and sitting room had no decoration to speak of. But the pillars were impressive, the tatami new, and the hearth spacious. The pot hook dangling over the hearth was decorated with a wooden carp so lustrous I wondered if it were made of gold. Set into the earthen oven were two huge pots, each big enough to cook half a bushel of rice. It was a solid, old house.

The master of the inn was a short-cropped, hard-to-read sort of fellow, who had a habit of keeping his hands tucked inside his cotton jacket even when sitting in front of a brazier. His wife, in contrast, was charming, the kind of person who says all the right things. She laughed cheerfully when my companion told the story about carrots and gourd shavings and prepared a meal of two kinds of dried fish and miso soup with bits of seaweed. I could tell by the way she and her husband acted that they had known the monk for a long time. Because of their friendship, I felt very much at home.

Eventually we were taken to our beds on the second floor. The ceiling was low, but the beams were huge, unmilled logs, two arm-spans in diameter. The roof slanted down at an angle so you had to be careful not to bump your head on the ceiling where the roof met the walls along the edges of the room. Still, it was comforting to know that even if an avalanche came tumbling down the mountain behind us, it would not disturb such a sturdily built structure.

I jumped right into bed, happy to see that our bed warmer had already been prepared for the night. In order to make the most of the heated coals, our bedding had been laid out at right angles so we could both take advantage of the warmer. The monk, however, pulled his futon around beside mine, intending to sleep without the comfort of the smoldering fire.

When he finally got into bed, he didn't even bother to remove his sash, much less his robe. Still wearing his clothes, he curled himself into a ball and quickly backed feetfirst into his quilts. As soon as his arms found the sleeves in his upper quilt, he pressed his hands to the mattress beneath him and lowered himself onto his pillow. Unlike you or me, the holy man slept facedown.

Before long he stopped stirring and seemed to be falling asleep. As I had told him many times in the train, I find it hard to get to sleep before the night grows late; and so I asked him, begging like a child, to take pity on me and tell me about some of the interesting things he had experienced on his many pilgrimages.

He nodded, and added that since middle age he had always slept facedown but that he was still wide-awake. Like me, he too had difficulty falling asleep. "So you want to hear a story? Then listen to what I'm about to tell you," he said. "And remember that what you hear from a monk isn't always a lecture or a sermon." It was only later that I learned he was none other than the renowned and revered Monk Shūchō of the Rikumin Temple.

3

"The owners of this inn mentioned that someone else might join us here tonight," the monk began. "A man from Wakasa, same as you. He travels around and sells lacquerware. He's young, but I know him to be a good, serious fellow, quite unlike a young man I once met when making my way through the mountains of Hida. This other person was a Toyama medicine peddler whom I happened to run into at a teahouse in the foothills. What a disagreeable, difficult fellow!"

I intended to make it all the way to the pass that day, and I had set out from my inn at about three o'clock in the morning. I covered fifteen miles or more while it was still cool. But by the time I made it to the teahouse, the morning mist had burned off and it was starting to get hot.

I had pushed myself at a fast pace and my throat was as parched as the road beneath my feet. I wanted to get something to drink right away but was told the kettle wasn't boiling yet.

Of course, there was no reason to expect the teahouse to be ready for business as so few pass by on such mountain paths. In a place as isolated as that, smoke from the hearth rarely rises while the morning-glory blossoms are still blooming. As I waited, I noticed an inviting brook running in front of the stool on which I had taken a seat. I was about to scoop up a handful of water from a bucket nearby when something occurred to me.

Disease spreads quickly in the summer months, and I had just seen powdered lime sprinkled over the ground at the village called Tsuji.

"Excuse me," I called to the girl in the teahouse. I felt a bit awkward asking, but forced myself to inquire. "Is this water from your well?"

"It's from the river," she said.

Her answer alarmed me. "Down the mountain I saw signs of an epidemic," I said. "I was just wondering if this brook comes from over by Tsuji."

"No, it doesn't," she replied simply, as though I had nothing to worry about.

I should have been happy to hear her answer, but listen—someone else was already at the teahouse. The young medicine peddler I just mentioned had been resting there for quite some time. He was one of those vulgar pill salesmen. You've seen them dressed in an unlined, striped kimono, a cheap sash, and the obligatory gold watch dangling in front. Leggings and breeches, straw sandals, a square medicine chest tied to the back with a pale yellowish-green cotton cloth. Add an umbrella or an oilskin slicker, folded up and tied to the pack with a flat Sanada string, and there you have it, the typical traveling salesman.

They all look the same—that serious, knowing look on their faces. But as soon as they get to their lodgings for the night, they change into loud, large-patterned robes. And with their sashes loosely tied, they sip cheap wine and try to get their feet onto the maids' soft laps.

"Hey, Baldy," he called, insulting me from the very start. "Forgive me for asking this, but I need to know something. Here you are. You know you're never going to make it with the ladies, so you shave your head and become a monk, right? So why worry about dying? That's a little odd, don't you think? The truth is, you're no better than the rest of us. Just like I thought. Take a look at him, miss. He's still attached to this floating world." The two looked at each other and burst into laughter.

I was a young man at that time, and my face burned red with shame. I froze there with the scoop of water still in my hands.

"What are you waiting for? Go ahead, drink till you drown. If you come down with something, I'll give you some of my medicine. That's why I'm here. Right, miss? It's going to cost you, though. My Mankintan's three *sen* a packet. It may be 'the gift of the gods.' But if you want it, you buy it. I haven't done anything bad enough to make me want to give it away. But maybe we can fix that. How about it, girl? Maybe I should have my way with you." He patted the young woman on the back.

I was shocked by the man's lewd behavior and quickly got away from there. Of course, someone of my age and profession has no business going on about the seduction of teahouse maids, but since it's an important part of the story. . . .

4

I was so furious I rushed down the road that led through some rice paddies in the foothills. I had gone only a short distance when the path rose steeply. Looking to the side, I could see it going up the side of the mountain like a rounded, earthen bridge. I had just started the climb, my eyes fixed upward upon my goal, when the medicine peddler I had encountered earlier came hurrying along to overtake me.

He didn't have anything to say this time. Even if he had, I doubt I would have responded. Thoroughly accustomed to looking down on other people, the peddler made a point of giving me a contemptuous glance as he passed by. He pressed forward to the top of a small hill, where he stopped, holding his opened umbrella in one hand. Then he disappeared down the other side.

I followed him, climbing the steep slope until I made it to the top. Then I proceeded ahead.

The peddler had already made it down the other side and was standing on the road, looking this way and that. I suspected he might be planning some mischief and was on guard as I continued in his footsteps. When I reached the spot, I could see why he had stopped.

The road forked at that point. One of the two paths was extremely steep and headed directly up the mountain. It was overgrown with grass on both sides and wound around a huge cypress tree four, maybe even five, spans around, then disappeared behind a number of jutting boulders that were piled one on top of the other. My guess was that this wasn't the road to take. The wide, gently sloping one that had brought me this far was, no doubt, the main road, and if I just stayed on it for another five miles or so, it would surely take me into the mountains and eventually to the pass.

But what was this? The cypress I mentioned arched like a rainbow over the deserted road, extending into the endless sky above the rice paddies. The earth had crumbled away from its base, exposing an impressive tangle of countless eel-like roots; and from there a stream of water gushed out and flowed over the ground, right down the middle of the road I had decided to take, flooding the entire area before me.

It was a wonder the water hadn't made a lake of the rice paddies. Thundering like rapids, the torrent formed a river that stretched for more than two hundred yards, bordered on the far side by a grove. I was glad to see a line of rocks that crossed the water like a row of stepping-stones. Apparently, someone had gone to a lot of trouble to put them there.

The water wasn't so deep that I would have to strip down and wade. Still, it seemed a bit too difficult to be the main road, as even a horse would have had a hard time of it.

The medicine peddler, too, had hesitated because of the situation.

But then he made his decision and started climbing the hill to the right, where he disappeared behind the cypress tree. When he reappeared he was five feet or so above me. "Hey, this is the road to Matsumoto," he called down, then sauntered another five or six steps. Half-hidden behind one of the huge boulders, he called out in a jeering tone. "Watch out or the tree spirits'll get you! They don't give a damn if it's still daylight!" Then he entered the shade of the boulders and eventually disappeared into the grass growing farther up the slope. After a while, the tip of his umbrella reappeared higher up the mountain, but then, just as it reached the same level as the treetops, it disappeared again into the undergrowth.

That was when I heard someone behind me. I turned to see a farmer hopping across the stones laid out across the flowing water, encouraging himself with a relaxed-sounding *Dokkoisho.* He had a short reed skirt tied around his waist and carried a shoulder pole in one hand.

5

Needless to say, from the time I left the teahouse until that moment, I hadn't met anyone but the medicine peddler. As the peddler went his way, I paused to consult my map—the one I was telling you about earlier. It occurred to me that even though the grass-grown path seemed like the wrong road, the peddler, who was a professional traveler after all, ought to know his way around these mountains.

"Excuse me," I said to the farmer.

"Yes," he replied. "How may I help you?" Mountain people are especially polite when talking with monks, as you know.

"Sorry to bother you about such an obvious matter," I said. "But this is the main road, isn't it?"

"You're going to Matsumoto?" he asked. "Then yes, this is the right road. We've had a lot of rain this year, and the whole place has turned into a river. But this is it."

"Is it like this all the way?"

"Oh, no. Just what you see here. It's easy enough to cross. The water goes over to that grove there. On the other side, it's a regular road. Up to the mountains, it's wide enough for two carts to pass each other with no problem. A doctor once had his mansion in that grove there, and this place, believe it or not, used to be a village. A flood came through thirteen years ago and washed everything away. Many people died. Since you're a monk, sir, maybe you could pray for the dead as you walk through."

The good man gave me more information than I had asked for. Now that I had the details, I was comforted to know which was the right road. Yet at the same time, his instructions meant that someone else had gone the wrong way.

"Then may I ask where this other road goes?" I inquired about the left fork that the medicine peddler had taken.

"That's the old road people used to take fifty years ago. It'll get you to Shinshū all right, and it cuts off a good seventeen miles overall. But you can't get through anymore. Just last year, a family on pilgrimage went that way by mistake. It was terrible. They were poor as beggars. But since every soul is precious, we felt we should try to find them. We got a search party together—three local constables and twelve people from the village—and went into the mountains to bring them back out. Sir, I wouldn't get too ambitious and decide to take that shortcut. Even if the longer road is more tiring and makes you spend a night under the stars, I wouldn't take the chance. Well, take care now and have a good trip."

I said goodbye to the farmer and started across the line of stepping-stones that had been set in the river. But then I stopped. What would become of the medicine peddler?

I doubted the old road was nearly as bad as the farmer had described. But if it were true, it would be like letting the man die before my very eyes. Anyway, as one who had renounced the world, I had no business worrying about whether I could find an inn before nightfall or not. And so I decided to go and bring the medicine peddler back. Even if I didn't find him and ended up taking the old road all the way, it wouldn't be as bad as all that. This wasn't the season for wild dogs prowling or for forest spirits lurking about. "So why not?" I thought. When I turned around, I saw that the kind farmer had already disappeared from sight.

"I'll do it," I said to myself and started up the steep path. It wasn't that I wanted to be a hero or that I was getting ahead of myself. Judging from what I've just told you, you might think I'm some sort of enlightened saint. But the truth is that I'm really a coward. I didn't even dare drink the river water. So you're probably wondering why I decided to take the dangerous path.

To tell the truth, I wouldn't have cared that much about someone with whom I'd exchanged only a few words of greeting. But because the peddler had been such a disagreeable person, I felt I would be purposely letting him take the wrong road. In short, my conscience made me do it.

The Monk Shūchō, still lying facedown, brought his hands together in prayer. "I just didn't think letting him die would be worthy of the *nenbutsu* I chant," he added.

6

"So, listen to this."

I walked past the cypress tree, then made my way through the boulders and ended up on the trail above them. Passing through a stand of trees, I entered a path in the thick grass that seemed to go on forever.

Before I knew it, I had climbed the mountain and was approaching another. For a while a meadow opened up, and the path sloped gently and became even wider than the main road I had just left—easily wide enough to accommodate a daimyo's procession. The two roads were running parallel to each other. One was slightly to the east and the other situated a bit to the west, with the mountain in the middle.

Even in this broad plain, though, I could see no sign of the medicine peddler, not even a speck the size of a poppy seed. Every once in a while, a small insect would fly across the baking sky. I felt even more insecure, walking in the open where everything was empty and unfamiliar! Of course, I had heard about travel in the Hida Mountains before—how few inns there were along the way, and how if you got millet-rice for dinner you were doing well. I was prepared for the worst, and because my legs were strong, I kept up the pace without flagging. As I made my way, the mountains began closing in until I was walled in on both sides and the trail before me rose steeply.

From here I knew I'd be crossing the notorious Amō Pass, and so I did what I could to prepare myself for the climb. Readjusting my straw sandals, I gasped for breath in the blistering heat.

Years later I heard about a wind cave in the pass that sends air all the way to the Rendai Temple in Mino; but at that time, of course, I had no desire to go see it. I was so intent on climbing that I was oblivious to the scenery and to whatever natural wonders might lie along the way. I didn't even know if it was cloudy or sunny. Concentrating only on getting to the top, I crawled up the incline.

Now this is the part I really want to tell you. You see, the trail got much worse. Not only did it seem impossible for a human being to climb, but there was something even more horrible: snakes. They were buried in the grass, their heads on one side of the trail and their tails on the other, writhing like bridges across my path. The first time I encountered one, my breath rushed from my lungs and my knees gave way beneath me. I crumpled to the ground, my sedge hat still on my head and my walking staff still in my hand.

I've always been afraid, or maybe I should say terrified, of snakes.

That first time, the creature did me the favor of slowly slithering away. It raised its head, then disappeared into the grass.

I got to my feet and continued ahead another five or six hundred yards, only to find another snake sunning its belly, its tail and head also hidden in the grass on either side of the path.

I shouted and jumped back, and this one, too, slithered away. But the third snake I encountered was in no hurry to move. You should have seen how big around it was! I guessed that if the thing started crawling, it would take a full five minutes before its tail finally appeared. Having no other recourse, I forced myself to step over its thick body. My stomach turned and I felt as though my hair and all my pores had turned into scales. I closed my eyes and imagined my face turning as pale as the creature's belly.

I could feel myself breaking out in a cold sweat. My legs lost their strength. Barely able to keep my feet under me, I stumbled down the trail, my heart pounding with fear. And again, another snake appeared.

This one had been cut in half. All that remained was the length from belly to tail. The wound was tinged with blue, and, as the snake twitched on the path, a yellow fluid ran from where it had been severed.

That was when I finally panicked and started running back the other way. But then I came to my senses and remembered the other snakes I had just passed. No doubt they were lying in wait for me. And yet I would rather be killed than jump over another one. I knew in my heart that if the farmer had said, even in passing, that there were snakes like this on the old road, I wouldn't have taken this way though it might have meant suffering in hell for abandoning the medicine peddler. Baked by the sun, I felt tears come to my eyes. "Save me, Merciful Buddha!" Even now the thought of that experience makes me shudder.

The monk pressed his hand to his forehead.

7

But losing control wasn't going to help, so I did my best to regain my composure. It was not the time to be turning back. I would only run into the severed body of the dead snake, about three feet long. This time I left the path, deep into the grass, in order to get around it. And as I did, I panicked again, fearing that the other half would appear and coil itself around me. My legs grew stiff and I stumbled over a stone. Apparently, that's when I twisted my knee.

From there I had to limp along the trail as best I could. I knew that if I collapsed on the road, I would be killed by the steamy heat. So I made up my mind that I was going to make it and pressed on.

The hot stench of the grass was menacing. And underfoot I was constantly stepping on what felt like large birds' eggs strewn about.

For the next five miles, the road twisted and turned up the mountain in a series of switchbacks. Reaching the heart of the mountain, I turned the corner around a huge boulder and worked my way through a tangle of tree roots. This was when I stopped to look at the map, for the trail had become impossibly difficult.

It was the same road, all right—whether you hear about it or see it on a map. There was no mistaking it was the old road, though knowing this was no consolation. The map was reliable, but all it showed was a sign for "wilderness area" with a red line drawn over it.

Maybe it was too much to ask for notations that would indicate the true difficulties of the trail—the snakes, the insects, the birds' eggs, and the suffocating odors of the grass. I folded the map, stuffed it into my kimono, took a deep breath, and, with the *nenbutsu* on my lips, started off again. I had the best of intentions, but before I had taken another step, another snake crossed my path.

"No use," I thought, wondering for the first time if this might not be the doing of the mountain spirits. I threw down my staff, got on my knees, and placed both hands on the baking earth. "I'm truly sorry to bother you," I fervently implored the gods. "But please let me pass. I'll go quietly, I promise. I won't disturb your afternoon nap. Look, I've already thrown away my walking stick." I was truly at wit's end.

When I raised my head, I heard a terrifying, rushing sound. This time, I thought, it must be a gigantic snake—three, four, five feet long, maybe more. Before my eyes, the grass moved in a straight line that gradually approached the ravine to my left. Then the peak towering above me, indeed the entire mountain, began swaying back and forth. With my hair standing on end, I froze in my tracks as a coolness pierced my bones. It was then that I realized it was not a giant snake at all but a mountain gale, and the sound I was hearing was the wind's echo. It was as if a whirlwind had originated deep in the mountains and had suddenly rushed out an opening it had created for itself. Had the mountain gods answered my prayer? The snakes were nowhere to be seen and the heat dissipated. Courage returned to my heart, and strength to my legs. Before long I learned why the wind had suddenly grown so chilly: just ahead was a deep forest.

There is a saying about the Amō Pass—that it rains there even on a cloudless day. People also talk about the remote forests that haven't been touched by an ax since the age of the gods. Up to this point there hadn't been many trees, but now—

Stepping into the cold, damp woods, I thought about how there would be crabs rather than snakes crawling around now. As I walked ahead, it became dark. Cryptomeria, pine, Chinese nettle—there was just enough light to allow me to tell the trees apart. Where the shafts of weak sunlight touched the earth, the mountain soil was pitch black. Depending on how the sun pierced the canopy of treetops, though, the light was also mottled blue and red. Some of the places were textured and very beautiful.

Occasionally my toes would get caught in the threadlike rivulets that had formed from the water dripping from the leaves. These drops had traveled from branch to branch, originating high up in the forest canopy. They were joined by the steadily falling evergreen leaves and the rustling of some other trees that I couldn't identify. Some leaves fell on my hat, and some landed behind me where I had just walked. They, too, had collected on the branches, and it was my guess that some had taken decades to reach the forest floor.

8

I don't have to tell you how despondent I was. But I suppose a dark place like that is better than daylight for strengthening one's faith and pondering the eternal truths, even for a coward such as myself. At least it wasn't as hot as before. My legs were beginning to feel much stronger, and so I walked much more quickly, thinking I was already three-quarters of the way through the woods. But just then something fell, apparently from the branches five or six feet above my head, and landed on my hat.

It felt like a lead sinker. Perhaps it was the fruit of a tree. I shook my head once, twice. But it stuck to my hat. I reached up and grabbed it. Whatever it was, it was cold and slimy.

In my hand it looked like a sliced-open sea slug with no eyes or mouth. It was alive, no question about that. And how repulsive! I tried to fling it away, but it only slid down and dangled from my fingers. When it finally fell off, I noticed bright red drops of blood dripping. Surprised, I brought my hand up to take a closer look and discovered another creature, similar to the first, dangling from my elbow. It was about half-an-inch wide and three inches long. It looked like an enormous mountain slug.

As I examined the creature in stupefied amazement, it sucked blood from my arm, swelling larger and larger from the tail up. It had brown stripes on its dull black skin, like a cucumber with warts. Now I could see it for what it was—a blood-sucking leech!

There was no mistaking it for anything else, though it was so huge that I hadn't recognized it at first. No rice paddy, no swamp, however famous for its grotesqueries, had leeches like this.

I gave my elbow a vigorous shake, but the animal was firmly attached and wouldn't let go. Even though it was the last thing I felt like doing, I grabbed the leech with my other hand and pulled until it finally came off with a sucking sound.

I couldn't bear the thought of the leech touching me a moment longer and immediately flung it to the ground. These dumb creatures had taken over the woods by the thousands, and the dank, sunless forest had been prepared especially for that purpose. When I tried to squash the thing under my foot, the ground was soft and the leech merely sank into the muck. It was impossible to crush.

Already my neck had started to itch. There was another one! I tried to brush it off, but my hand only slipped over its body. Meanwhile, another had worked its way into my kimono and was hiding on my chest. I examined it with horror and discovered still another on my shoulder.

I jumped up and down. I shook my entire body. I ran out from under the large branch in order to get away. As I ran, I frantically grabbed at the ones that were sucking away at my blood. I was under the impression that the leeches had fallen from one particular branch, but when I looked back at the tree, I saw that the whole thing was swarming with them. On the right, on the left, on the branch in front—they were everywhere!

I lost control and shouted out in terror. And then what do you think happened? Even as I stood there watching, a shower of thin, black leeches began raining down on me.

They covered the tops of my sandaled feet and piled themselves one on top of the other. They stuck to the sides of my feet and made my toes disappear beneath their disgusting mass. As I watched those blood-sucking creatures squirming and pulsing and heaving, I started to feel faint. It was then that the strangest thought occurred to me.

These terrifying mountain leeches had been gathered there since the age of the gods, lying in wait for passersby. After decades and centuries of drinking untold quantities of human blood, they would have their fill and disgorge every ounce! Then the earth will melt. One by one, the mountains will turn into vast, muddy swamps of blood. And at the same time, all these enormous trees, large enough to block out even the midday sun, will break into small pieces that will then turn into even more leeches. Yes. That's exactly what will happen!

9

The destruction of mankind will not come with the rupture of the earth's fragile crust and with fire pouring down from the heavens. Nor will it come when the waves of the ocean wash over the land. Rather, it will begin with the forests of Hida turning into leeches and end with the black creatures swimming in blood and muck. Only then will a new generation of life begin.

It was true that nothing had seemed so unusual about the forest when I first entered it. But once I had, conditions were as I've just described. If I continued on, I would discover that the trees were rotting from the roots up and had turned into leeches, every one. There was no hope for me! It was my fate to be killed in the woods!

Suddenly it occurred to me that such are the thoughts of those who sense the approach of death. If I was going to perish anyway, I thought, I might at least try to reach the shore of this vast swamp of blood and muck, to see with my own eyes a place that ordinary people couldn't imagine in their wildest dreams. The decision made, I became oblivious to the ghastliness of my situation. The leeches stuck to my body like beads to a rosary; but my hands found them and plucked them off one after another. With arms flailing and legs marching, I made my way like a madman dancing through the forest.

At first my body swelled and the itching was unbearable. But then I felt as though I'd been reduced to pain-racked skin and bone. As I pressed on, the attack of the blood-sucking leeches continued.

My sight grew dim and I felt as though I was about to collapse. But just as I reached the height of my tribulations, I caught a faint glimpse of the distant moon, as if I had reached the end of a tunnel. At last, I emerged from the leech-infested forest.

When I saw the blue sky above me, I threw myself down on the road and began smashing the creatures to pieces. I wanted nothing more than to reduce them to the dust of the earth. I rolled on the ground, not caring if it were covered with gravel or needles; and after scraping off more than ten, I tumbled ahead another thirty feet before I stood up with a shudder. My friend, those creatures had had their way with me. Here and there in the surrounding mountains, the evening cicadas were chirping against the backdrop of this forest that was so intent on turning itself into a great swamp of blood and muck. The sun was low in the sky. The bottom of the ravine was already dark with shadows.

There was a chance I might become food for wild dogs, but even that would be an improvement over being sucked to death by leeches. The road sloped gently downhill. Carrying my bamboo walking stick on my shoulder, I made a hasty escape.

If only I hadn't been suffering such indescribable torment—at once so painful, itchy, and ticklish—I would have danced down the road through the Hida Mountains, chanting a sutra as my accompaniment. But I had recovered enough to be able to think about chewing one of my Seishintan pills and applying the paste to my wounds. I pinched myself. Yes, I really had returned from the dead. Even so, I wondered what had become of the medicine peddler from Toyama. My guess was that he was in the swamp behind me, long since reduced to blood, his corpse nothing but skin and a skeleton, lying in some dark spot in the woods with hundreds of the filthy, disgusting creatures still sucking on his bones. It would be useless to try to dissolve them with vinegar. With my mind filled with such thoughts, I continued down the slope, which went on for some distance.

When I finally reached the bottom, I heard the sound of running water. There, in the middle of nowhere, I came upon a small earthen bridge.

With the music of the water in my ears, I immediately thought of how wonderful it would feel to throw my sucked-over body headfirst into the river below and to soak it there. If the bridge collapsed as I tried to cross over, so be it.

Giving no thought to the danger, I started across. The bridge was a bit unsteady, but I made it. On the other side, the trail rose steeply again. Yet another climb. Is there no end to human suffering?

10

Tired as I was, I didn't think I could make it over one more hill. But then, coming from up ahead, I heard the echoing sound of a neighing horse.

Was it a packhorse driver on his way home? Or a horse passing by? Not much time had passed since my chance meeting with the farmer that morning, yet I felt as though I had been denied the company of my fellowmen for at least several years. If that was a horse I heard, there should be a village nearby. Given new courage by the thought, I pushed ahead.

Before I knew it, I was standing in front of a secluded mountain cottage. As it was summer, all the sliding doors had been left open. I couldn't locate a front gate, but directly before me was a dilapidated veranda. On it sat a man. What kind of man, I couldn't really tell.

"Excuse me. Excuse me." I called out in a pleading voice, as if imploring him to help me.

"Excuse me," I said again, but received no reply. He looked like a child. His head was cocked to one side so that one ear almost touched his shoulder. He stared at me with small, expressionless eyes. He was so listless it seemed he couldn't even be bothered to move his pupils. His kimono was short, the sleeves only coming to his elbows. His vest was properly starched and tied in front, but his stomach protruded from the kimono like a huge, smooth drum, and his belly button stuck out like the stem of a pumpkin. He fingered it with one hand, while waving the other in the air as if he were a ghost.

His legs were sprawled out as if he had forgotten he had them. Had he not been seated squarely on the veranda, I'm sure he would have toppled over. He appeared to be about twenty-two or -three years old. His mouth hung open, his upper lip curled back. His nose was flat and his forehead bulged. His hair had grown out and was long like a cockscomb in front, flipped all the way back to his collar and covering his ears. Was he a mute? An idiot? A young man about to turn into a frog? I was surprised by what I saw. He presented no real danger to me, but what a bizarre sight!

"Excuse me," I said again.

Despite his appearance, I had no choice but to try to communicate with him. My words of greeting, though, made little difference. He only stirred slightly and flopped his head over so it now rested on his left shoulder, mouth still agape.

I couldn't anticipate what he might do. But I did feel that if I weren't careful he might suddenly grab me, and then, while fiddling with his navel, lick my face instead of answering my inquiries.

I stepped back. But then I thought that no matter how out-of-the-way this place might be, no one would leave such a person alone. I stood on tiptoe and spoke a little louder.

"Is anyone home?"

I heard the horse whinny again. The sound came from behind the cottage.

"Who is it?" It was a woman's voice, coming from the storage room. My goodness! Would she come slithering out, scales on her white neck, trailing a tail behind her? I fell back another step.

And then she appeared—a petite, attractive woman with a clear voice and a gentle manner. "Honorable Monk," she greeted me.

I let out a huge sigh and stood still. "Yes," I finally said, and bowed.

She sat down on the veranda and leaned forward, looking at me as I stood in the evening shadows. "Is there something I can do for you?"

She didn't invite me to stay the night, so I assumed her husband was out. It seems they had decided not to take in any travelers.

I quickly stepped forward. If I didn't ask now, I might lose my chance.

I bowed politely. "I'm on my way to Shinshū. Can you tell me how far it is to the next inn?"

11

"I'm afraid you still have nineteen miles or more to go."

"Then perhaps you might know of a place nearby where I could stay the night?"

"I'm afraid I don't." She stared into my eyes without blinking.

"I see. Well, actually, even if you were to tell me that I could find lodging nearby, and that they'd put me up in their best room and fan me all night as an act of piety, I really don't think I could take another step. Please, I beg you. Even a shed or the corner of a horse stall would be fine." I said this because I knew that the horse I had heard couldn't possibly belong to anyone else.

The woman considered my request for a moment. Suddenly she turned, picked up a cloth bag, and started pouring rice from it into a pot at her side. She emptied the bag as if it were filled with water. With one hand steadying the pot, she looked down and scooped up the rice with the other.

"You can stay here tonight," she said at last. "We have just enough rice. Mountain cottages like this get cold at night, but it's summer and you should be fine. So, please. Won't you come in?"

As soon as she said this, I plunked myself down on the veranda. The woman got to her feet. "But, Sir. There is one thing I have to ask of you."

She was so forthright that I expected her to set down some impossible condition. "Yes," I said nervously. "What is it?"

"Nothing that important. It's just that I have a bad habit of wanting to know what's going on in the city. Even if you're not in the mood to talk, I'll keep asking you question after question. So you mustn't tell me anything, not even by a slip of the tongue. Do you understand what I'm saying? I'll keep pestering you if you do. So you mustn't say anything. Even if I beg you, you have to refuse. I just wanted you to know that."

There seemed to be some hidden reason behind her request. It was the sort of thing you might expect to hear from a woman living in an isolated cottage where the mountains are tall and the valleys immeasurably deep. As it seemed an easy enough request to fulfill, I nodded.

"That's fine. Whatever you say."

With this, the woman immediately became friendlier. "The house is a mess but please come in. Make yourself at home. Should I get you some water so you can wash up?"

"No, that won't be necessary. But I could use a washcloth. And would you mind getting it wet and wringing it out for me? I ran into a little trouble along the way. I feel so sticky I'd like to wash up, if I could trouble you for that."

"You do look hot. It must have been hard traveling on a day like this. If this were an inn, you could take a bath. They say that's what travelers really appreciate most. I'm afraid, though, you won't get even a cup of tea, let alone a tub of hot water. If you don't mind going down the cliff behind the house, though, there's a beautiful stream. You could go there and wash."

Hearing those words, I was ready to fly to the river. "That sounds perfect."

"Then let me show you where it is. I have to wash the rice anyway." The woman picked up the pot, placed it under her arm, then put on her straw sandals. Stooping over, she looked under the veranda and pulled out a pair of old wooden clogs, which she clapped together to shake off the dust. She set them down on the ground for me. "Please, wear these. Leave your straw sandals here."

I pressed my hands together and thanked her. "That's very kind of you."

"Your staying here," she said, "must have been determined by a former life. Don't hesitate to ask for what you need."

My friend, she was a most hospitable woman.

12

"Please follow me." With the rice pot in her hand, the woman tucked a small towel into her narrow sash. Her rich, lovely hair was tied up in a bun and held in place with a comb and an ornamental hairpin. I noticed she had a beautiful figure.

I quickly removed my sandals and put on the old clogs. When I stood up from the veranda and looked around, there was Mr. Idiot still staring in my direction and babbling some sort of nonsense. "Sister, dis, dis." He slowly lifted his hand and touched his tousled hair. "Monk. Monk?"

A smile formed on the woman's face. She gave him quick nods.

The young man said "Mmm," then grew limp and started playing with his navel again.

Out of sympathy for the two, I didn't raise my head but merely stole a glance at the woman. She didn't seem to be bothered at all. Just as I was about to follow her, an old man appeared from behind a hydrangea bush.

He had come around from the back. A carved ivory netsuke dangled from a long pouch string tied around his waist. Holding a pipe in his teeth, he came up to the woman and stopped. "Well, if it isn't a monk."

The woman looked over her shoulder at the man. "May I ask how it went?"

"Oh, you know. He's one stupid jackass, all right. Nobody but a fox could ever ride that horse. But that's where I come in. I'll do my best to get a fair price. A good deal should fix you up for two or three months."

"That would be nice."

"So where you headed?"

"Down to the water."

"Don't go falling in with the young monk now. I'll be on the lookout here." He leaned over and sat down on the veranda.

"Listen to him talk." She looked at me and smiled.

"Maybe I should go by myself." I stepped to the side and the old man laughed.

"Hurry up and get going, you two."

"We've already had two visitors today," she said to the old man. "Who knows? Maybe we'll have another. If somebody should come while Jirō's here alone, they won't know what to do. Maybe you could stay and make yourself comfortable until we get back."

"Sure." The man moved over to the idiot and whacked him on the back with his enormous fist. The idiot looked as if he might cry, but then grinned.

Horrified, I turned away. The woman didn't seem to be bothered by it at all.

The man laughed. "While you're away, I'm going to steal this husband of yours."

"Good for you," she said and turned to me. "Well then. Shall we go?"

I had the feeling that the old man was watching us from behind as I followed the woman along a wall leading away from the hydrangeas. We reached what seemed to be the back gate. To the left was a horse stable. I could hear the sound of a horse kicking at the walls. It was already starting to get dark.

"We'll take this path down. It's not slippery, but it is steep. Please be careful."

13

A grove of extremely tall, slender pine trees, their trunks clear of branches for about fifteen or twenty feet from the ground, marked the path that we were apparently going to take down to the river. As we passed through the trees, I spotted something white in the treetops far above. It was the thirteenth night of the new month, and though it was the same moon I had always seen, tonight it made me realize how far from the world of human habitation I had come.

The woman, who had been walking ahead of me, disappeared. When I looked down the hill, holding onto one of the trees, I spotted her below.

She looked up at me. "It gets a lot steeper here so please be careful. Maybe I shouldn't have given you those clogs. Would you like my sandals?"

She obviously thought I was lagging behind because of the steepness of the path, but really, I was more than willing to tumble down the slope to get that leech filth off my body.

"I'll come down barefoot if I have to," I said. "I'm fine. Sorry to make you worry, Miss."

"Miss?" She raised her voice slightly and laughed. It was a charming sound.

"That's what I heard the man call you. But maybe you're married?"

"Either way, I'm old enough to be your aunt. Now, come. Quickly. I'd give you my sandals but you might step on a thorn. They're soaking wet, anyway. You wouldn't like the way they felt on your feet." She turned away and quickly lifted the hem of her kimono. I could see her white ankles in the darkness. As she walked ahead they disappeared like the frost at dawn.

We were making good progress down the hill when a toad sluggishly emerged from a clump of grass on the wayside.

"Disgusting!" She lifted her heels and jumped to the side. "Can't you see I have a guest? Let go of my feet. Back to your bugs!" She turned to me. "Come right along. Don't pay attention to him. In a place like this, even the animals want attention." She turned back to the toad. "To think I'd be flattered to know you. Go away!"

The toad slowly moved back into the grass, and the woman started ahead.

"You'll have to climb up here. The ground's too soft." In the grass appeared the trunk of a tree, round and huge. I got up on it and had no trouble walking, even in my clogs. As soon as I had reached the end, the sound of rushing water was in my ears, although the river was still a distance away.

When I looked up I could no longer see the pine trees. The moon of the thirteenth night was low on the horizon, nearly half-covered by the mountain. Yet it was so brilliant I thought I could reach out and touch it, even though I knew its height in the heavens was immeasurable.

"It's this way." She was waiting for me, just a bit farther down the slope. There were boulders all around and pools created by the water flowing over them. The stream was about six feet across. As I approached it, the flowing water was surprisingly quiet, and its beauty was that of jewels broken from their string and being washed away. From farther downstream came the terrifying echo of the water crashing against other boulders.

On the opposite bank rose another mountain. Its peak was hidden in the darkness, but its lower reaches were illumined by the moonlight spilling over the crest of the mountain across the way. I could see boulders of various sizes and shapes—some like spiral seashells, others angular and truncated, and still others resembling spears or balls. They continued as far as the eye could see, forming a small hill at the water's edge.

14

"We're lucky the water's high today. We can bathe up here without going down to the main stream." She dipped her snow-white feet into the water that covered the top of a boulder.

The bank on our side was much steeper than the other, and tight against the river. We were apparently standing in a small, boulder-filled cove. It was impossible to see either directly upstream or downstream, but I could make out some water winding tortuously up the rock-strewn slope across from us. The stream gradually grew narrower, each bend bathed in moonlight so its water gleamed like plates of silver armor. Closer to where we stood, its waves fluttered white like a shuttle being taken up at the loom.

"What a beautiful stream."

"It is. This river begins at a waterfall. People who travel through these mountains say they can hear a sound like the wind blowing. I don't suppose you heard something along the way?"

I had indeed, just before I entered the leech-filled forest. "You mean that wasn't the wind in the trees?"

"That's what everyone thinks. But if you take a side road from where you were and go about seven miles, you come to a large waterfall. People say it's the largest in Japan. Not even one in ten has ever made it that far, though. The road is steep. So, as I was saying, this river flows down from there.

"There was a horrible flood about thirteen years ago," she continued. "Even these high places were covered with water, and the village in the foothills was swept away—mountains, houses, everything was leveled. There used to be twenty homes here at Kaminohora. But now they're gone. This stream was created then. See those boulders up there? The flood deposited them."

Before I realized it, the woman had finished washing the rice. As she stood and arched her back, I caught a glimpse of the outlines of her breasts, showing at the loosened collar of her kimono. She gazed dreamily at the mountain, her lips pressed together. I could see a mass of moonlit rocks that the flood had deposited halfway up the mountainside.

"Even now just thinking about it frightens me," I said as I stooped over and began washing my arms.

It was then that she said, "If you insist on such good manners, your robes will get wet. That's not going to feel very good. Why not take them off? I'll scrub your back for you."

"I wouldn't—"

"Why not? Look how your sleeve is getting in the water." She suddenly reached from behind and put her hand on my sash. I squirmed, but she kept going until I was completely naked.

My master was a strict man, and, as one whose calling it is to recite the holy sutras, I had never taken off my clothes, not even the sleeves of my robes. But now I was standing naked in front of this woman, feeling like a snail without a shell. I was too embarrassed even to talk, let alone run away. While she tossed my clothes onto a nearby branch, I hunched my back and stood with my knees together.

"I'll put your clothes right here. Now. Your back. Hold still. I'm going to be nice to you because you called me 'Miss.' Now don't be naughty." She pulled up one of her sleeves and held it between her teeth to keep it out of the way.

Without further ado, she placed her arm on my back. It was as smooth and lustrous as a jewel. For a moment, she only looked. "Oh, my."

"Is something wrong?"

"These bruises all over your back."

"That's what I was saying. I had a terrible time in the woods." Just remembering the leeches made me shudder.

15

She looked surprised. "So you were in the forest. How awful! I've heard travelers talk about leeches falling from the trees. You must have missed the detour and gone right through their nesting grounds. You're lucky to still be alive. Not even horses and cows make it. It must really itch."

"Now it only hurts."

"Then I shouldn't be using this cloth. It'll make your skin peel." She touched me gently with her hands.

She poured water over my body and stroked my shoulders, back, sides, and buttocks. You would think the cold river water would have chilled me to the bone, but it didn't. True, it was a hot time of the year, but even so. Perhaps it was because my blood was aroused. Or maybe it was the warmth of her hand. Anyway, the water felt perfect on my skin! Of course, they say that water of good quality is always soothing.

But what an indescribable feeling! I wasn't sleepy, but I began to feel drowsy. And as the pain from my wounds ebbed away, I gradually lost my senses, as if the woman's body, so close to mine, had enveloped me in the petals of its blossom.

She seemed too delicate for someone living in the mountains. Even in the capital you don't see many women as beautiful. As she rubbed my back, I could hear her trying to stifle the sounds of her breathing. I knew I should ask her to stop, but I became lost in the bliss of the moment. Was it the spirit of the deep mountains that made me allow her to continue? Or was it her fragrance? I smelled something wonderful. Perhaps it was the woman's breath coming from behind me.

Here Monk Shūchō paused. "Young man, since the lamp's over there by you, I wonder if you could turn up the wick a bit. This isn't the kind of story to be telling in the dark. I'm warning you, now. I'm going to tell it just as it happened."

The monk's outline showed darkly beside me. As soon as I fixed the lantern, he smiled and continued his story.

Yes, it was like a dream. I felt as if I were being softly enveloped in that warm flower with its strange, wonderful fragrance—my feet, legs, hands, shoulders, neck, all the way up to my head. When the blossom finally swallowed me completely I startled and collapsed on the boulder with my legs out in front of me. Immediately, the woman's arms reached around me from behind.

"Can you tell how hot I am? It's this unbearable heat. Just doing this has made me sweat."

When she said that, I took her hand off my chest. I broke away from her embrace and stood up straight as a stick. "Excuse me."

"Not at all. No one's looking," she said coolly. That was when I noticed she had taken off her clothes. When, I don't know. But there she was, her body softly shining like glossy silk.

Imagine my surprise.

"I suffer from the heat because I'm a little overweight. It's embarrassing," she said. "When it gets hot like this, I come to the river two or three times a day. If I didn't have this water, I don't know what I would do. Here. Take this washcloth." She handed me a wrung-out towel. "Dry your legs."

Before I knew what was happening, she had wiped my body dry.

"Ha, ha." The monk laughed, seeming a bit embarrassed. "I'm afraid this is quite a story I'm telling you."

16

With her clothes off, she looked very different. Her figure was voluptuous and full.

"I had some business to take care of in the shed back there," she said, "and now I've got horse's breath all over me. This is a good chance to wash up a bit." She spoke as if confiding in a brother or sister.

She raised one hand to hold back her hair, and wiped under her arm with the other. As she stood and wrung out the towel with both hands, her snowy skin looked as if it had been purified by this miracle-working water. The flowing perspiration of such a woman could only be light crimson in color, the shade of mountain flowers.

She began combing her hair. "I'm really being a tomboy. What if I fell into the river? What would the people downstream think?"

"That you were a white peach blossom." I said what came to my mind. Our eyes met.

She smiled, as if pleased by my words. At that moment, she seemed seven or eight years younger, looking down at the water with an innocent shyness. Her figure, bathed in the moonlight and enveloped in the evening mist, shimmered translucent blue before a huge, smooth rock that was being moistened black by the spray from the opposite bank.

It had grown dark, and I had trouble seeing clearly. But there must have been a cave somewhere nearby, for just then a number of bats, creatures as large as birds, began darting over our heads.

"Stop that. Can't you see I have a guest?" the woman suddenly cried out, and shuddered.

"Is something wrong?" I asked calmly. I had put my clothes back on.

"No," she said as if embarrassed, and quickly turned away.

Just then a small, gray animal the size of a puppy came running toward us. Before I could shout out, it jumped from the cliff, sailed through the air, and landed on her back. With the animal hugging her like that, she seemed to vanish from the waist up.

"Beast! Can't you see my guest?" Now there was anger in her voice. "What insolence!" When the animal peered up at her, she struck it squarely on the head. It let out a shriek, jumped backward into the air, and dangled by its long arm from the branch where she had hung my clothes. Then it did a somersault, flipped itself on top of the branch, and scampered up the tree. A monkey! The animal jumped from branch to branch, then climbed to the very top of the tall tree, sharing the treetops with the moon that had risen high in the sky and was showing through the leaves.

The woman seemed to be in a pout because of the monkey's misbehavior, or rather because of the pranks of the toad, the bats, and the monkey. The way her mood soured reminded me of young mothers who get upset when their children misbehave.

As she put her clothes back on, she looked angry. I asked no questions. I hid in the background and tried to stay out of the way.

17

She was gentle yet strong, lighthearted yet not without a degree of firmness. She had a friendly disposition but her dignity was unshakable, and her confident manner gave me the impression that she was a woman who could handle any situation. Nothing good could come of getting in her way if she were angry. I knew that if I were unfortunate enough to get on her wrong side, I would be as helpless as a monkey fallen from its tree. With fear and trembling, I timidly kept my distance. But, as it turned out, things weren't as bad as all that.

"You must have found it odd," she said, smiling good-naturedly, as if recalling the scene. "There's not much I can do about it."

Suddenly she seemed as cheerful as before. She quickly tied her sash. "Well, shall we go back?" She tucked the rice pot under her arm, put on her sandals, and quickly started up the cliff. "Give me your hand."

"No. I think I know the way now." I thought I was prepared for the ascent; but once we started the climb, it was a lot farther to the top than I had expected.

Eventually we crossed over the same log. Lying in the grass, logs have an amazing resemblance to serpents, especially pine trees with their scalelike bark. With the cliff towering above us, it seemed as though the fallen tree was indeed a slithering snake. Judging from its girth, the serpent's head would be somewhere in the grass on one side of the path and its tail on the other. There it was, its contours brightly lit by the moonlight. Remembering the road that had brought me here, I felt my knees begin to quiver.

The woman was good enough to keep looking back to check on me. "Don't look down when you cross over. Right there in the middle, it's a long way to the bottom. You wouldn't want to get dizzy."

"No, of course not."

I couldn't stand there forever, so I laughed at my timidity and jumped up on the log. Someone had cut notches into it for traction, and as long as I was careful I should have been able to walk on it even wearing clogs. Nevertheless, because it was so like the back of a boa—unsteady, soft, and slithery beneath my clogs—I shouted out in fear and fell, straddling the log.

"Where's your courage?" she asked. "It's those clogs, isn't it? Here, put these on. Do as I say."

By that time I had already developed a sound respect for her. For better or worse, I decided to obey, no matter what she wanted. I put on the sandals, just as she asked.

And then, listen to this, as she was putting on my clogs, she took my hand.

Suddenly I felt lighter. I had no trouble following her, and before I knew it we were back at the cottage.

As soon as we arrived the old man greeted us with a shout. "I thought it'd take a little time. But I see the Good Brother's come back in his original form."

"What are you talking about?" she said. "Anything happen while we were gone?"

"Guess I've done my time here. If it gets too dark, I'll have trouble on the road. Better get the horse and be on my way."

"Sorry to make you wait."

"Not at all. Go take a look. Your husband's fine. It's going to take more than I've got to steal him away from you." Pleased by his own nonsense, the old man burst into laughter and plodded off toward the horse stall.

The idiot was sitting in the same place, just as before. It seems that even a jellyfish will keep its shape if kept out of the sun.

18

I could hear neighing, shouts, and the sound of the horse's hooves stomping the ground as the man brought the animal around front. He stood with his legs apart, holding the animal by its halter. "Well, Miss, I'll be off. Take good care of the monk."

The woman had set up a lantern near the hearth and was on her knees, trying to get a fire started. She glanced up and placed her hand on her leg while holding a pair of metal chopsticks. "Thank you for taking care of everything."

"It's the least I could do. Hey!" The man jerked back on the animal's rope.

It was a dappled horse, gray with black spots. The muscular stallion with a straggly mane stood there with nothing on but a halter.

I found nothing particularly interesting about the animal. Yet when the man tugged on the rope I quickly moved over to the veranda from where I was sitting behind the idiot and called out, "Where are you taking that horse?"

"To an auction over by Suwa Lake. Tomorrow you'll be taking the same road."

"Why do you ask?" the woman suddenly interrupted. "Are you planning to jump on and ride away?"

"Not at all," I said. "That would be a violation of my vows—to rest my legs and ride while on pilgrimage."

"I doubt you or anybody else could stay on *this* animal," the old man said. "Besides, you've had your share of close calls already today. Why don't you just rest easy and let the young lady take care of you tonight? Well, I'd better get going."

"All right, then."

"Giddap."

The horse refused to move. It seemed to be nervously twitching its lips, pointing its muzzle in my direction, and looking at me.

"Damned animal. Hey now!"

The old man pulled the halter rope to the left and right, but the horse stood as firm as if its feet were rooted in the ground.

Exasperated by the creature, the old man began to beat it. He closely circled around the horse two or three times, but the animal still refused to move forward. When the man put his shoulder against its belly and threw his weight against the horse, it finally lifted one of its front feet, but then planted all four again.

"Miss! Miss!" The man wailed for help.

The woman stood up and tiptoed over to a soot-blackened pillar, where she hid herself from the horse's eyes.

The man pulled out a dirty, crumpled towel from his pocket and wiped the sweat from his deeply wrinkled brow. With new determination on his face, he placed himself in front of the horse and, maintaining his calm, grabbed the rope with both hands. He planted his feet, leaned back, and threw his whole weight into it. And guess what happened next?

The horse let out a tremendous whinny and raised both its front hooves into the air. The old man stumbled and fell to the ground on his back; and the horse came down, sending a cloud of dust into the moonlit sky.

Even the idiot saw the humor of this scene. For once and only once, he held his head straight, opened his fat lips, bared his big teeth, and fluttered his hand as if fanning the air.

"What now?" the woman said, giving up. She slipped on her sandals and stepped into the dirt-floored area of the cottage.

"Don't get it wrong," the old man said to her. "It's not you. It's the monk. This horse has had its eye on him from the start. They probably knew each other in a former life, and now the beast wants the Holy Man to pray for its soul."

I was shocked to hear the fellow suggest I had any connections with the animal. It was then that the woman asked me, "Sir, did you happen to meet anyone on your way here?"

19

"Yes. Just before I reached Tsuji, I did meet a medicine peddler from Toyama. He started out on the same trail, a little ahead of me."

"I see." She smiled as if she had guessed something right, then glanced over at the horse. She looked as if she couldn't help but smirk.

She seemed to be in a better mood, so I spoke up. "Perhaps he came by this way."

"No. I wouldn't know anything about that." She suddenly seemed to distance herself again, and so I held my tongue. She turned to the man, who was standing meekly before the horse, dusting himself off. "Then I guess I don't have much of a choice," she said in a resigned tone and hurriedly untied her sash. One end of it dangled in the dirt. She pulled it up and hesitated for a moment.

"Ah, ah." The idiot husband let out a vague cry. As he reached out with the long, skinny arm that was constantly fanning the air, the woman handed him her sash. Like a child, he placed it on his lap, then rolled it up and guarded it as if it were a precious treasure.

She pulled the lapels of her kimono together and held them with one hand just below her breasts. Leaving the house, she quietly walked over to the horse.

I was struck with astonishment as she stood on tiptoe. She gracefully raised her hand in the air, then stroked the horse's mane two or three times.

She moved around and stood directly in front of the horse's huge muzzle, seeming to grow taller as I watched. She fixed her eyes on the animal, puckered her lips, and raised her eyebrows as if falling into a trance. Suddenly her familiar charm and coquettish air disappeared, and I found myself wondering if she were a god, or maybe a demon.

At that moment, it was as if the mountain behind the cottage and the peak directly across the valley—in fact, all the mountains that surrounded us and formed this world that was set apart from all others—suddenly looked our way and bent over to stare at this woman who stood facing the horse in the moonlight. Turning ever darker, the deep mountains grew more lonely and intense.

I felt myself being engulfed in a warm, moist wind as the woman slipped her kimono off her left shoulder. Then she took her right hand out of its sleeve, brought it around to the fullness of her bosom, and lifted her thin undergarment. Suddenly she was naked, without even so much as the mountain mist to clothe her.

The skin on the horse's back and belly seemed to melt with ecstasy and drip with sweat. Even its strong legs became feeble and began to tremble. The animal lowered its head to the ground and, blowing froth from its mouth, bent its front legs as if paying obeisance to her beauty.

At that moment, the woman reached under the horse's jaw and

nimbly tossed her undergarment over the animal's eyes. She leaped like a doe rabbit and arched her back so she was looking up at the ghastly, hazy moon. Threading the undergarment between the horse's front legs, she pulled it from its eyes as she passed beneath the belly of the horse and stepped off to the side.

The old man, taking his cue from her, pulled on the halter. And the two started walking briskly down the mountain trail and soon disappeared into the darkness.

The woman put on her kimono and came over to the veranda. She tried to take her sash from the idiot, who refused to give it back. He raised his hand and tried reaching for her breasts. When she finally brushed off his hand and gave him a scornful look, he shrank back and hung his head.

All this I witnessed in the phantasmal flickering of the dimming lantern. In the hearth, the faggots were now aflame, and the woman, in order to tend to the fire, rushed back into the cottage. Coming to us from the far side of the moon, the faint echoes of the horseman's song reverberated in the night.

20

It was time for dinner. Far from mere carrots and gourd shavings, the woman served pickled vegetables, marinated ginger, seaweed, and miso soup with dried wild mushrooms.

The ingredients were simple but well prepared, and I was practically starving. As for the service, it couldn't have been better. With her elbows resting on the tray in her lap, and her chin cupped in her hands, she watched me eat, apparently gaining great satisfaction from it.

The idiot, tired of being left alone, started crawling limply toward us. He dragged his potbelly over to where the woman was seated and collapsed into a cross-legged position. He mumbled as he kept pointing and staring at my dinner.

"What is it?" she asked him. "No. You can eat later. Don't you see we have a guest tonight?"

A melancholy look came over the idiot's face. He twisted his mouth and tossed his head from side to side.

"No? You're hopeless. Go ahead, then. Eat with our guest." She turned to me. "I beg your pardon."

I quickly set my chopsticks down. "Not at all. Please. I've put you through too much trouble already."

"Hardly. You've been no trouble at all." She turned to the idiot. "You, my dear, are supposed to eat with me, after our guest finishes. What am I going to do with you?" Saying this to put me at ease, she quickly set up a tray identical to mine.

Good wife that she was, she served the food quickly, without wasting a single movement. Yet there was also something refined and genteel about her.

The idiot looked up with dull eyes at the tray set before him. "I want that. That," he said while glancing goggle-eyed around the room.

She looked at him gently, in the way a mother might look at her child. "You can have that any time you want," she said. "But tonight we have a guest."

"No. I want it now." The idiot shook his entire body. He sniveled and looked as if he was about to burst into tears.

The woman didn't know what to do, and I felt sorry for her. "Miss, I know next to nothing about your situation here," I said. "But wouldn't it be better just to give him what he wants? Personally, I'd feel better if you didn't treat me like a guest."

"So you don't want to eat what I've fixed?" she asked the idiot. "You don't want this?"

She finally gave in to him, as he looked as if he was about to cry. She went over to her broken-down cupboard, took something from a crock, and put it on his tray, though not without giving him a reproachful look.

"Here you go." She pretended to be peeved and forced a smile.

I watched from the corner of my eye, wondering what kind of food the idiot would be chewing in his huge mouth. A blue-green snake stewed with vegetables in thick soy and sugar? A monkey fetus steam-baked in a casserole? Or something less grotesque, like pieces of dried frog meat? With one hand the idiot held his bowl. With the other he picked up a piece of overpickled radish. It wasn't sliced into pieces either, just chopped into a big chunk so the idiot could munch on it as if eating a cob of corn.

The woman must have been embarrassed. I caught her glancing over at me. She was blushing. Though she hardly seemed like an innocent-minded person, she nervously touched a corner of her towel to her mouth.

I took a closer look at this young man. His body was yellow and plump, just like the pickled radish he had just devoured. By and by, satisfied with having vanquished his prey, he looked the other way, without even asking for a cup of tea, and panted heavily with boredom.

"I guess I've lost my appetite," the woman said. "Maybe I'll have something later."

She cleared the dishes without eating dinner.

21

The mood was subdued for a while after that. "You must be tired," she finally said. "Shall I make up your bed right away?"

"Thank you," I replied. "But I'm not the least bit sleepy. Washing in the river seems to have revived me completely."

"That stream is good for any illness you might have. Whenever I'm worn out and feel withered and dry, all I have to do is spend half a day in the water and I become refreshed again. Even in the winter, when the mountains turn to ice and all the rivers and cliffs are covered with snow, the water never freezes in that spot where you were bathing. Monkeys with gunshot wounds, night herons with broken legs, so many animals come to bathe in the water that they've made that path down the cliff. It's the water that has healed your wounds.

"If you aren't tired, maybe we could talk for a while. I get so lonely here. It's strange, but being all alone in the mountains like this, I even forget how to talk. Sometimes I get so discouraged.

"If you get sleepy, don't stay up on my account. We don't have anything like a real guest room, but, on the other hand, you won't find a single mosquito here. Down in the valley they tell a story about a man from Kaminohora who stayed the night there. They put up a mosquito net for him, but since he had never seen one before he asked them for a ladder so he could get into bed.

"Even if you sleep late you won't hear any bells ringing, nor any roosters crowing at dawn. We don't even have dogs here, so you can sleep in peace."

She looked over at the idiot. "That fellow was born and raised here in the mountains. He doesn't know much about anything. Still, he's a good person, so there's no need to worry on his account. He actually knows how to bow politely when a stranger visits, though he hasn't paid his respects to you yet, has he? These days he doesn't have much strength. He's gotten lazy. But he's not stupid. He can understand everything you say."

She moved closer to the idiot, looked into his face, and said cheerfully, "Why don't you bow to the monk? You haven't forgotten how, have you?"

The idiot managed to put his two hands together on the floor and bowed with a jerk, as if a wound-up spring had been released in his back. Struck by the woman's love for the fellow, I bowed my head. "The pleasure's mine."

Still facing down, he seemed to lose his equilibrium. He fell over on his side, and the woman helped him back up. "There. Good for you."

Looking as if she wanted to praise him for what he had done, she turned to me and said, "Sir, I'm pretty sure he could do anything you asked of him. But he has a disease that neither the doctors nor the river can heal. Both of his legs are crippled, so it doesn't do much good to teach him new things. As you can see, just one bow is about as much as he can tolerate.

"Learning something is hard work. It hurts him, I know, so I don't ask him to do much. And because of that he's gradually forgotten how to use his hands or even how to talk. The one thing he still can do is sing. Even now he still knows two or three songs. Why don't you sing one for our guest?"

The idiot opened his eyes wide and looked at the woman, then at me. He seemed shy as he shook his head.

22

After she encouraged and cajoled him in various ways, he cocked his head to one side and, playing with his navel, began to sing.

Even the summers are cold
On Mount Ontake in Kiso.
Let me give you
A double-lined kimono
And tabi socks as well.

The woman listened intently and smiled. "Doesn't he know it well, though."

How strange it was! The idiot's voice was nothing like you might expect, having heard his story. Even I couldn't believe it. It was the difference between the moon and a turtle, clouds and mud, heaven and earth! The phrasing, the dynamics, the breathing—everything was perfect. You wouldn't think that such a pure, clear voice could emerge from the throat of that young man. It sounded as though his former incarnation was piping a voice from the other world into the idiot's bloated stomach.

I had been listening with my head bowed. I sat with my hands folded in my lap, unable to look up at the couple. I was so moved that tears came to my eyes.

The woman noticed I was crying and asked me if something was wrong. I couldn't answer her right away, but finally I said, "I'm fine, thanks. I won't ask any questions about you, so you mustn't ask about me either." I mentioned no details, but I spoke from my heart. I had come to see her as a veritable Yang Gui-fei, a voluptuous and alluring beauty who deserved to be adorned with silver and jade pins for her hair, gossamer gowns as sheer as butterfly wings, and pearl-sewn shoes. And yet she was so open and kind to her idiot husband. That was the reason I was moved to tears.

She was the sort of person who could guess the unspoken feelings of another. She spoke up as if she immediately understood exactly what I was feeling. "You're very kind." She gazed at me with a look in her eyes that I cannot begin to describe. I bowed my head and looked away.

The lantern dimmed again, and I wondered if this perhaps was the idiot's doing; for just then, the conversation lagged and a tired silence overcame us. The master of song, apparently bored, yawned hugely, as if he were about to swallow the lantern before him.

He started to fidget. "Want sleep. Sleep." He moved his body clumsily.

"Are you tired? Shall we go to bed?" The woman sat up and, as if she had suddenly come to her senses, looked around. The world outside the house was as bright as noon. The moonlight poured into the cottage through the open windows and doors. The hydrangeas were a vivid blue.

"Are you ready to retire?"

"Yes," I said. "Sorry to inconvenience you."

"I'll put him to bed first. Make yourself comfortable. You're right out in the open here, but in the summer this bigger room will be better for you. We'll sleep in the inner room, so you can get a good rest. Wait just a moment," she started to say and stood up. She hurriedly stepped down onto the earthen floor. Because her movements were so vigorous, her black hair, which had been twisted into a bun, fell down over the nape of her neck.

With one hand touching her hair and the other on the door, she looked outside and said to herself, "I must have dropped my comb in all the excitement."

She was obviously talking about when she had passed beneath the horse's belly.

23

The monk paused as he told his story. The night was still, and we could clearly distinguish slow, quiet steps in the hallway downstairs. It sounded like someone going to the bathroom. One of the rain shutters opened with a rattle; then came the sound of hands being washed. "The snow's piling up," came a voice. Most surely, it was the owner of the inn.

"I guess the merchant from Wakasa found some other place to spend the night," the monk said. "I hope he's having sweet dreams."

"Please, finish your story. What happened next?" I urged Monk Shūchō to continue.

Well, the night grew late, he resumed. As you can understand, no matter how tired a person gets, when you're in an isolated cottage in the middle of mountains like that, it's hard to fall asleep. Besides, I was bothered by something that kept me from dozing off. In fact, I was wide awake. I kept blinking my eyes, but, as you might expect, by that time I was so exhausted that my mind had become clouded. All I could do was wait for dawn to brighten the night sky.

At first I listened, out of habit, for the morning temple bells. Will they ring now? Are they about to ring? Surely enough time had passed since I had retired for the night. But then I realized there wouldn't be any temples in a place as isolated as this, and suddenly I became uneasy.

Then it happened. As they say, the night is as deep as a valley. As soon as I could no longer hear the sound of the idiot's slovenly breathing, I sensed the presence of something outside.

It sounded like the footsteps of an animal, one that hadn't come from very far away. At first I tried to comfort myself, thinking that this was a place where there was no scarcity of monkeys and toads. But the thought did little to reassure me.

A bit later, when it seemed the animal had stepped up to the front of the house, I heard the bleating of a sheep.

My head was pointed in its direction, which meant that the beast must have been standing right beside my pillow! A bit later I heard the sound of beating bird's wings just to my right, under the spot where the hydrangea was blooming.

Then came the sound of another animal crying *Kii, kii* on the rooftop. I guessed it was a flying squirrel or some such thing. Next a huge beast, as big as a hill, came so close I felt as though I were being crushed by it. It bellowed like a cow. Then came another two-legged creature that sounded as if it must have come running from far away with straw sandals on its feet. Now all kinds of creatures were circling and milling around the house. Altogether, there must have been twenty or thirty of them, snorting, beating their wings, some of them hissing. It was like a hellish scene from the Realm of Suffering Beasts. In the light of the moon, I could see the silhouettes of their ghastly figures cavorting and dancing in front of the house. Were these the evil spirits of the mountains and rivers?

The leaves on the trees shuddered. I held my breath. From the room where the woman and the idiot were sleeping came a moan and then the sound of someone drawing a long breath. It was the woman, overcome by a nightmare.

"We have a guest tonight," she cried out.

A few seconds passed before she spoke again, this time in a clear, sharp voice. "I said we have a guest."

I could hear the woman tossing in bed, and a very quiet voice that said, "We have a guest." Then followed more tossing.

The beasts outside stirred and the entire cottage began to shake back and forth. Frightened out of my senses, I began reciting a *dharani.*

He who dares resist the heavens
And vainly tries to block truth's route,
May his head be split in seven
Like the young arjaka sprout!
His sin is worse than parricide,
His crushing doom without relief,
His scales and measures telling lies
Like Devadatta, we despise
Offenders of belief!

I chanted the sacred words with heart and soul. And suddenly the whirlwind twisting in the trees blew away to the south and everything became still. From the couple's bed came not a sound.

24

The next day at noon, I ran into the old man who had gone off to sell the horse. I was standing by a waterfall not far from a village, and he was on his way back to the cottage. We came upon each other just at that moment when I had decided to give up my life as a monk, to go back to the mountain cottage and spend the rest of my days with the woman.

To tell the truth, ever since I had left her earlier that morning this single idea dominated my thoughts. No snakes spanned my path, and

I encountered no leech-filled forests. Still, though the way might continue to be hard, bringing tribulation to my body and soul, I realized that my pilgrimage was senseless. My dreams of someday donning a purple surplice and living in a fine monastery meant nothing to me. And to be called a living Buddha by others and to be thronged with crowds of worshippers could only turn my stomach with the stench of humanity.

You can understand why I haven't given you all the details of my story, but after the woman put the idiot to sleep, she came back out to my room. She told me that rather than going back to a life of self-denial, I ought to stay by her side in the cottage by the river, there where the summer is cool and the winter mild. Had I given in to her for that reason alone, you'd probably say that I had been bewitched by her beauty. But in my own defense let me say that I truly felt sorry for her. How would it be to live in that isolated mountain cottage as the idiot's bed partner, not able to communicate, feeling you were slowly forgetting how to talk?

That morning when we said goodbye in the dawning light, I was reluctant to leave her. She regretted never being able to see me again, spending the rest of her life in such a place. She also said that should I ever see white peach petals flowing upon a stream, however small, I would know that she had thrown herself into a river and was being torn apart bit by bit. She was dejected, but her kindness never failed. She told me to follow the river, that it would lead me to the next village. The water dancing and tumbling over a waterfall would be my sign that houses were nearby. Pointing out the road, she saw me off, walking along with me until her cottage had disappeared behind us.

Though we would never walk hand in hand as man and wife, I kept thinking I could still be her companion, there to comfort her morning and night. I would prepare the firewood and she would do the cooking. I would gather nuts and she would shell them. We would work together, I on the veranda and she inside, talking to each other, laughing together. The two of us would go to the river. She would take off her clothes and stand beside me. Her breath upon my back, she would envelop me in the warm, delicate fragrance of her petals. For that I would gladly lose my life!

Staring at the waterfall, I tortured myself with these thoughts. Even now when I think back on it, I break out in a cold sweat. I was totally exhausted, both physically and spiritually. I had set off at a fast pace and my legs had grown weary. Even if I was returning to the civilized world, I knew that the best I could expect was some old crone with bad breath offering me a cup of tea. I could care less about making it to the village, and so I sat down on a rock and looked over the edge at the waterfall. Afterward, I learned it was called the Husband and Wife Falls.

A large jagged rock, like the gaping mouth of a black killer shark, stuck out from the cliff, dividing in two the quickly flowing stream that rushed down upon it. The water thundered and fell about fifteen yards, where it reformed, white against dark green, then flowed straight as an arrow toward the village downstream. The branch of the waterfall on the far side of the rock was about six feet wide and fell in an undisturbed ribbon. The one closest to me was narrower, about three feet across, caressing and entangling the huge shark rock in the middle. As it tumbled, the water shattered into a thousand jewels, breaking over a number of hidden rocks.

25

The smaller stream was trying to leap over the rock and cling to the larger flow, but the jutting stone separated them cleanly, preventing even a single drop from making it to the other side. The waterfall, thrown about and tormented, was weary and gaunt, its sound like sobbing or someone's anguished cries. This was the sad yet gentle wife.

The husband, by contrast, fell powerfully, pulverizing the rocks below and penetrating the earth. It pained me to see the two fall separately, divided by that rock. The brokenhearted wife was like a beautiful woman clinging to someone, sobbing and trembling. As I watched from the safety of the bank, I started to shake and my flesh began to dance. When I remembered how I had bathed with the woman in the headwaters of this stream, my imagination pictured her inside the falling water, now being swept under, now rising again, her skin disintegrating and scattering like flower petals amid a thousand unruly streams of water. I gasped at the sight, and immediately she was whole again—the same face, body, breasts, arms, and legs, rising and sinking, suddenly dismembered, then appearing again. Unable to bear the sight, I felt myself plunging headlong into the fall and taking the water into my embrace. Returning to my senses, I heard the earthshaking roar of the husband, calling to the mountain spirits and roaring on its way. With such strength, why wasn't he trying to rescue her? I would save her! No matter what the cost.

But then I thought that it would be better to go back to the cottage than to kill myself in the waterfall. My base desires had brought me to this, to this point of indecision. As long as I could see her face and hear her voice, what did it matter if she and her idiot husband shared a bed? At least it would be better than enduring endless austerities and living out my days as a monk.

I made up my mind to go back to her, but just as I stepped back from the rock, someone tapped me on the shoulder. "Hey, Monk."

I had been caught at my weakest moment. Feeling small and ashamed, I looked up, expecting to see a messenger from Hell. What I saw instead was the old man I had met at the woman's cottage.

He must have sold the horse because he was alone. He had a small string of coins hanging from his shoulder and was carrying a carp. The fish had scales of brilliant gold and looked so fresh that it seemed alive. It was about three feet long and dangled from a small straw cord threaded through its gills. Unable to think of a word to say, I could only look at the man while he stared into my eyes. Finally, he chuckled to himself. It wasn't a normal laugh but a gruesome sort of snicker.

"What are you doing here?" he asked me. "You should be used to this kind of heat, or did you stop for something else? You're only twelve miles from where you were last night. If you'd been walking hard, you'd be in the village giving thanks to Jizō by now.

"Or maybe you've been thinking about that woman. Your earthly passions are stirred, aren't they? Don't try to hide it. I may be a bleary-eyed old man, but I can still tell black from white. Anyone normal wouldn't still be human after a bath with her. Take your pick. Cow? Horse? Monkey? Toad? Bat? You're lucky you're not going to be flying or hopping around for the rest of your life. When you came up from the river and hadn't been turned into some other animal, I couldn't believe my eyes. Lucky you! I guess your faith saved you.

"Remember the horse I led off last night? You said you met a medicine peddler from Toyama on your way to the cottage, right? Well, he's what I'm talking about. The woman had that lecher turned into a horse long before you showed up. I took him to the auction and cashed him in. With the money I bought this carp. Oh, she loves fish! She'll eat this one tonight! Tell me. Who do you think she is anyway?"

"Yes. Who *was* she?" I interrupted the monk.

26

Monk Shūchō nodded. "Listen to this," he murmured. "It must have been my fate. Remember the farmer I met at the crossroads, where I took that trail into the haunted forest? Remember how he told me that a doctor once had his house there where the water was flowing over the road? Well, it turns out that the woman was his daughter."

In the high mountains of Hida, where life is always the same and nothing strange ever happens, something extraordinary occurred. To this country doctor was born a daughter who, from the moment of her birth, was as beautiful as a jewel.

Her mother had fat cheeks, eyes that slanted down, a flat nose, and breasts of the most disgusting sort. How could she raise a daughter who was so beautiful?

People used to gossip, comparing their situation to ancient tales where a god desires someone's daughter and shoots a white-feathered arrow into the roof of a house, or a nobleman who is hunting in the countryside, sees a country maiden and demands her for his mistress.

Her father, the doctor, was a vain, arrogant man with jutting cheekbones and a beard. During threshing season, farmers often get chaff in their eyes; and because infections and other diseases are common, he had gained some proficiency as an eye doctor. As an internist, though, he was an utter failure. And when it came to surgery, the best he could do was mix a little hair oil with water and apply it to the wound.

But you know what they say about how some can believe in anything or anybody. Those of his patients whose days were not already numbered eventually recovered; and as there were no other quacks around, her father's practice flourished.

When his daughter came to be sixteen or seventeen, in the bloom of her youth, the people in the area came to believe that she was Yakushi, Healer of Souls, and that she had been born into the doctor's family in order to provide help to the needy. And provide she did. Both men and women came pleading for her healing touch.

It all began when she started showing interest in her father's patients. "So your hands hurt? Let me see." She pressed the soft palm of her hand to the fingers of a young man named Jisaku—he was the first one—and his rheumatism was cured completely. She stroked the belly of another patient who had drunk tainted water, and his stomachache went away. At first it was the young men who benefited from her healing powers, but then the older men started going to her, too, and later women. Even if they weren't cured completely, the pain was always less than before. When someone had a boil to be lanced, they screamed and kicked as the doctor cut with his rusty knife. But if his daughter pressed her chest up against their backs and held their shoulders, they could bear the pain.

Now, near the grove where the doctor had his house there was an old loquat tree; and in the tree, a swarm of bees had built a frighteningly huge hive. One day, a young man named Kumazō, the doctor's apprentice, found it. His duties were mixing medicine, cleaning the house, taking care of the garden, and transporting the doctor by rickshaw to the homes of patients living nearby. He was twenty-four or -five at the time, and had stolen some syrup from the doctor's medical supplies. Knowing the doctor was tightfisted and would scold him if he ever found out, Kumazō hid his own jar of the syrup on a shelf with his clothes and, whenever he had a few minutes of spare time, would satisfy his sweet tooth by secretly sipping from it.

Kumazō found the bees' hive as he was working in the yard and came over to the veranda to ask the doctor's daughter if she wanted to see something interesting. "Pardon me for asking, but if you could hold my hand, I'll reach into a bees' hive and grab some. Wherever you touch me won't get hurt even if the bees sting. I could try driving 'em away with a broom, but they'd scatter and get all over me. It'd be sudden death." She hesitated, but smiled and let him take her hand. He led her to the hive, where the bees were making a horrifying drone. In went his left hand. And out it came unharmed, even with seven or eight bees on it, some fanning their wings, some moving their legs, others crawling between his fingers.

Well, after that incident, her fame spread like a spider's web. People began saying that if she touched you, even a bullet would cause no pain. And it was from about that time that she herself became aware of her power. When she went off to live in the mountains with the idiot, her powers grew even more wondrous. As she grew older, she became able to summon the most astounding magical powers at will. In the beginning, she needed to press her body against you. Then it was a touch of her foot or a caress of the fingertips. Finally, she didn't need to make physical contact at all. With a puff of her breath, she could turn a lost traveler into the animal of her choice.

The old man drew my attention to the creatures I had seen around the cottage—the monkey, the toad, the bats, rabbits, and snakes. All of them were men who had bathed in the river with her! When I heard that, I was overwhelmed with memories of the woman and the toad, of her being embraced by the monkey and attacked by the bat, and of the evil spirits of the forest and mountains that circled the cottage that night.

And the idiot? The old man told me about him, too. At a time when the daughter's fame had spread throughout the region, he had come to her father as a patient. He was still a child, accompanied by his father—a brusque, taciturn man—and by his long-haired older brother, who carried him down the mountain on his back. The boy had a bad abscess on his leg, and they had brought him to the doctor's house for treatment.

At first they stayed in a room in the doctor's house, but the boy's leg turned out to be more serious than originally thought. They would have to let his blood, and, particularly because the boy was so young, they would need to build up his strength before anything could be done. For the time being, the doctor prescribed that he eat three eggs a day. And to put his father's mind at ease, a plaster was put over the infection.

Whenever the plaster had to be removed, whether by his father or brother or by someone else, the scab would get pulled off, and the boy would cry out in pain. When the doctor's daughter did it, though, he endured silently.

As a matter of practice, the doctor used the poor physical condition of his patients as an excuse to put things off whenever he knew he couldn't do anything to help. After three days passed, the boy's hardworking father left his older son to look after the younger one and returned to the mountains. Bowing and scraping, he excused himself and backed out to the entrance of the doctor's house. He slipped on his straw sandals, got down on the ground and bowed again, imploring the doctor to do what he could to save his son's life.

The boy didn't get any better, though. On the seventh day, the older brother also returned to the mountains, saying that this was harvesttime and by far the busiest season of the year. Bad weather was moving in, and if the storms continued for very long, the rice crop, their very source of life, would rot in the fields and their family would starve. Because he was the oldest son and the strongest worker in his family, he couldn't afford to stay away any longer. "Don't cry now," he said softly to his brother, and left him behind.

After that, the boy was alone. According to official records he was six years old, but actually he was eleven. The army wouldn't draft a son whose parents were already sixty. And so the boy's parents had waited five years before they registered his birth. Having been born and raised in the mountains, he had difficulty understanding people in the valley, but he was a bright and reasonable child, who understood that his diet of three eggs a day was producing the extra blood that was to be drained. He would whimper from time to time. But because his brother had told him not to cry, he bore his burden well.

The doctor's daughter felt sorry for the boy and invited him to eat with them, though he preferred going over to a corner of the room to chew on a pitiful chunk of pickled radish. On the night before the operation, after everyone had gone to sleep, the doctor's daughter got up to use the bathroom and heard him weeping quietly. Out of pity, she took him to her bed.

When it came time for the bloodletting, she held him from behind as she usually did for her father's patients. The boy perspired profusely and bore the pain of the scalpel without moving, but—was it because the doctor had cut the wrong place?—they couldn't staunch the flow of blood. As they watched, the boy lost his color and his condition became critical.

The doctor himself grew pale and agitated. By the grace of the gods, the hemorrhaging stopped after three days; and the boy's life was saved. Still, he lost the use of his legs and from that point on was a cripple.

All the boy could do was drag himself around and look pathetically at his lifeless limbs. It was an unbearable sight, like seeing a grasshopper carrying its torn-off legs in its mouth. When he cried, the doctor, irritated by the thought that his reputation might suffer, glared angrily at him, making the boy seek refuge in his daughter's arms. The doctor had wronged his patients many times before. But this time he admitted his mistake and, though feeling it was inappropriate for a woman his daughter's age to be letting the boy bury his face in her bosom, he just folded his arms and sighed deeply.

Before long, the boy's father came to get him. He didn't complain to the doctor but accepted what had happened to his son as fate. Because the boy refused to leave the young woman's side, the doctor, finding an opportunity to make amends, sent his daughter to accompany them home.

As it turns out, the boy's home is the very mountain cottage that I've been telling you about. At the time, it was one of about twenty houses that formed a small village. The doctor's daughter intended to stay only one or two days, but lingered because of her affection for the child. On the fifth day of her stay, the rain came pouring down in an unrelenting torrent, as if waterfalls had been unleashed on the mountains. Everyone wore straw raincoats even inside their homes. They couldn't open their front doors, let alone patch the holes in their thatched roofs. Only by calling out to each other from inside were they able to know that the last traces of humanity had not been wiped off the face of the earth. Eight days passed as if they were eight hundred. On the ninth, in the middle of the night, a great wind began to blow; and when the storm reached its peak, the mountains and village turned into a sea of mud.

Strangely enough, the only ones who survived the flood were the doctor's daughter, the young boy, and the old man who had been sent from the village to accompany them.

The doctor's household was also annihilated by the same deluge.

People say that the birth of a beautiful woman in such an out-of-the-way place is a harbinger of a new era. Yet the young woman had no home to which to return. Alone in the world, she has been living in the mountains with the boy ever since. You saw for yourself, he said, how nothing has changed. From the time of the flood thirteen years ago, she's cared for him with utter devotion.

Once the tale had been told, the old man sneered again. "So now that you know her story, you probably feel sorry for her. You want to gather firewood and haul water for the woman, don't you? I'm afraid your lustful nature's been awakened, Brother. Of course, you don't like to call it lust. You'd rather call it mercy or sympathy. I know you're thinking of hurrying back to the mountains. But you'd better think twice. Since becoming that idiot's wife, she's forgotten about how the world behaves and does only as she pleases. She takes any man she wants. And when she tires of him, she turns him into an animal, just like that. No one escapes.

"And the river that carved out these mountains? Since the flood, it's become a strange and mysterious stream that both seduces men and restores her beauty. Even a witch pays a price for casting spells. Her hair gets tangled. Her skin becomes pale. She turns haggard and thin. But then she bathes in the river and is restored to the way she was. That's how her youthful beauty gets replenished. She says 'Come,' and the fish swim to her. She looks at a tree, and its fruit falls into her palm. If she holds her sleeves up, it starts to rain. If she raises her eyebrows, the wind blows.

"She was born with a lustful nature, and she likes young men best of all. I wouldn't be surprised if she said something sweet to you. But even if her words were sincere, as soon as she gets tired of you, a tail will sprout, your ears will wiggle, your legs will grow longer, and suddenly you'll be changed into something else.

"I wish you could see what the witch is going to look like after she's had her fill of this fish—sitting there with her legs crossed, drinking wine.

"So curb your wayward thoughts, Good Monk, and get away as quickly as you can. You've been lucky enough as it is. She must have felt something special for you, otherwise you wouldn't be here. You've been through a miracle and you're still young, so get on with your duties like you really mean it." The old man slapped me on the back again. Dangling the carp from his hand, he started up the mountain road.

I watched him grow smaller in the distance until he disappeared behind the mass of a large mountain. From the top of that mountain, a cloud rapidly blossomed into the drought-cleared sky. Over the quiet rush of the waterfall, I could hear the rolling echoes of clapping thunder.

Standing there like a cast-off shell, I returned to my senses. Filled with gratitude for the old man, I took up my walking staff, adjusted my sedge hat, and ran down the trail. By the time I reached the village, it was already raining on the mountain. It was an impressive storm. Thanks to the rain, the carp the old man was carrying probably reached the woman's cottage alive.

This, then, was the monk's story. He didn't bother to add a moral to the tale. We went our separate ways the next morning, and I was filled with sadness as I watched him begin his ascent into the snow-covered mountains. The snow was falling lightly. As he gradually made his way up the mountain road, the holy man of Mount Kōya seemed to be riding on the clouds.

One Day in Spring

(*Shunchū* and *Shunchū gokoku,* 1906)

Part 1

"Who, me?"

The still of the spring day, no doubt, had made it possible for the reply to come so quickly, like an echo to the wanderer's "Excuse me, sir." How else could it be? The old man, wearing a loosely fitting headband on his wrinkled forehead, had a sleepy, almost drunken expression as he calmly worked the soft ground warmed by the sun. The damp and sweaty plum blossoms nearby, a flame ready to flutter away into the crimson sunset, swayed brilliantly with the chatter of small birds. Their voices sounded like conversation, but the old man, even in his rapturous trance, must have known that the sound of a human voice could only be calling for him.

Had he known the farmer would answer so promptly, the passerby might have thought twice about saying anything. After all, he was just out for a walk and could have decided the matter by dropping his stick on the road: if it fell north, toward Kamakura, he would tell the old man; and if it toppled south he would continue his walk without saying a word. Chances are the old man wouldn't hear him anyway, and then he'd soon be on his way again. But he had to say something, even if it was none of his business.

"Who, me?"

Surprised by the prompt response, the wanderer stepped over to a low lattice fence and slowly stretched his back as he glanced behind him. There wasn't a blade of grass between him and the man. The three rows of earth the farmer had so industriously spaded gave forth a pleasing, joyful smell. And yet there was something lonely about the field, the clumps of milk vetch showing here and there, and the green, dust-covered fava-bean sprouts, severed from their roots and returned to the soil.

The wanderer put a hand to his tweed hunting cap. "Is that yours, the house on the corner?"

The old man turned slowly, his wizened face catching a full measure of sunlight. Against the shadowed plum blossoms, the roof tiles of the house across the way rose high into a midday sky that was baking the wheat fields with its brightness. "Which house?"

"The one with two stories."

"That's not mine." The answer seemed a little abrupt, but the farmer didn't seem as though he meant to cut him off. The old man moved his shoulders, turned his hoe upside down, and set it down on the ground. Then he looked over at the passerby.

"Well, then, sorry to have bothered you," the wanderer said, ready to move on.

The old man pulled off his headband. "No trouble at all. Are you looking for something? The front gate's shut, but they're not renting if that's what you're asking." The old man hiked up the skirt of his kimono and tucked it and his neckerchief under his sash. He kept his fingers stuck there, making it look as though he didn't intend to let the wanderer get away easily.

"It's nothing so important."

"What's that?"

"I said, if that *was* your house, I was going to tell you something, and not because I'm looking for a place to rent either. I know it's not empty. I heard voices coming from inside."

"Two young ladies live there." The farmer nodded.

"Well, it's about those two. As I was walking past their house, by that stone wall along the gutter, I saw it crawling there—a long one."

1

The sun shone brightly on the old man's forehead as he knit his eyebrows. Without looking down, he produced a tobacco pouch from his sleeve.

"You don't say."

"I've never been one for snakes, really." The wanderer laughed and tried to smile. "That's why I stopped and watched. It crawled halfway through the fence and flopped its tail right into the gutter. Then I'll be damned if it didn't stick its head right into the clapboards. I thought it might be headed for the bathing area, or maybe the kitchen. Anyway, I could hear voices, and I was afraid somebody might be in for a scare. A snake like that could easily squirm its way into a sitting room or pantry. No terrible thing, maybe. But what if it curled up on the floor somewhere and someone stumbled over it? I know, it's really none of my business. But then I saw you, and the house was right there. So I thought, well, if that's your place, I should say something. On the other hand, maybe you people don't think anything of a snake or two."

"Garden snake most likely." The old man opened his mouth to laugh, and the gentle rays of sunlight poured onto his tongue. "Wouldn't say it's nothing to worry about, though. Those people are from Tokyo and had quite a little scare just a while back. I'll go take a look. Most likely the snake's long gone by now, but I'm good friends with the girls who work in the kitchen."

"By all means. Sorry for the trouble, then."

"Not at all. The day's long. Not much else happening anyway."

By the time the two men parted, the snake seemed to have vanished like a dragon, beyond the limits of the common imagination. When the wanderer turned around he heard the noise of weavers at work, their shuttles sounding like the beating of chicken's wings. He followed the road along the fence, passing beneath some plum trees and by a few farmhouses where two women were working at their looms. One was eighteen or nineteen, and the other was about thirty.

He glimpsed the younger woman's profile through the half-opened *shōji* of her workroom. She wore a scarf on her head, and the whiteness of her arm flashed as she threw her shuttle. The older woman had spread a reed mat on the dry ground in front of the house and was sitting with her back to the road. She quickly lifted her feet from the pedal and her loom sang its gentle song—*kiri, kiri, kiri.*

That was all he saw as he passed by. It was a nostalgic sight, the kind one rarely sees anymore except in illustrations of nineteenth-century romances such as "The Women of Imagawa." He wanted to stop and look, but there was no one else around, not even children. They were probably out in the fields with everyone else. Thinking the women might be embarrassed by the sight of a stranger, especially a man, he decided to keep walking. He let the road take him back to where he had seen the snake and turned at the corner where the two-story house stood. To his left was a wheat field. It sloped down and opened toward the beach, where white waves fluttered delicately upon the pale-green wheat, and a large, Western-style villa stood vividly against a cloudless sky. Considering how the people here branded foreigners "Blue Goblins" and "Red Goblins" because of the bright paint they put on their houses, a man like himself, though lacking the required beard, would also be considered one of the hat-wearing bourgeoisie.

If the villagers thought of Europeans as blue and red monsters, they no doubt thought of boat sails whenever a butterfly passed by. The area had long since opened its beaches to the modern pursuit of recreational swimming, but the mountains to the right were the same as before—pure black, like the wings of huge hawks piled on top of each other, the foothills stretching down from the peaks, one here and another there, encroaching on the fields of rice seedlings, squeezing the narrow valleys between them. Far up one of these valleys, where it dead-ended in darkness, he saw a simple thatched roof and a window that looked like the mountain's open eye, as if a giant toad had crawled up from the dawning sea and had made that his hiding place for the sunlit hours.

2

Continuing his walk, he saw a hillside kiln climbing higher than the tops of the houses. He passed an unidentified shrine, an abandoned graveyard, camellia blossoms falling one after another, huge leeches in the rice paddies. Here on the Shōnan coast, in the small bays tucked into the meandering mountain range, white sails rode upon the waves of the floating world. For a brief moment, so long as the sea still harbored no thoughts of rushing up the valleys and flooding the land, the villagers turned their backs to the water and worked their fields in twos and threes. The young woman throwing her shuttle and the older woman stepping on the pedal of her loom also faced the mountains, unafraid of the menacing ocean.

These seven or eight homes that were clustered around the two-story house on the corner formed the center of the village. Farther up the valley the houses became scattered; and a few hundred yards closer to the ocean they disappeared altogether. Crowded together on both sides of the crooked lane, these homes, plus another seven or eight that were spaced farther apart, formed a neighborhood.

The wanderer came to a field of rape blossoms, where the sunlight was dazzling. The green of the cliff to his left and the blue-green mountain across the valley were the only suggestions that the field of pure yellow did not extend forever. Even the small stream, flowing at the wanderer's feet, did little to cut the color's brilliance.

To his dazzled eyes, it was as if the two weavers at their looms had been vaguely copied onto a piece of white paper, and that the remaining space around them had been painted yellow. The contrast between the rape blossoms and the colors of the two women—their kimonos, their scarves, even the pieces of fabric they were weaving—made them stand out in his mind. Of course, he couldn't say if this method of highlighting was effective or not. But the image did hold him spellbound as he imagined a line of gold on red, the tip of a weaver's shuttle leaping in a circle, searing his eyes, flying into the grass by the stream's edge, disappearing like an extinguished flame.

That was when he saw a second snake, shining brightly as it slithered among the rape plants. He shuddered and turned. Immediately before him, hidden by the treetops, a flight of stone steps led steeply up to a thatched temple roof hovering like a cloud in the sky. Blooming near the top of the roof, against the peak's hair of green and black, was a patch of purple irises, seeming close enough to touch.

This is what our wanderer had come to see: the temple of the Kunoya Kannon. But as he stood at the bottom of the stairway, ready to go up to the main hall, a huge, shaggy face appeared from the dense undergrowth that surrounded the path. The animal was nearly as wide as the trail itself; and, as if that weren't surprising enough, there were more than one of them. Mane after mane, belly after belly, for about five or six meters, nothing but solid horse.

Immediately, the wanderer planted his stick and stood back. He found himself enclosed in a triangle formed by a line that connected the snake at the corner house, the snake in the rape field, and this herd of horses.

How very strange! But then again, as it says in the *Lotus Sutra:*

> *If beset by savage beasts*
> *Armed with claws and sharp, mean teeth,*
> *Lizards, snakes, and scorpions, too,*
> *Their fiery breath a poison dew,*
> *Oh come! Thou One Who Sees Them All!*

3

A horseman appeared alongside the horse, one of three animals that swaggered single file down the mountainside.

"Thanks for waiting," the first horseman said.

"Sorry to be in your way," said the second.

"Excuse us," said the third.

The three horsemen greeted him as they passed. Trying to get out of the way, the wanderer stood at the stream's edge, feeling as though his eyes were being blanketed with horsehide.

The path narrowed even more, but he found footing on the soft grass. With the sounds of the weavers lost in the distance, he came to the base of the steps, where the blue sky seeped down through the trees. The long flight was in poor repair, and the horses were hauling new stones to the back gate of the priest's quarters near the bottom of the steps.

Climbing those steps was like crawling up an unsteady ladder. Some stones were missing, the corners of others worn away. Because the earth crumbled beneath his feet, the wanderer was forced to crawl up the hill. He progressed slowly, but the fields and paddies below grew steadily smaller and more distant, and the waves appeared blue as the surrounding mountains embraced the sea and closed in around his feet, everywhere the same.

In the woods' deep shadows, among the green, mossy stones of the stairway, grew lavender firefly gowns, relatives of the Chinese bell flower. The early spring blossoms seemed to dampen the wanderer's mind. He felt hot and sweaty, as if he were climbing up where boiling water had once flowed down. Yet with the slightest breeze, he suddenly felt chilled.

He finally reached the top of the stairway. The temple grounds were rather cramped. Behind the main hall with its thatched roof, wrapped around the walkways on either side, the mountain rose like a curtain, its undergrowth black as sumi ink, the wind moaning through the pines growing there. Or was the noise coming from somewhere else?

Down the mountain, the snow-tipped waves were spreading on the shore below, coupling with the beach and vanishing into the cliffs, their sound still faintly audible. Sadly gone, however, was the *kiri hatari* of the weaver's looms. From the vantage point of the mountain, he no longer saw the two weavers among the yellow rape blossoms. Now they were floating upon the waves, outlined by the blue of open sea.

But first, let us pray.

The temple, perched as high as a horse's back, was approached by five stone steps that had long since lost the balustrade's shadow. In its day, the building must have been marvelous to behold, with its vermilion-lacquered pillars, lintels carved with flower patterns, and beams painted Prussian blue. But now the golden dragons had a forlorn look, and the midday moonlight fell upon the temple's thatched roof, leaking down in butterfly patterns upon the Chinese-style doors. The building resembled an ancient painting done in the flamboyant Tosa style. Though not dazzling, it did possess a certain depth, a fineness, a feeling of nostalgia.

The dark interior of the hall appeared through the open lattice doors. To the side of the small shrine, draped with curtains, white lotus blossoms stood with their faces held high. Positioning himself before them, the wanderer bowed his head and withdrew, first one step and then another. With peace in his heart, he looked up at the coffered ceiling, carved in red and white peonies. The fading blossoms of Chinese whites were scattered among the crimson, making him feel as though he were in a dream, gazing upward at a garden of flowers.

Pasted over the flowers, the rounded pillars, the pedestals for the offerings, the paneled doors, and on the outer Chinese-style doors and crossbeams, wherever he looked were the small paper stickers that named the various pilgrims who had come to the temple. One read "Engraver Hori." Another read "Fishmonger Masa." There was "Yasu the Roofer," "Tetsu the Carpenter," "Goldsmith Sakan." One was from Tokyo's Asakusa District, another from Fukagawa. Others were from places far away—Suō, Mino, Ōmi, Kaga, Noto, Echizen, Kumamoto in Higo, Tokushima in Awa. They were like birds from distant inlets and bays, the wagtail, the cuckoo. These stickers had been left behind by unseen visitors, all of them virtuous men and women who had stayed in cheap lodgings with nothing but the cold night for a pillow, who had traveled rainy nights on rush-roofed boats and had found a home for their dreams here. Even today, the spirits of those pilgrims must come back to frolic, here where the stickers served as doorplates to their spiritual homes.

4

For such pilgrims, this sacred spot was a place of equanimity and divine favor, an engaging garden of flowers. Those who heard the temple's call were willing to travel any distance—ten, one hundred, one thousand miles, even from the ends of the sea. At first chance, they came to watch the flowers falling through the air. They came to worship the moon in her robes of white. The fevered of mind drank droplets of dew from the riverbank willows. Those suffering from love sought to touch the supple hand of Kannon, wanting to be held in her embrace. For those who had lost their way, there were green tiles and jeweled fences of cinnabar, gilded pillars and red balustrades, agate stairways and flower-patterned Chinese doors. The visitors fantasized about jeweled chambers and golden palaces, about phoenixes dancing in the dragon's shrine, giraffes frolicking among the peonies, the morning light shining upon the lion's throne, even about mothers and children sleeping together, cherry blossoms for a quilt, moon-bright pearls for a pillow. Whatever the dream, the all-merciful, all-suffering Kannon would not find fault.

"Engraver Hori," "Fishmonger Masa." Simply by looking at the names the pilgrims had left behind, proof that their spirits had passed this way, one could imagine which were men and which were women. One could guess their appearance, their deportment, their presence. If the donations published in the newspapers and the lists of donors posted at the temples were realism, these name tags were romanticism.

Smiling, the wanderer inspected them one at a time.

Looking back toward the door and the large, wooden donation coffer, he spotted a piece of tissue paper pasted to a huge, cracked, mortarlike pillar. On it was a poem written in a woman's flowing hand:

In a nap at midday
I met my beloved,
Then did I begin to believe
In the things we call dreams.
Tamawaki Mio

It was gently and beautifully written.

"You'll want to come over here, sir."

The wanderer had not seen the priest standing right beside him, the sleeves of his linen robe overlapping, his straw sandals visible beneath the hem of his skirt.

He turned, and the priest greeted him with a smile.

"Follow me."

The priest walked past the donation box and leaned back toward the latticed doors. Standing directly before the shrine, he pulled his robe to the sides, produced a match from his sleeve, then reached up and lit a candle. He brought his hands to his forehead and pressed his palms together. Then he opened a door just in front of the wanderer, who was still standing in the main hall.

A four-mat room was situated on the other side of its thick, worm-eaten threshold, built wide and set up a level from the hall floor. The wanderer could see trees through the cracks in the walls, but the unbordered tatami mats were new and green. The priest entered and sat down in front of a small table, its top completely cleared. Then he slid forward on his knees and pushed an ash-covered smoking box toward his guest. It contained a charcoal holder but no tobacco.

"Please. Make yourself comfortable."

Again, the priest rustled his sleeves as he began searching for something. "Oh, here they are!" He laughed and produced a box of matches from beneath the table.

"Thank you very much." The visitor stepped over the threshold and sat down. He lit his pipe and blew a puff of smoke that was darker in shade than that place where the ocean meets the sky. "Really an impressive temple you have here. What a view!"

"I'm afraid everything's in a shambles. I hate to say it, especially in front of the Buddha here, but I just can't keep up with everything by myself."

5

"You must get a lot of visitors." The wanderer said the first thing that came to mind.

The priest seemed to nod as he moved in front of the table and put his legs to one side. "I wish I could say we did, but these days we don't get many. At one time this temple was part of a huge complex. You know that place you just passed? You can see it from here. From the foot of that hill there, all the way to those rape fields. Once there were seven temples lined up one after another. It's written down somewhere. This place, the Cliff Palace Temple, was the first to be built here in Kunoya. We're the second stop on the Bandō Circuit, a famous holy place though now just a shadow of what once was.

"Strangely enough, most of our visitors come from quite a distance. The closest are from Kazusa and Shimōsa; and some come all the way from Kyushu, hearing of us by word of mouth. They say that when they ask the local people for directions, a lot of them don't even know where we are. Our visitors have the worst time trying to find us."

"I can imagine."

"Oh, yes." The priest laughed and cut his own sentence short.

There was something solicitous about the way the priest spoke, and the wanderer was not sure at first what to make of him. Emptying the ashes from his pipe, he noticed how sooty the smoking box was, how the charcoal bowl was stuffed with the remains of burned matches. It reminded him of the dormitory at Shinshū University in Sugamo, where the students were waiting for the advent of Miroku, the Buddha of the Future. This place wasn't exactly equipped for entertaining visitors either, but maybe that actually fostered the open sharing of one's feelings. Anyway, that was how he felt.

He filled his pipe and enjoyed another round of tobacco. Blowing the smoke toward the edge of the mountains, he fancied himself as the Taoist wizard Tekkai, a man who could blow an image of himself into the air.

"It must be nice and cool here in summer."

"Yes. It hardly ever gets hot. As you can tell, the main temple here is quite pleasant. But the temporary lodging down the hill is even cooler. It's nothing but a thatched hut, but stop in on your way back and rest your feet. I could build a little fire and make you a cup of tea. It's definitely rustic. You might see the teakettle sprout a tail and turn itself back into a badger. But that's the charm of the place." The priest laughed again.

"It's nice here. I really envy you."

"Oh, I wouldn't say that. It's lonely living alone, you know. You saw how I came hurrying out when I saw you. By the way, do you mind if I ask where you're staying?"

"Me? I'm living near the station."

"Since—"

"The month before last."

"Then you're staying at an inn?"

"No. I'm renting a room. I do my own cooking."

"I see. This may sound rude, but maybe you'd be interested in making use of our hut. I know this is all very sudden, but just last summer, under very similar circumstances, I provided accommodations for a fellow much like yourself. Couples are fine, too. There's plenty of space for two."

"Thanks, anyway." The wanderer smiled. "I was just passing by. Didn't expect to find a place like this. This is really a fine temple."

"Come by as often as you like. Come take a stroll."

"That would be a waste. No, I'll come to worship."

The wanderer didn't mean anything in particular by it, but the priest eyed him suspiciously.

6

The priest put a hand on his knee. "I guess I didn't expect to hear you say that."

"Why not?" his visitor asked, though it wasn't hard to guess the answer.

The priest was a small man with cheeks that puffed out when he smiled. "Isn't it obvious?" he replied. "Young people these days, you know—" He laughed. "Not that I'm that old myself."

"Oh, no. I understand," the visitor said. "You're talking about teenagers, students, right? No need to hold back. That's what's wrong. That's just your problem." He found himself rearranging his legs little by little. "I agree that the teachings of Buddhism have grown stale," he continued. "I don't even know which sect you belong to here. But, as you say, the people who come are usually well along in years. Salvation is difficult for people who've been to college. They don't think they need Kannon.

"But really, these days it's the old people who are dishonest and wicked. They stop right in the middle of chanting a sutra to nag their daughters-in-law. They recite prayers with their shirts off and while holding eel skewers between their teeth. It wasn't always that way. There's plenty of room for argument, I know, but I think things were a little better back when people lived with some idea of heaven and hell in their heads. These days, we go around thinking we gain enlightenment on our own. In the worst cases, someone looks at a painting of hell and blurts out, 'Not bad at all.'

"But it's the young people, you know," the wanderer continued. "The ones you don't expect to come to the temple. They're the ones who are most attracted to the teachings. They're desperate for peace and life. Some go insane. Some even commit suicide in their searching.

"It doesn't matter who it is. You might think, 'Now there's a real twentieth-century person,' but go right up to him and say, 'Hail, Amida, Giver of Light and Truth,' and see what happens. Whether it's a man or a woman, some of them will faint, some will say they want to shave their heads and follow the Way, and still others will clap their hands and gain enlightenment on the spot. Some might even want to die because they see the light.

"It's true. I'm not kidding. That's how powerful the teachings of

Buddha are. Now is the time for Buddhism to shine. Why do people like you vacillate and withdraw?"

"I see. Yes. Certainly." The priest listened carefully. "Well, I do hear about how our intellectuals are going through great turmoil these days, how there are those who claim to have seen God, some who have been visited by the Buddha, others who say they are the Savior, and even others like the Divine Wind group in Kumamoto who recently staged uprisings for the sake of religion. Be that as it may, these are matters of lofty argument and research, not about these things we priests look after, these . . . idols." He looked over at the small shrine and continued. "If a statue is well made, the world thinks it's an object of art, a piece of sculpture. Maybe, as you say, Buddhism will flourish in the future. But what about these idols? What do you do with them? If we all became believers, what would happen to those who say they worship the *image* of Buddha? Now that's the crucial point. Naturally, we'd appreciate it if people like you thought about the difference between Buddhism and idol worship. I was of the opinion that you thought of them as works of art. That's why I invited you to come and take a stroll."

"But how could we possibly do without idols?" the wanderer responded. "Without images, what would we have to believe in? Your mistake, sir, is in calling them idols. They have names, every one of them. Shaka, Monju, Fugen, Seishi, Kannon. They all have names."

7

"It's the same with people," the wanderer continued. "If they're strangers, they mean nothing to us. But let's give them names. With a name a person becomes father, mother, brother, sister. And in that case, would you still treat them like strangers? Idols are no different. If they're just idols, they mean nothing to us. But the one here in your main hall is Kannon. And so we believe in it, don't we?"

He pointed to the main hall. "You could say a carved figure is nothing but wood or metal or earth, decorated with gold, silver, and gems to add color. But what about people? Skin, blood, muscle, the five organs, the six organs, join them together, add some clothes, and there you have it. Never forget, sir, that even the most beautiful woman is nothing more than this."

He faced the priest. "You might say that people have spirits and idols don't. But, sir, it's precisely our understanding of the spirit that causes us either to lose our way or to find it, to feel threatened or to gain peace. To worship, to believe. How can you practice archery without a target? Even acrobats and jugglers have to study. So to those who say they don't need idols I have to ask, 'Is it enough to yearn for your beloved, to love and to pine for someone without ever thinking you'll be together someday? Is it all right never to see her? And if you do see her, then is it acceptable never to speak to her? And if you speak to her, wouldn't you want to touch her hand? And if you touch her hand, would it matter if you never slept together?' Ask them that.

"The truth is that you'd want to embrace the one you love even if it could only happen in your dreams. Come now. Even if it were a fantasy, you'd still want to see the gods, wouldn't you? Shaka, Monju, Fugen, Seishi, Kannon. Tell me that you aren't thankful for their images."

The priest's face became animated and his eyes shone so that the wanderer could almost count the points of stubble around his smile. "Well said. Most interesting."

The priest put a hand on his knee and touched the other to his forehead. "In a nap at midday I met my beloved. Then did I begin to believe in the things we call dreams." He quietly mumbled the lines of the verse pasted on the pillar.

The wanderer looked over to where the spiderwebs framed the brush's brilliant trace.

"Now that you've spoken I feel embarrassed, and unless I explain why you'll never understand. It's about this poem. 'In a nap at midday. . . .' "

"Poem?"

"That's right. See those things over there? Those are all name tags that visitors to my temple have put up. Some of them are advertisements—for medicine and for whatever. It's a custom, so I don't mind. I don't know how they put them up, or when. But that one, over there on the pillar—"

"You mean the poem?"

"Then you saw it."

"Just a while ago, when you called to me."

"It caught your eye, no doubt. I know who wrote it."

"A woman, right?"

"That's correct. Apparently it's an old poem. Ono no Komachi's my guess."

"Yes, I think that's right."

"Well, the woman who put it up there was just as beautiful as Komachi."

"You mean the Tamawaki lady?" The wanderer's voice was clear and steady, but in spite of himself he revealed his interest.

"I see. When you brought up the subject of lovers a while ago, I didn't fault you as your purpose was clear. Like 'the moon shining faintly upon the edge of Bright Mountain,' perhaps you were using a metaphor to link the desire for Kannon with this ancient poem—'Then did I begin to believe in the things we call dreams.'

"There are plenty of examples of rare beauties who accept the Buddha and receive Nirvana. Some might be quick to condemn the woman for going around scribbling love poems. But that, too, depends on your point of view. Even in the sutras it says, 'If a woman seeks a man, Kannon will give help,' so we shouldn't be trying to find fault. And yet, a man died because of that poem."

The wanderer's surprise was even greater than when he saw the snake in the field of yellow blossoms.

8

"You probably won't believe it. It's such a bizarre story." The priest touched his cheek, looked down at the floor, and thought for a moment. "If you don't want to blame the poem, I guess you could say he died from delusion."

"But that's a shocking thing to say! Tell me, what happened?" The wanderer had already started to edge forward on his knees. Eager to hear more of what promised to be a good story, he removed his hunting cap from the bosom of his kimono and set it aside. Outside, the spring wind sounded in the pines, not as it swept down from the sky but as it rose, lighter than a human being, to gently caress the heavens.

The priest looked at the votive lamp standing before the Kannon statue. "Well then, since you asked. It was the man I was telling you about, the gentleman who came to stay in the hut down the hill. I guess you could say he died of longing for the woman who wrote that poem about dreaming. Or maybe we should call it lust. That's the gist of it."

"Amazing. I didn't know that sort of thing still happened. What sort of man was he?"

"He was a man like you."

"What!" The priest didn't seem to be trying to trick his visitor, and yet he had served up more than just tea. It was like getting whacked on the back thirty times by a Zen master. "That's quite a comparison." The wanderer laughed it off.

"I shouldn't have said that, considering your remarks, and how similar your circumstances are with the other—"

"Don't worry about that. I've always wanted to die of love anyway. Heaven knows, a man doesn't get many chances these days to go down in battle. So if I'm going to die in bed, let it be from love. 'Born into a wealthy family, he died of passion.' What more could you ask for? We all want romance, even if it means the agony of separation. The only real problem is that dying of lust is even harder than saving money."

"Quite a sense of humor, I must say." The priest laughed.

"No, I'm serious. That's why it sounds like a joke. I envy that fellow's luck, actually. Being able to find someone like that, a woman you'd kill yourself for."

"She is beautiful. There's no question about that. And not that hard to find, either. You wouldn't have to dive to the bottom of the sea or climb to heaven in order to meet her."

"So she's still alive."

"Yes. She lives right here."

"Here?"

"That's correct. Right here in Kunoya."

"In Kunoya?"

"Sir, on your way here today, you must have passed right by her house."

"Her house?" As he asked, the sight of the young weaver woman working amid the brilliant yellow of the rape blossoms flashed before his eyes. "You mean the young woman in the farmhouse?"

"No, no. I'm talking about a very wealthy man's wife."

"So it's not her," the priest's guest mumbled to himself. Then of the priest he asked, "A rich man's wife, is she? A flower with an owner."

"That's right. That's *why,* sir."

"Oh, I get it. An affair. So she's really that attractive, is she?"

"Definitely. In the summer months we get thousands of visitors from Tokyo, and some of the women are very striking. But not one of them comes close."

"So you're saying that if I saw her, I'd fall in love with her too, is that it? Sounds dangerous."

"Why?" the priest asked in a serious tone of voice.

"I'll have to be careful on the way home, I guess. So where is it? This rich man's house."

"It's on the corner, the two-story one."

"What?" The visitor shuddered.

9

The hut's thatched roof blended into the rape blossoms far below. The waves showed their white tips as the pine-blowing wind blew in a faint banner of mist. Down the mountainside, nothing jutted higher than the thatched roof of the hut, tucked among the soft crimson of plum blossoms.

"That's where the woman lives." Suspecting nothing, the priest continued. "She moved in last fall, just about the time I rented the hut out to the gentleman I mentioned to you. I won't reveal his name."

"That's fine with me."

"He was staying at that hut when he died one night in the ocean."

"Drowned?" the visitor asked.

"It seems so. His body washed up on the shore. Was it an accident? A suicide? Of course, everyone suspected suicide when they first heard of it. But, as I said, it seems his death was connected with that poem—"

"No kidding."

"Just two months after the gentleman passed away, she moved in over there." The priest pointed down the mountain toward the two-story house, his sleeves forming a veil of blackness. "At the time of the incident, the family was still living together in a house down by the water. That's the main residence, even now. But they also have a large store in Yokohama where the husband spends most of his time. Here in Kunoya, the wife lives quietly with a few other young women."

"So that's their second home."

"Actually, no. It gets a bit complicated. That two-story house *is* the main residence. That's where her husband was born. Back then, though, the family was just barely making it, and the house was nothing like it is now, just a leaky thatched roof that let in the rain and the moonlight. Tamawaki's father passed away a while ago. He was a tenant farmer. But extremely frugal. After saving up for a number of years, he was able to rent a small plot of land adjoining the back gate of our hut. This used to be quite a complex. I understand the head priest's retreat was there.

"Anyway, it was spring, time to plant beans—warm enough for the gentle heat waves to be rising from the paddy levees. Carrying a hoe on his shoulder, Tamawaki's father came to a spot at the bottom of the hill he was reclaiming. I heard it happened around noon, when his son came to call him in for lunch.

"It was cold when he set out early that morning, wearing a padded cotton coat, but the weather was good and he worked straight through. By noon he was hard at it, stripped to the waist, a towel wrapped around his head. As he had already taken care of his rented land, he was trying to increase his acreage by hacking away at the hill. When his boy showed up to call him in, he said, 'Let me take a smoke,' and hacked one last time at the mountainside. Then guess what happened? The earth suddenly grew soft, and his hoe sank deep into the ground. When he pulled it out, the hoe was wet and covered with something sticky and red."

"A corpse?" the visitor broke in.

"Oh, no." The priest shook his head. "Just what the doctor ordered."

"I see. Hidden treasure."

"That's right. When you're out on the ocean, the sight of red fish scales is startling indeed. And of all the colors that seep from the earth, the most surprising of all, more than purple or yellow or blue, is red.

" 'My god!' the old man thought, getting excited. Another two or three hacks, and suddenly he had a hole. He lay down against the mountain, and looked in like this."

10

"The red earth gaped like the open jaws of a huge snake. He could see something black inside. Reaching in with his hoe, he pulled it out. It was an urn.

"Apparently, the lid was broken, and the jar was completely filled with a red, shiny jelly. It was useless to him, so he thought nothing of smashing the jar into pieces. There was still another one inside the hole, lined up next to where the other had been. And this time it was the real thing.

"He hurriedly put the half-opened lid back on, and looked suspiciously over both shoulders. He glanced sharply at his son, who had been able to see everything because of where he was standing.

"Without even taking the time to put his clothes back on, he wrapped the urn in his padded coat and hefted it to his bare shoulders. Using his hoe for a walking stick, he carried the urn like a baby on his back. As the two walked together, he said to his son, 'Shut your mouth, now. Don't say nothin'. Don't you go talkin' to nobody.' When they got home, he closed all the shutters, spread a bamboo mat in front of the Buddhist altar, and poured the gold out in a pile! The coins had tarnished with age, but from that night on their little shack glowed even in the middle of the night. Or so the neighbors said.

"The jelly in the other urn was cinnabar of highest quality. From the broken vessel it spread over the mountainside, as brilliant as the rare cluster amaryllis, and finally disappeared in the spring rain.

"A few days passed, and the father, who had gone up to Tokyo on village business, visited a money changer at Shibaguchi. From his battered tobacco pouch he produced just one coin, covered with bits of tobacco. Wanting to see what he could get for it, he watched as the fingernails of the money changer's hand turned yellow as soon as he touched it. The coin was genuine all right. The offer was seven *ryō*, but Old Man Tamawaki received seven *ryō*, one *bu* for it. And that was how things got started.

"He visited various shops and patiently cashed in the gold, buying a secondhand boat that he used to transport firewood and charcoal. Eventually he got into the lumber trade. And when he had purchased seven boats, he sold them all off and bought land. Next, he enlarged his shop and went into the construction business.

"Now with a base established, he started renting his land and was able to make his money sitting down. He also lent money at high interest. The lush mountain forest was cut down, and the timber stacked in front of his shop kept disappearing and turning into money. Everything went just as planned. The renters would borrow on credit to buy up parts of the mountain. Then they would use up their capital to cut down the trees. Using the lumber as collateral, they would borrow more money. Soon they'd owe interest on what they had borrowed, so they'd cut down even more trees and use up more capital. Then they'd borrow again, and again there would be more interest to pay. The people borrowing from him would work hard cutting the trees and stacking them in front of his shop. When they started getting behind on their payments, they'd sell the lumber off at bargain prices, and the old man would get everything for a song and make even more money. People were always coming and going, never passing by without leaving something at his shop.

"His fortune grew, and everyone was astonished at how he had gained control of the entire mountain. Behind his back, though, they talked about how he had carried the urn home in his coat, and about how the treasure would someday bring trouble to his family."

"Envious people like that never find gold." The wanderer and the priest looked at each other and laughed.

"It's all up to fate. No matter how you try to hide things, somebody always finds out. And there's a story about that, too." The priest looked as though he had just remembered something.

"Now listen to this. The boy, Seinosuke, who was never to tell a soul about the money, went around saying, 'My father went out to work, and came home carrying Tempō coins without holes.' What do you think of that?" He laughed.

"Tempō coins without holes," the visitor repeated. "You mean, solid gold."

"Exactly. And that boy is now owner of the Tamawaki fortune. He's a member of parliament. Upper tax bracket. Tamawaki Seinosuke. And his wife, Mio, is the woman who wrote that poem. How's that for a story?"

11

"Here's your tea. As I said, it's nothing fancy. I can't even offer you a saucer, but then again, there's not much cleaning up to do. Make yourself at home. In the fall, you should see our persimmons and chestnuts. We chase the crows away and pick the persimmons. We shake the chestnuts down and scare away the shrikes. I'd be happy to give you some. Please, make yourself at home."

The priest took off his robe and hung it on a nail. The shadows of the plum trees played on the hut's *shōji,* showing through the white paper like corrections on a manuscript page. The priest brushed his robe.

Looking uphill from the hut, they could see the flight of stone steps hidden among the treetops, the roof of the main hall floating and sinking into the clouds of green, and the skirts of the yellow-green mountains crowding the veranda. The two of them relaxed beside a mosquito net, while butterflies fluttered about the rim of a stone-cold hibachi.

"I really couldn't relax up there in the main hall. But having tea like this after listening to your story is a nice touch. I must say, I do miss looking at that poem, though."

"With the stairway here, the sexy Buddha's just a dash away." The priest laughed. "To tell you the truth, I felt a little funny, too, as if I were making a confession. Here we can relax. As you can see, I really let down as soon as I get away from there. Shouldn't be like this, I guess. But anyway, we were talking about the man who used to live here."

"What kind of a person was he?"

"I can't say. Not that I didn't get a close look at him. He used to talk to me about the books he was reading. And I know how he made a living and all that sort of thing. But misinterpreting the scriptures is a sin, let alone gossiping about a man's life. I'd hate to spread false information about a dead man as that would be like passing judgment on him. I can tell you what I know about his relationship with Tamawaki's wife, though.

"It started one evening, the hottest time of the year. He had returned from a walk along the beach. 'My friend,' he said.

'Go down to the shore and take a look. I met the most beautiful woman.'

" 'Is that so? Where?'

" 'At the place where you get that wonderful view of the bay with Mount Fuji in the distance. You take the sandy road through the pines, cross the bridge, and the house is right there.'

"Do you know the place?" the priest asked the wanderer.

"Yes. I go there almost every day."

"There, by the bridge, where the pines grow on the sandbank in the middle of the river. That's the Tamawaki mansion. A huge front gate, a stone-covered entrance, and a large garden. It's modeled after some of the villas built here by the city people. The husband's very outgoing and likes to entertain a lot. Since the Kunoya house is a bit too far from the water, which is the main attraction around here, he took all his nicest things to the other place and made that into his main residence. He got married just last summer. So of course his wife was living with him there.

"Well, crossing the bridge, the gentleman suddenly saw the round bay. The water was as shiny as glass, as if he were looking at it through a telescope. And between the blue of the water and the white of the mountains was the pink of the woman's dress, a faint rainbow, waving before his eyes.

"It was Tamawaki's wife, though at the time he didn't know who she was. Neither did I. I jokingly pursued the matter, listening to his reports while fanning myself to keep cool.

"He took off his bathing cap. Sitting there on the veranda in his swimsuit, the gentleman said to me, 'Well, whoever she is, she's truly extraordinary.' "

12

"She must have seemed very dignified, to hear the way the gentleman talked about her," the priest continued. "He told me, 'There was another young woman following her, probably one of her helpers. She had on the same summer gown, and her sash was carefully tied. The two passed by together, and I only got a quick look. Her features were delicate, her complexion pale, and her lips very red.

" 'She was well dressed. But she seemed totally at ease, like just another person from the neighborhood. She wore a cap over her eyes and was looking down, letting the visor protect her face from the sun. As we passed each other, moving over to let the other by, she glanced up. Her eyelashes were dark. She looked at me coolly. It was as if the great Sesshu had dipped his brush into Murasaki Shibiku's inkwell—a portrait of the subtlest shading, lovelier than words can express. I, on the other hand, am a portrait of a more foolish sort for telling you all these things. Maybe after dinner tonight I'll get dressed and go out looking for melons in the moonlight.'

"That was all that happened that first night, sir. The next day he went out for a walk and returned at about the same time. I asked him jokingly, 'So how was Sesshu's brush today?'

" 'I couldn't tell,' he said. 'The cloudy weather kept her in, I guess.'

"Two or three days later I talked with him again, 'Doesn't clear up, does it? I suppose the clouds are still getting in the way.'

" 'Well, there's no "As I Crossed the Komatsu Bridge" chapter in *The Tale of Genji,* but today, as a matter of fact, on that bridge—'

" 'Then congratulations!' I said, and laughed.

" 'This time she was so dressed up she looked like a different person. Just as I was crossing the bridge, she came up the other side. This time she had three boys with her—the oldest about thirteen, another about ten, and another about seven or eight. She was patting the youngest on the shoulder, bending over and smiling at him, when they reached the top of the bridge.

" 'Her hair was done up in a full flower-moon coiffure that any woman would envy. She wore a pale, sky-blue singlet, almost transparent and covered with a medium-sized pattern. She looked good in a kimono.

" 'Her sash was silk gauze, sky blue and white. I didn't recognize the pattern, but she had it tied so it bulged out like a drum in the back, the white part of the sash meeting her waistband as if embracing the summer snow. I was struck by her beauty as she passed. And she, seeming to notice me, let both arms go limp and moved her shoulders ever so slightly.

" 'Don't ask me why, but as she passed by me I sat down on the bridge railing. Maybe I thought I was going to fall over. I knew that there was a river below, and if I fell in I was a dead man. The water wasn't that deep or fast, but I knew I wouldn't be able to get a rescue boat. And no one would help me even if I did call out. They'd think I was joking and let me die before their very eyes. I don't swim, you see.'

"I think the gentleman smiled when he said that," the priest continued. "But it later turned out to be true. Isn't it strange? When it comes to love's agony, we on the outside are more than willing to laugh and let a person die before our very eyes. From the start, I didn't take him seriously enough. I kept teasing him—'How's you-know-who?'—not realizing how perilous the matter was really becoming. You'd probably do the same."

How was the wanderer supposed to answer? He tapped the ashes from his pipe. "Well, I wonder. No, I don't think I'd have taken him that seriously either. When a young woman has her problems, there's always someone she can talk to. But a man? He probably just wanted to catch a fish in the river."

"Ha, ha, ha! That's a good one." The priest gave his knee a slap.

13

"Speaking of fish, there happened to be a man squatting on the far bank with his line out in the water. He made his living selling pots and pans at a shop on the riverbank. Looking at his trim figure, you'd have thought he was quite a tidy person. But in fact he was a little 'loose in the loincloth,' if you know what I mean. His fishing compulsion was most likely the result of something he had done in a former life. What a shameful sight!

"People around here call him Plate Head, because the bald spot in the middle of his head looks like an unglazed plate. Teeny Plate Head of the Riverbank. And it just so happened he was fishing there, right at that moment.

"The gentleman, sitting on the bridge railing, was watching the woman walk away—her forelocks trailing delicately, the nape of her neck white as snow. She was about to tap one of the boys on the back, the ten-year-old, who playfully grabbed her around the waist. As her fingers arched back like small fish, there came a booming voice. 'Young Master! You dropped your handkerchief!' It seems that Plate Head, content to let the fish take his bait, also had his eye on the woman.

"The oldest of the boys yelled something and ran back to get the white handkerchief. He picked it up off the bridge, stuffed it in the bosom of his kimono, and, without saying a word, ran back to Yamawaki's wife. As children do, he didn't bow or say a word of thanks.

"But the woman herself was grateful. She puckered her lips and almost touched her chin against her shoulder as she looked back and stared at the gentleman with her cool eyes, mistaking him for Plate Head. That's really when the two of them met for the first time.

"Caught up in the moment, he bowed back to her. And that was it. She eventually disappeared from sight. And when he looked, sir, there was Plate Head, staring at him.

"The gentleman broke out in a cold sweat. And no wonder. How embarrassing it must have been! I know it doesn't sound like much, but add a touch of the erotic and see what you get. First of all, there was the coarseness of the voice she had heard, and then the undignified way Plate Head called the boy 'Young Master' when he wasn't connected with the boy's father in any way. And stopping them like that was hardly what you'd call a show of refinement. Even Plate Head seemed a little embarrassed, having done the gentleman a favor. A strange situation, indeed. And, of course, the gentleman was in no position to thank him.

"From my point of view, it seemed that the incident had a dampening effect on the gentleman. He stayed in the hut for the next four or five days. Only then did he give me the details. As it turned out, that misunderstanding became the beginning of their relationship. They both exchanged greetings the next time they met. Imagine how happy that made him. Apparently that was exactly what he wanted.

"Oh, what a terrible thing to lose one's way! How heartless! Any fool would know better. The third time, he—"

"He met her?" the visitor asked, anticipating the answer.

"That's right. But this time it was the other way around. He was returning from the beach, and she was on her way there. They met at the place I described earlier, where you suddenly come onto the water.

"It was already quite dark. The hottest time of summer had just passed and the days were starting to grow shorter. He was coming back later and later from his walks. Tired of swatting mosquitoes, I had come up here and was sitting inside my mosquito net. When he got back and came to see me, he often said that he'd eaten somewhere else.

"So, this third time, it was already evening. He saw her face in the dim moonlight. It was she, he was sure, but this time accompanied by five men, one of them her husband. She was the only woman, surrounded by these fellows, noisily hurrying toward the beach. They were with her, and the gentleman was the only outsider. How could the two of them even have hoped to exchange glances? Now about those five men—"

14

"One had thick eyebrows and flared nostrils. Another, glaring downward, had a wide forehead and a pointed jaw. Still another man had his nose in the air and an unlit cigar sticking out of his mouth. And there was one who defiantly spun around and tapped the woman on her bottom with his fan. They were all dressed like commoners, each man wearing a thin summer kimono. That was fine, but one had on a light-yellow waistband, the knot tied casually and the ends of it hanging down to his calves. And someone else had a crimson under-sash wrapped high around his chest. How preposterous! The yellow waistband was the man's own, but the fellow with the crepe under-sash had stolen it from one of the young women. He was drunk, and it was his trophy.

"Needless to say, these men rubbed the gentleman the wrong way. Silhouetted against the sunset and the steadily growing waves, he imagined red and green demons leading a frail, helpless woman down to hell. Surrounded by them, she seemed dismal and desolate, and the sadness of it made him want to risk his very life for her salvation. He could imagine now what her life at home must be like, and he told me how uneasy it made him feel. But, sir, you must know how senseless it was for him to think that way.

"Have you ever seen pictures of angels descending from heaven into hell? They're quite marvelous, I think, because they give the impression that even the starving demons are going to be saved. And yet there's no need to feel sorry for someone like Benzaiten when she's surrounded by snakes because the serpents are really her servants. I'm afraid it was nothing but the gentleman's delusion."

The wanderer folded his arms. "You know, when a woman finds

out her lover has a beautiful wife, she gets jealous. But with a man it's the other way around."

"I see," said the priest. Now it was the wanderer's turn to philosophize.

"Men don't get jealous like that. If a man's lover forms a match with some other person—say the flower of Ono no Komachi and the moon of Ōe no Chisato—he seems relieved. On the other hand, the man with the light-yellow waistband and the one with the crimson undersash do make you wonder. If a Christian hears that his wife has dreamed about being embraced by Jesus, that's hardly the same as if she were seduced by a genie. Neither one is good, but if he had to pick, he'd pick the first, right? So you were saying, the woman was surrounded by these unsavory characters—"

"It was all because of the way Tamawaki's father got his money, carrying it home in his tattered coat, using the handle of his hoe for a walking stick. Tamawaki came to live as well as anyone. And though he was never cheap in his dealings with others, people of quality preferred to keep their distance. The sad truth is that he always associated with these questionable types."

"So what kind of a person is his wife?"

The priest nodded and cleared his throat. "Good question. She's about twenty-three or -four. Maybe twenty-five."

"With three children? You said the oldest one was thirteen."

"Yes. But none of them is hers."

"Stepchildren?"

"That's right. All three from a previous marriage. There's a story about Tamawaki's first wife, too, but we won't go into that. He married this one called Mio about two or three years ago.

"Now here's the thing. No one knows anything about her—where she was born, where she grew up, whose daughter or sister she might have been. Did Tamawaki acquire her as security for a loan? Did he buy her? Some said she was the daughter of an aristocrat who had run into hard times. Others said she came from a wealthy household that had fallen apart. Some were convinced she was a high-ranking geisha, or that she had once been a high-class prostitute. There was no end to the rumors flying about, including one theory that she was the guardian spirit of some bottomless lake. Nobody knew who she really was."

15

"I surely couldn't learn much about her when I saw her. Of course, a priest isn't supposed to have much of an eye for that sort of thing anyway—the shape of a woman's eyebrows, her eyes, and so forth. I didn't think she was that charming, but her mouth was well shaped, hardly the kind that looked as if it would utter a word of false praise. And she did seem intelligent, as though she understood the vanity of life and the true nature of love.

"Her body and face expressed a lot of feeling. She wasn't the kind of woman who would give the cold shoulder to a man, whether a boatman or a horseman or even a priest. Even if she didn't allow a relationship to develop, she would at least answer her suitor with an appropriate poem. The knot of her sash, the hem of her sleeve—with the slightest touch, a man's bones would melt with the dew of human passion.

"She was refined. But you'd have to say her face was more striking than angelic. She had the looks of a woman who would dress in a crimson skirt and read by candlelight in a dark castle keep, the dew dripping from her sleeves, her hair too fine to be washed with ordinary water. She was like a woman swimming alone in a mineral spring, far removed from any sign of human life, wringing her long black hair, her skin like snow. She didn't fill me with longing so much as with the impression that she possessed a boundless power that could bewitch a man in a single glance. In her was heaven and hell and this world of dust, making me think that both her sins and her punishments were profound.

"Anyway, to the gentleman who fell in love with her, those other men, the one with the yellow belt and the other with the crimson undersash, were mercenaries from hell dragging her to the beach at the witching hour. And that's why he ended up over at the Tamawaki mansion.

"At that spot where the river curves away from the beach road and runs along the back gate of the mansion, he stood in the shade of a reed fence and watched her and the men walking among the pine trees on the other side. She stood among the three men as they moved in a line together. He could see her face clearly but, because of the fence, her sash and skirt and everything from her shoulders down was hidden. The four moved among the flowing grass and Chinese bell flowers. Gradually, they disappeared, leaving him to wonder if they had sensed his presence and had led her off to some other part of the mansion. The fiendish-looking one in the lead seemed to be saying to him that he would never get to see the woman again, at least not until the next life. But then again, maybe all they were doing was enjoying the miniature hill that had been recently built in the garden.

"Finally, as if realizing he would have to meet her under different circumstances, he went and stood among the trees on the other side of the river. This, too, was Tamawaki's property, and he had begun clearing away some of the timber. There was a large tidal lake and an area of green grass, surrounded by the thick stand of pine. Right now the violets are in bloom. Come summer, there will be Chinese pinks. And in the fall, the bush clover. It's a quiet spot. You ought to go take a look."

"Sounds a little gloomy."

"Not at all. There's plenty of light. The perfect place to take a walk and read a book."

"What about snakes?" the wanderer suddenly asked.

"You don't like snakes?"

"Not really."

"Why not? I never understand why snakes have such a bad reputation. Take the time to look at them closely and you'll see they're very gentle creatures. Yes, they rise up and stare at you when you pass by on the road. But look back over your shoulder, and you'll see how they lower their heads and turn away in embarrassment. They're hardly what you'd call hateful animals." The priest laughed. "They have feelings, too, you know."

"That's even worse."

"I wouldn't worry. Snakes don't like salt water, so you won't find them near the lake. These days Tamawaki's wife isn't staying at the mansion, anyway. And all those holes in the ground? They're dark and empty and as numerous as the chambers in a wasp's nest. They're holes for crabs, actually, not for snakes. And they're so small you could never get your foot stuck in one."

16

"But to the gentleman, those holes must have seemed like eyes in a skull. He walked around the lake and then toward the river. No doubt the Tamawaki mansion began to seem like a prison for the woman he now loved.

"The tide ebbed and flowed almost imperceptibly. There against the dull-gray cliff, neither floating nor sinking, were five or six water-soaked logs, doomed eventually to fall apart and turn into hundreds of carp. No doubt he thought he could make them into a boat if he had a saw; or that he could fashion them into a raft if he only had rope enough to tie them together. But he had neither saw nor rope; and without them, how could he cross love's abyss? He could never do it, at least not while he was still alive. Only his soul would be able to make that journey.

"Before the gate, surrounded by the pine groves, he stood on tiptoe. To the butterflies, he must have seemed like a fickle man, wandering among the young trees, able to see the others only from the shoulders up, feeling that he himself had lost his legs and his feet, that he had become a bat fluttering about at midday.

"From the bosom of his kimono he produced a book and began to read.

Flames of tapers, hung on high,
Emblaze the gauze-screened air.
In the flowery chambers at night
Men crush the cinnabar-fed geckos.

The elephant's mouth puffs incense forth.
My Persian rug is warm.
The Dipper hangs o'er the walls.
I hear the water clock's gong.

Cold creeps through the eave-hanging net
As palace shadows darken.
The brilliant simurghs on lintels of blinds
Wear the scars of frost.

"Here in Japan, the image would probably be of a frog crying at the moon from where it sits beneath a balustrade. A few lines later, the poem reads "lock up this poor Chen," because Lady Chen, a favorite of Emperor Wen of Wei, later fell out of favor and was imprisoned.

In dreams I pass through the gates of my home,
Up past the sandy isles.
The River of Heaven curves down through the air
To meet the road on Long Island.

Chen is released from the palace and rides upon the back of a fish. Splaying the waves, she makes her escape.

"Quietly intoning the poem, the gentleman started to weep; his eyes watched the logs sink and rise and flap their fins as they approached the gate. He stared at them. He glared at them. Something was happening. The poem, by the way, is in the T'ang Collection, isn't it?"

"I wouldn't know," the visitor replied. "How did you say it went? She sees herself returning home in a dream, up past the sandy isles? It's almost as if her soul were wandering in a desert. 'The River of Heaven curves down through the air to meet the road on Long Island.' What a sad poem. It even makes *me* think she's being held prisoner. So, tell me, what happened next?"

"Next? Well, his face got thinner," the priest continued. "His eyes grew sunken. He turned pale. Then one day he finally got up enough energy to go into town and get a shave. And that's when it happened.

"He had his hair shampooed, and, for the first time in a long while, he felt refreshed. He walked out of the shop and saw, right across the street, one of those country mercantiles where they sell everything from tobacco to kitchenware. The ground in front of the shop door was sprinkled with water, and a lantern was hanging from the eaves. Someone had laid a porchlike platform over the gutter and into the street, and there two people sat facing each other playing *shōgi.* They were using thin slices of wood for missing pawns. A common practice, as you know.

"As he had nothing else to do, the gentleman went over and stood on the side of the road to watch the men. Both players were taking each other's castles one after another, slapping their pieces on the board, and shouting each time they triumphed. One of the players was tending his child, probably while his wife was at the bathhouse, holding the little boy on his lap and chewing on his pipe, cup facing down.

"Each time he shouted, it looked as though the pipe was going to hit the child on the head. The boy, his brow more wrinkled than his father's, was trying his best to grab it. Fortunately, the pipe wasn't lit, so while the father was moving around, trying to save his castle from being taken, the boy was in no danger of getting burned. The son would reach out. The father's castle would escape.

"Just as the child started drooling, his father suddenly shouted out his victory. Witnessing the fall of the opponent's general, a tall, barrel-chested, ruddy-faced Zen priest, who had been looking on with the corners of his huge mouth turned down, reached over and playfully grabbed the bridge of the winner's nose with his crowbar of a thumb. 'Good game!' " He laughed.

17

"Then the man sneezed, and the boy finally got a thump on the forehead. The tobacco fell out of the pipe, and the child began to cry. The laughter of a loser. The slobber of a babe. The monk who had pinched the father's nose now looked at his fingers in disgust.

" 'Time to go,' the gentleman thought, glancing back at the post office that was sandwiched between the mercantile and the reed screen of the adjoining house. That was when she emerged. Apparently a train had arrived at the station, because a horse-drawn carriage and five or six empty rickshaws rattled past on their way to pick up passengers. Tamawaki's wife stood looking out at the street from beneath the eaves of the post office, and her eyes squarely met the gentleman's.

"She saw him and drew back into the blind's shadow. As she retreated, he felt captivated by her eyes, which were still looking his way. He watched her there behind the screen. Her hair was piled on top of her head and held with a straight pin. Maybe that was why her eyebrows seemed longer than before. She wore a light summer kimono and had a golden chain, which looked as if it jingled as it quivered, dangling from her sash. As she continued to look back at him through the reed screen, his heart began to pound. Then her face showed at the edge of the screen, as though veiled in a mist. Dazzled by the sight of her, he bowed.

"She looked down at the ground, and just then, sir, the telephone rang. She had been waiting for the call.

"She disappeared into the telephone booth. But because the phone was close to the entrance, he could hear what she said.

" 'Hello. Yes, it's me. What happened? Why didn't you come? Yes, I do resent it. I can't sleep at night. I know the trains don't get here in the middle of the night. Still, I was wondering if you could come now.

" 'Me?' she continued. 'You should know. So what if you're far away? I can still hear your voice, even without a phone. But you can't hear me. That's right. So what? I know it's my fault. Don't come because you feel obligated. A little, maybe. No, you're not being ungrateful to your parents. It's a matter of life and death. Tonight, I'll wait up. No, don't say that. You know I won't sleep anyway. I do resent it. Then I'll meet you in my dreams. No, I can't wait.'

"Did she call her Mii-chan? Or Mitsu? It was a woman's name. 'Mii-chan, I'll meet you in my dreams,' she said, then hung up the receiver."

"I see." The wanderer was absorbed in the story.

"When the gentleman returned to the hut that night he was in a fine mood. I was, in the words of Shikō, 'dangling my legs from the veranda, in the cool of evening.' He jumped into the wooden bathtub by the well, and we chatted while he soaked in the hot water. Both of us had to talk loudly. But as we don't have neighbors, it didn't matter. It was a lot like talking on the phone.

" 'Well, priest,' he said to me, 'the spider's slid down his thread, shining in the moonlight, down from the plum leaf, down through the steam.' Oh, what a fine mood he was in!

" '*Banzai! Banzai!*' I said. 'So tonight you're incognito?'

" 'Of course,' he answered, soaking his head and looking up at the sky. He didn't have the slightest trace of shame on his face. Judging from his everyday behavior, I didn't think he seemed like the kind of man who would be interested in someone else's wife, no matter how desperately in love he might have been. I doubted that he was actually going to see her.

"We finished a meal of tofu garnished with greens and shared a fragrant white melon for dessert. Tightening his sash, he announced, 'I'm going over there.'

"I was shocked. And then he left, not down the steps toward the ocean, but up the hill toward the temple."

Although the sunlight was full around the priest and his visitor, a thin cloud lightly waved upon the mountain grass like the wings of a butterfly. Looking out past the eaves of the thatched hut, the wanderer could see that the mountain peak had become dark, hazy, and unbearably hot.

18

Rain? They say that when a snake comes out into the sunshine, there's sure to be a storm. And hadn't the wanderer already seen two snakes that day? Was it the covering of clouds that made the air feel so close? Perhaps that would explain the sound of flutes and drums coming from so far away, like the chirping of frogs from the other side of the mountain. And yet the sound also seemed close enough to touch—dreamy, muffled, like a gramophone playing in the fog, echoing in the distance.

The wanderer and the priest could hear something—a vague noise, with no distinguishable voices. It sounded as if the village's shutters, pillars, doors, paper screens, pots and pans were all stretching and yawning, bored by the lengthening days. It was still before noon, yet the sounds of people laughing excitedly and the occasional lowing of cattle carried to the hut on the gentle wind.

The wanderer listened attentively, and the priest commented, "Things are happening in the village today."

"A festival or something?"

"I thought you said you were staying near the station. It's right there in your neighborhood. They've remodeled the place for the emperor's visit."

People had been talking about the event for the past month, and the inauguration ceremony for the expansion was being held that day. A stage had been built at the station, actors from Tokyo had come, and some of the local people were also joining in the performances. The dumpling-tossing ceremony had already been held, and last night's celebrations had lasted until the early hours. When he set out this morning, the wanderer had had to work his way through the crowds in order to get away, but somehow he had completely forgotten about the festivities.

"I guess I got caught up in your story. Or maybe it's because this is such a quiet place. I forgot all about the celebration in town. In fact, the reason I came here was to get away from all the noise. But it looks like rain, don't you think?"

The priest looked up and out past the eaves of the thatched hut. "It's getting a little sticky. I doubt it will be much of a rain, though. I could lend you an umbrella, if you want. Stay as long as you like. That is, if you're not planning to see the play tonight. Strange, isn't it? You wanted to come visit the temple, but the music's so powerful it just won't let you ignore it. When it trails away you start feeling as though you've been cut off from the rest of the world. Strange. Gloomy. Sad."

"That's it, exactly."

"You know, people used to say that whenever they dug a well they could hear sounds coming from inside the earth—dogs and chickens, people's voices, the creaking of oxcart wheels. Maybe it was a little like what we're hearing now, coming from the beach down there, beneath the fog. See? You can just make out that spot of light down in the valley. What an unearthly noise! Like a band of badgers at night. Which reminds me of our gentlemen's story—"

The priest took a quick gulp of tea, then set down his cup.

"As I was saying, when evening came the gentleman dashed up the stone steps. It wasn't inspiration that drove him, only passion. Having lived here for a while, he was more than used to the steps. He quickly climbed to the main hall, where the moonlight shone on the pillars and wooden planks, and looked out at the burning clouds on the ocean's horizon, shimmering crimson, the chaos of twilight, water and mountains all absorbed into one huge lake, the light of the setting sun leaking through the eaves, wisps of clouds gradually disappearing like a scattering of red and white lotus blossoms. Had he stayed there on the veranda, aboard the Vessel of the Law, he wouldn't have had to drown in that sea of passion. But then a most unusual thing happened. He heard the sound of flutes and drums coming from behind the temple. Listen. Hear that? It came from exactly the opposite direction."

The priest stood and stuck a hand out past the eaves, pointing to the mountain to the left of the main hall. He got up so suddenly that his black robes blinded the wanderer's eyes, his sleeves covering the white paper doors like sumi ink flowing up to heaven.

19

"He passed before the temple and went off to the left, between the two cliffs that rise on both sides to make a tunnel to the sky. He continued through a grove of trees and came out on the back side of the mountain. The valley stretched below. Toward the water, the hills tapered off, revealing a road and a train passing by. In the other direction, the valley rose to meet the mountains that gradually accumulated, peak after peak, beneath a steadily thickening cover of clouds. Here and there, the ridges of the peaks clustered together like tree roots. In other places they surrounded broad fields, and in still others they encircled the small, charcoal-makers' huts.

"The road on which he stood ran along the crest of a cliff and seemed like the top of a giant levee. He followed it, passing through the darkness of thick woods, occasionally catching a glimpse of an island or white sails upon the water. It's different now, but at the time the grass grew so thick it was almost impenetrable. Nightingales sounded in the valley. Small, white-eyed birds sang on the peaks. At the base of the deep-blue cliffs, where violets bloom in the spring and gentians in the fall, the narrow mountain path, softly bubbling with springwater, was like the bottom of a boat. He passed through the grass growing on both sides and, after continuing for a little over a mile, came to the end of one range. Here the mountain became a cliff and marked the beginning of a new province, where the ocean takes on a different look.

"There on the ridge, facing away from the temple on this side of the mountain, sat a huge statue of Jizō. It's known as the Rock Jizō, bold-looking, and very roughly carved. In fact, it's more like a natural rock that just happens to look like a statue. Its face is very severe, very frightening when you're praying to it.

"The hall was still standing but badly neglected and tilting toward the cliff. The floor was so rotten your feet went right through it. The roof and pillars were tangled with spiderwebs, and the temple grounds were completely overgrown. The area was flat and open so he could stand and look out over the valley. Any mountain climber who accidentally stumbled onto such an eerie place would be terrified, I'm sure.

"The path that led down to the valley was a far cry from our stone steps. It was so steep, the gentleman had to dig his toes in and crawl down backwards. For a short distance the trail zigzagged down a slope covered with countless stone statues, each about a foot to a foot and a half tall, certainly no taller than three, lined up one after another like trees reaching for the sky. Showing their age, some had fallen over on the side of the path. But fortunately the gentleman didn't have to step over any on his way down. Though some were leaning, they were still lined up in straight rows.

"There's a saying about those statues: that a woman's name is carved on each, along with the year of her birth and an age. Some time ago, women came from all over the country and imbued the figures with their prayers. From standing in the dew and rain, the statues' black hair turned to frost and evaporated, their sleeves and skirts were transformed into moss, leaving only shadows. The ones with narrow, pointed faces are said to have been female at one time. There's no such thing as a Jizō with a woman's body, of course, but just hearing that makes them seem more sinister.

"I've told you too much about the gentleman already, but having thought things over, I must say that where he went wrong was in wandering down that mountain path, separating himself from the Kannon here at the temple."

"Oh, I see," the visitor said. "He was led on by those pagan stone statues." He sighed and looked the priest in the eyes.

"No, no. That's not what I mean. He wandered down that path, to the left of the temple and between the two cliffs, because of something else. Music! Close enough to reach out and touch! The villagers were stirring below, and the pounding of their drums rolled deeply into the mountains. He must have thought that if he could get around to the other side, he'd be able to get a view of the festivities. He wanted to look down and see everything.

"The moonlight was on the trees as he entered beneath them, pushing the grass aside and pressing ahead. Here and there window-like openings appeared where woodcutters and harvesters of mountain roots had cut paths down the mountainside to connect the main trail with the village below.

"When he turned on to one of the smaller paths, he found himself with a view in every direction. To the left, he saw the eaves of a beach house. Turning right, he saw a thatched roof. He turned off the trail at two or three other places to take stock of the situation. But no matter where he looked, he couldn't see anything that resembled a festival. Below him, the ocean was bright, the valley filled with mist."

20

"The music told him that if he could get past just one more clump of grass or one more stand of trees, he would be able to tell where the sounds were coming from. Two steps became three, five became ten. He advanced deeper and deeper into the woods, feeling that, having come this far, it would be a shame to go back. And somehow he also felt that the path ahead of him was brighter than the one behind. He started to hurry, and the trail began getting steeper and steeper until he found himself climbing into the darkness, tugging at the grass, pulling himself up to a flat area on top of a hill. It seemed as though the place had been leveled for construction; or maybe it was a graveyard. It was too dark to tell. Where was the moon? Hidden behind the clouds? Fallen into the sea? In one direction was the path that had brought him here and in the other, a cliff, or maybe a valley. He couldn't tell. The entire area was covered with haze. Far in the distance he saw color, as if someone had started a bonfire below. There was a spot of red deep in the valley; but from somewhere much closer came the sounds of pounding drums, whistling flutes, and shouting voices.

"What a lively procession! And yet it was impossible to say exactly where it was. Standing on the peak, the gentleman felt as though he had reached the Mino-Ōmi line, where the houses on either side are so close together that you can lie in bed and talk to someone across the border. He was prepared to witness a festival of some illusive kingdom where all emotions and customs and tales bore no resemblance to anything he knew. It was far too lively to be the evening before the main festival, so he thought that this must be the final night, even though the crowds had already peaked.

"As he stared into the darkness, his mind began to wander. There was something lonely about it all. He had come a long way. He was tired. But as soon as he thought of going back, the fire-brightened haze seemed to move as if coaxed by a wind, rising from the bottom of the valley, its color gradually gaining strength along the foothills until the mist-hidden mountain across the way flared before his eyes.

"It was then that he made up his mind. Walking straight ahead over the leveled area, he looked down the side of the mountain.

"Goodness! There it was, stretching all the way back toward the village at the bottom of the valley, the lights gradually brighter down the hill, where they reached a vivid glow. The entire procession was headed straight toward the spot where he was standing!

"Between him on one side and the mountain on the other was another flat place, shaped like a winnowing basket. Without losing his step, he quietly descended the hill until he was standing on level ground. One side of the area led to the road along which the procession was fast approaching. Closer to the valley, eight tatami mats had been laid out on a spot that had been worn bare of grass and was stained dark with oil."

The priest paused and pushed the porcelain hibachi toward the veranda. Looking down, he put the edge of his hand to the tatami.

"Standing on that bare ground, the gentleman thought he could make out the shape of someone sitting there."

The priest shifted his legs and put his hand on his knee. Glancing outside, his visitor noticed that the clouds had rolled up the mountain and were almost touching the eaves of the hut.

"The dark figure reached out and waved a hand, inviting him to come closer. The gentleman slowly stepped forward and stopped when he was five or six yards away. He observed the man, who, without looking up at him, reached over, took up the wooden clappers that were resting on the ground beside his knee, and knocked them together. *Kachi, kachi.* The sound echoed loudly, making him clench his teeth. And then—"

"What?"

"A curtain opened. It was nothing but a dirty, torn piece of cotton sail."

"A curtain?"

"That's right. He could see it through the haze, stretched out on the hillside across the way. The man sitting on the ground pulled the rope that opened it. Or so it seemed.

"There was a tomb carved into the hillside, quite a large one apparently, the opening about two yards across. That's not unusual around here. Tombs are all over in these mountains. The farmers use them for storing pickles or for growing vegetables. Anyway, when the curtain opened, he could see a stage."

21

"That made sense, as he had noticed what looked like coins scattered among the leaves on the ground. With the curtain open, he could see the shallow cavity carved straight back into the hill. No decorations. No props. And then there was something about the stage that made him want to look away. He felt a chill run through his body. No one else was there except the other man. Still, he couldn't just turn and walk away, so he nestled his hand inside the bosom of his kimono and watched.

"*Kotsu, kotsu.* Again came the gloomy, wet sound of the clappers knocking against each other. As he suspected, there was a rope running from the man's hand to the cave. Against the hillside, to the left and right of the stage, were more curtains, two strands of white mist that drifted toward the opening, then disappeared like smoke curling up in a whirlwind.

"Next there appeared a number of crudely carved caves, like blackened windows or boxes, forty or fifty in number, all in a row, and each one containing the figure of a woman. Some were sitting, some were upright, others were posed informally with one knee to the ground. Some were wearing only crimson underslips. Some had blood on their faces. Still others looked as if they had been bound. He glanced at them once, and suddenly they disappeared into the distance, becoming smaller and smaller until their faces were lilies blossoming in the valley.

"He shuddered. But before he could run away, the wooden clappers sounded again—*kon, kon.*

"It was then, sir, that someone emerged from one of the compartments that trailed off into the valley. It was a tiny figure of a woman who walked toward him without making a sound. By the time she finally reached the stage, she had grown to regular height.

Actually quite tall, she looked back over her sloping shoulders and stared seductively at the gentleman. What an exquisite sight! Tamawaki Mio."

22

"She wore a robe and a sash that was wrapped several times around her waist. Her bare feet were as white as frost, and she, still facing away, bent her knees, as if collapsing to the stage.

"Again the wooden clappers sounded. *Kan.*

"The gentleman stood transfixed. Then someone quickly stepped forward, brushing his back as he passed. It was a black shadow.

" 'Is someone else here?' he thought. But how could it be? And yet the shadow staggered onto the stage and sat down, back to back, with the woman. When it looked his way, the wanderer saw his own face. It was he."

"It was who?"

"The gentleman himself. Later he told me, 'If that had really been me on that stage, I should have died there.' I remember how he sighed and turned pale.

"He couldn't stop looking. His flesh was leaping and his blood on fire. He saw himself twisting around and looking rapturously at Tamawaki Mio's back. He saw himself use the tip of his finger to trace a peak and then a line, making a triangle on her pale robe.

"The gentleman's heart was filled with ice, his body soaked with cold sweat. The woman, Tamawaki, kept her head bowed.

"Next, he drew a square. I mean, he watched himself draw a square. His finger touched her knee and began to tremble.

"Then he drew a circle, a round line on her back; and just as he was completing the figure, the wind gusted, sweeping the earth and gouging the sky. The torch light down in the valley vanished completely, leaving a bright, delicate pink. Was that the beach? Or the color of the ocean? As he stood looking, he heard the rustle of leaves and scattered coins swirling in the wind. He realized that four or five people were huddled together, sitting close behind him, and that they, too, had been watching.

"The color of the woman's face shone through her bangs, making her look all the more attractive. A smile formed on her lips as she leaned back, resting against his leg, using his knee for a pillow. Her black hair flowed down as she looked up, and the white of her bosom appeared. Under her weight, the man fell back, and the stage slipped down and down into the earth.

"When the gentleman came to, he was still standing in the same place. He heard a voice that sounded all the way from the tops of the mountains to the valley. Losing his senses, he started running back to the temple. When he finally returned, I was sleeping inside my mosquito net. He embraced me and called out, 'Water, please!'

"His body was covered with cuts and drenched with dew. From that moment until daybreak, he confessed everything to me. The next day he slept straight through. In the afternoon, when Tamawaki's wife came to the temple with two of her young women, I did what I could to keep the gentleman from finding out she was here. Believe me, sir, it was hot, but I kept these doors shut tight.

"And that was when the poem appeared.

"For the next two or three days, the gentleman secluded himself, bound by his own terror, shut away from the world of delusion. I, of course, cared for him constantly. But when I took my eyes off him for one brief moment, he disappeared. A woodcutter came by just as it was getting dark. 'I just passed your visitor,' he said. 'Over there. By the Snake Cavern.'

"The Snake Cavern is on the other side of this mountain, two hills over. It's an ancient cave, filled with water. If you shout into the hole, it echoes back with a bottomless sound, stretching for twenty-five miles into the heart of the range. They say the water is connected with the ocean. But who really knows? The gentleman probably wanted to see a performance like the one he had seen a few nights before. We found his body in the ocean."

A storm came from the direction of the two-story house. It approached only as sound, dressed in robes and traveling up the path, not even dampening the grass. It had obviously been lured out by the woman's ghost. With cloud-black hair and peach-colored robes, the storm came to the garden, accompanied by the butterflies that had been fluttering above the field of rape blossoms. Standing alongside the shimmering waves of heat, it peered in softly through the window.

Part 2

The rain soon stopped and left a misty brocade of butterflies and flowers on the velvet moss of the garden and mountainside. The fragrance of rape blossoms lingered everywhere—in the hut, in the sitting room, on the sleeves of the priest and his visitor.

When the first rays of sunshine broke through, the priest offered to show the wanderer to the Snake Cavern on the other side of the mountain. But having heard the gentleman's story, the wanderer wasn't in the mood for walking the hills behind the temple. He'd pay his respects some other day, he thought, and finally took his leave.

He had no particular thoughts about the priest's story, neither judgments to make nor opinions to give. He had simply taken in all that had been said, filling his mind until his heart, too, had become full. Walking quietly alone, he felt the need to run the story through his mind again in an attempt to understand it. There was probably nothing to be suspicious about, as the story came from a priest; and he had no reason to doubt the man, even though the priest's parting words had seemed a bit abrupt: "See you."

He put the long flight of stone steps behind him and, seeing the two-story house ahead, let out a sigh. "In a nap at midday. . . ." He tried to mumble the lines of the poem, turning his head slightly to the side as he approached the house. His walking stick was getting in the way, so he tucked it under his arm, looking like a young kabuki actor who, after the curtain falls, makes an unhurried exit down the raised walkway. Though the sky had cleared and the sun was shining brightly, he walked very deliberately alongside the rape blossoms, not wanting to slip and fall.

"In a nap at midday, I met my beloved." He returned to the poem. "Then did I begin to believe in the things called dreams."

He raised his head slightly. An oak tree was growing horizontally from the cliff to his left. Looking at it from a distance, he saw that the leaves of the tree blotted out the bottom of the stone stairway. The hut would be just behind it and to the right.

He had just seen a dream, but then—

What about dreams? he thought. He felt as though he were seeing one now. If you wake up and realize you were asleep, then you know you were dreaming. But if you never wake up, how could it be a dream? Didn't someone say that the only difference between the mad and the sane is the length of one's periods of insanity? Like waves that grow wild in a blowing wind, everyone has times of madness. But the wind soon calms, and the waves end in a soothing dance. If not, then we begin to lose our minds, we who ply the seas of this floating world. And on the day that we pray for repose yet find no reprieve from the winds, we become seasick. Becoming seasick, we quickly go mad.

How perilous!

We find ourselves in the same situation when our dreams don't stop. If we can wake up, it's a dream. If we can't, then it's our reality. And yet, if it is in our dreams that we meet the people we love, why wouldn't we dream as much as we could? If the world asks, 'What's gotten into him?' The dreamer answers, 'Here I am,' fluttering in tandem with another butterfly, enjoying his enlightenment. Judging from what the priest had said, the gentleman who had been living in the hut must have had complete faith in his dreams.

The wanderer was consumed by these thoughts as he continued yielding to the butterfly's enticements. As the thread of his life stretched out along the quiet field of rape, suddenly from the side came a snow-white arm, a crimson collar, a figure with toes bent back and arms stretched out, riding upon a black horse, flying through the blue sky, shooting past the brim of his cap aboard a great wave, dancing over the rainbow in one stride.

When his flight of fancy ended, he realized he had just passed the spot where he had earlier encountered the snake in the rape field, and also the small house where the two women were working at their looms. This time he didn't hear the welcome sound of their shuttles at work, but rather the beating of drums coming from the distant train station. Like the second hand of a giant clock, the din reverberated in his chest.

It looked as though someone was waiting there beside the lattice fence just up ahead. Ah, it was the kind old man, slowly standing his hoe up, and smiling at him.

"On your way home?" the farmer greeted him.

"Oh, hello. Sorry about a while ago."

23

Smiling, the farmer let go of his hoe and pressed his hands together. "Thanks to you, I got a lot of praise."

"I hope I didn't put you out." The wanderer spoke calmly, seeming to enjoy his elevated status. The farmer, of course, was the man he had met on the way to the temple earlier that day.

"No trouble at all. The women in the house thanked me over and over. They really appreciated my going over there to tell them."

"So you took care of it, did you?"

"I pinned the snake down with a bamboo stick and tossed it into the woods over there by the hill. The young ladies told me not to kill it."

"Good thing you didn't. It would eventually have come around to me, since I was the one who pointed it out."

The old man laughed. "Forgive me for saying so, but you sure don't like snakes, do you? When the ladies there heard about it they almost broke down the door. I went in from the garden. They led me down the veranda to the kitchen, and I looked for it there. But, as you said, the snake was in the bathing area, over in the west corner, its tongue flicking from its mouth. It was bigger than I expected.

" 'Hey!' I said to it, 'If you want to take a bath, then make like a frog and *"jump into the ancient pond!"* What are you doing in the ladies' room? Powdering your face?' I pinned him down so he couldn't move and stood there thinking about what I should do with him. All the ladies were on tiptoe, trying to keep away. 'Don't kill it,' they said. 'Please, take it out. The lady of the house is ill and she worries about this sort of thing.' It wasn't a pretty sight, but since I didn't have any reason to kill it, I let it go in the bamboo grove on the hillside.

"Tamawaki's wife was sleeping upstairs. She wasn't feeling well. But just after the shower cleared, right there beneath that peach tree, where the drips were falling bigger than raindrops, she came out the back door and opened her purple parasol. 'Thank you,' she said to me. 'I hear the man who reported the snake went up to the temple. I don't suppose he's come back yet?'

" 'That I don't know,' I said. 'I didn't go inside for long. And I don't think the rain would have chased him home. My guess is he hasn't come back yet.'

" 'If you do see him, be sure to give him my thanks,' she said, then hopped over the gutter and started down the road."

It was the same road the wanderer was on.

"That's right. She went off toward the valley."

The old man turned toward the junction where the road from the temple led off toward the village of Kashiwabara. He moved with such energy that the wanderer couldn't help looking that way. It was the very road he would have to take to get home. He was trapped.

"Look. You can see it, there. On top of the bank."

It showed above the inviting grass, flowing like an embroidered sash, like the outline of a purple moon nestled in a thin mist stretched by the rain along the foot of the mountain, or like a bouquet of violets. It was an iris, a lavender silk umbrella, just the sort of thing you would expect an attractive woman to have.

When the wanderer saw it, he immediately felt the mist begin to wrap itself around his arm.

Here and there, tangled in the knot of spring scenery, the old man's finger pointed boorishly like a horseradish root. "There. In the shade of that umbrella." He laughed. "She's waiting for you."

24

Toppled onto the grass, the parasol caught the sunlight and glowed like the golden wings of insects gathered around a purple aster. From beneath the parasol's shadow, the woman's supple train stretched over the embankment. Its waving lines of silk crepe were coquettishly set off against the greenery, and the thin hem of her skirt, lying over the grass between her and the muddy road, flowed in soft curls down to her ankles. She had drawn her feet back in a modest pose, though her silk undergarment was exposed at the knees. She had taken off one of her sandals and left it on the road. One of her legs was bent back gracefully over the grass.

The wanderer tried to get past her, but felt himself slow to a halt. It was as if he had turned into that famous horseman who crossed the Uji Bridge at the witching hour of dusk, spurring his horse on and betting on the outcome. His approaching footsteps did not create the slightest echo against her purple shield or against the striking crimson skirts she had so nonchalantly thrown onto the embankment.

Feeling his chest tremble, he came to a standstill. He raised his shoulders and swung his stick, drawing a magic figure in the air in order to protect himself. Again he tried to get by.

The road at that point was so narrow that he was forced to step over the shoe she had taken off. It was a three-way junction. In one direction was the ocean, in another Kashiwabara village, and in the other the temple he had just visited. It was as if the road, because he was afraid to pass by the place where she was waiting, had turned into a monster's wooden bell hammer.

He turned and faced the wheat field, his back toward her, his face burning as if he had drunk too much wine. Oh, dear god! She actually spoke to him as he tried to step by.

He stood his ground, not breaking from his position, most likely feeling regret, as the tail of his horse, painted thickly with oil, slipped through the goblin's grasping claws.

He looked back at her. "Did you say something?"

What he actually saw wasn't a grinning, bald-headed goblin, but a face brightened by the parasol's purple-tinted sunlight, a violet lunar brilliance on a folding screen, her locks like clouds, her hairpin like a star, her lips a red blossom, the corners of her eyes like hollyhocks. Leaning back like a willow upon the grass, she was a dandelion with its skirts floating in the air.

She adjusted her collar, and her fish-white finger showed against bluish-purple. Her eyes caught his. "Pardon me," she said, smiling.

He looked for a path of escape.

"I was calling to you." She sat forward from her position on the embankment where she had been leaning back.

"What is it?" He looked directly at her. "What do you want?" His expression went blank.

"They said it was someone like you. Someone who was worried about us."

She pulled her sandal toward her with one foot; and as the silk of her kimono fluttered, its floral pattern appeared before his eyes and filled the air with its scent.

The woman got to her feet.

"You saved us from disaster." She bowed, revealing the nape of her neck.

The wanderer, conqueror of goblins, held his stick beneath his arm. He removed his helmet and said vaguely, "I'm afraid I don't know what you're talking about."

The woman laughed in a friendly way. "I see. Well, I'd call it a disaster. What if that snake had gotten into the sitting room and someone had found it there? We would have had to evacuate the entire house and go live somewhere else. But thanks to you we didn't have to."

"So how did you know it was me?" He blurted out the question, which didn't come out quite as planned.

"What's that?" She asked him to repeat what he had just said.

25

"I assume you're talking about the snake. But what I want to know is how you knew it was me. You took me by surprise." Ready to retreat quickly, he turned his horse around and smiled.

"See for yourself. We're in the middle of nowhere. No one ever comes through here. Since this morning, you're the only one I've seen who looks like you. And I know about what happened this morning."

"Then you heard it from the old man."

"I saw you from the second floor when you passed by the stone wall."

"So you saw the snake—"

"No. You were standing in the way, so I didn't have to." She tilted her head slightly, as if remembering something.

"But, you're supposed to be—" he blurted out.

"To be what?" She encouraged him to continue, but he had come to a dead end. He fiddled with his stick. He blinked. He pressed his lips together. "What is it?" She pursued the question. "You can ask me."

"Didn't they say you weren't feeling well? I thought you were supposed to be sleeping." He seemed flustered.

"Basking in the sun like this?"

"What?"

She peered into his eyes and then looked away, lightly touching the palm of her slender hand to her cheek. He heard the sound of her crimson undergarment moving against her snow-white arm, and the rustling of her kimono. "The truth is, I *was* sleeping."

"You were?"

"But at the time I wasn't asleep. I was awake." Her voice grew a bit louder. "I guess I'm not making much sense, am I?"

Her voice gained a tone of familiarity. Suddenly she turned away, showing the nape of her neck as she looked at the ground. One foot came back as she tried to maintain her balance.

"No. I wasn't sleeping. I saw you and then I started feeling ill. That's when I went to bed."

"Oh, really." Risking everything, he drew a step closer. "I guess you would have preferred to see the snake instead, right? So why did you stop me? To thank me for saving you from a 'disaster'? You know, at first I thought the snake was none of my business. But when I heard you were living alone in that house, I felt bad about not saying something even though I was just now trying to get away from you. When you make it seem like you owe me so much, it not only makes me feel bad but it looks bad, too. I'm no ghost. I'm not a spirit that goes around spreading some curse. I have a body. I have a shape. And your saying that you got sick after seeing me seems a bit cruel, I must say. If you hate to see me go out of my way to help you, just say so. I'd like to get by here anyway. Do I have to pretend I'm Benkei? If I can't, I'll try something else. Maybe I should go back to the temple and escape through the mountains."

He decided to fight back and sit himself down on the grassy embankment. But because he had been staring into the face of this demon, he lost his balance and, rather than sitting to the side, slipped and fell to the ground.

"Careful! You'll hurt yourself."

Did she speak too quickly?

Before his eyes, dazzling colors appeared through the mist. Her silk kimono opened at the knees, and, without fixing her skirts, she knelt lightly on one knee. The strap on his sandal was broken. She pushed it over to him and tried to help him get back to his feet. Both her hand and the colored handkerchief it held shone in the sunlight, releasing a fragrance as she gently touched him on the back.

26

Kannon, Goddess of Mercy! The wanderer silently prayed for help. His defenses had all come to naught.

"Your stockings are all covered with mud. Why don't you take them off and let me have them cleaned? I live right over there."

He hastily pulled back from her fingers as they reached for his leg. He collapsed onto the embankment, then sat up, the nape of his neck hot because of the warm grass. He was sweating. His face was flushed. His eyes were blinded by the intense spring light.

"Forget about my stupid stockings." His words sounded like something a second-rate storyteller would say. He shuddered. When his vision finally became clear, the woman was picking up his walking stick. She held it gracefully with both hands and stood before him in a relaxed fashion.

Her sash was tied with its ends hanging freely. Her lined kimono fit loosely on her shoulders. With the slight movement of her body, the crimson silk slipped down slightly over the edge of her sky-blue sash. The style of her clothing hardly matched the walking stick. She looked pitiful, crushed by love's burden, as if she had been taken prisoner and was being held captive in place of her husband.

"Thank you so much." Again, she took the initiative. "I'm not sure what I should do." Her eyes were half closed in thought. She seemed worried and weighed down with sadness, like the blind when they sigh. "I shouldn't have said that. I really didn't mean it that way. I didn't want to say I began feeling ill *because* I saw you. Even if that were true, how could I say such a thing? I saw you. And *then* I started to feel ill. . . ."

She repeated what she had just said, whispering to herself. "Please. I know you understand what I'm trying to say." She came closer and sat down. Leaning back, she spread her sleeves out on the embankment. She parted the green spring grass with her shoulder. Their skirts spread out toward the wheat field before them.

"I didn't mean to insult you. You understand that, don't you?"

"Yes."

"You do?"

He nodded, but he still seemed to be bothered by something.

"You're mean for getting mad at someone because of the way they talk," she said.

What a disagreeable woman! He looked at her, feeling as if he had to defend himself. "You should talk. I didn't get mad at you for the way you said it. You're the one with a bad temper. All I was doing was repeating what you said to me."

"Yes, and you lost your temper."

"No I didn't. I was going to apologize."

"But you should have known what I really meant. It's a matter of expression, you know. Like a morning-glory leaf. From the top it looks thin and flat, but underneath it's quite full. You should listen to the underside of language."

"The underside of language? Now just wait a minute." He closed his eyes, tilted his head back, and took a breath. "You're trying to tell me you meant the opposite of getting your feelings hurt. Which is this: that after you saw me, you felt better, right? So why don't you just leave me alone? It's perfectly clear that you're just playing around." He took her to task but laughed as he did.

She stared at him coolly. "You're such a complicated man. What did I say to make you talk that way to me? You shouldn't pick on people who are weaker than you. Can't you see I'm suffering?"

She put her hand on the grass and moved her knee. "Listen to what I have to say. All right?" She smiled as if enraptured. Her mouth was so seductive it seemed as though her teeth had been dyed black. "Let's suppose there's someone I dream about all the time, someone I long for. Can you imagine that?"

27

"Well, there is someone, and we can't be together. But I stay awake nights thinking of him. I'm distracted because of him. I even wonder if I'm not losing my mind. And if I can't be with him, then what about someone who looks like him? Suppose I heard that such a person had come from Tokyo, but that I hadn't had the chance to meet him yet. And then—how many years has it been? how many months?—I get a glimpse of someone who looks just like him. What would you think?"

She tried to pluck the tall horsetail that was casting a shadow near her hand. "That was a distressing moment for me. Afterward I had to lie down. I really don't know how to describe how I felt. But it was a bad feeling, as I told you. I don't know any other way to say it."

For a while, he said nothing. "So there *is* someone." He searched for a way to avoid the conversation.

"As if you didn't know."

Now she had him!

"What?"

"I said, 'As if you didn't know.' "

"Now look. You and I met just a minute ago. I don't even know your name. Why should I know anything about this man you're in love with?"

But from the poem—"In a nap at midday I met my beloved . . ." —he did know the name Mio. And, yes, he did want to know more about "those things called dreams."

"How did you know I wasn't feeling well?" she asked.

"That farmer mentioned it. He said you were upstairs when he went to catch the snake, and that you weren't feeling well. But he didn't say anything about your getting sick after seeing me. Why should I know anything? He did say you wanted to thank me, and then I really didn't know what to do. You see, my problem is that I can't get home without passing through here. If I had known it was going to be like this I would have crawled into a hole somewhere so I wouldn't have to meet you. How was I supposed to know you saw me from your window?"

"There you go again. If you doubt me that much, then I'll have to spell it out for you. See this glorious grass? These trees? They have blood and passion. They're hot beneath the sun's red light, and the earth is warm like skin. The light penetrates the bamboo grove, and the blossoms are without shadows. They bloom like fire, and when they flutter down onto the water, the stream becomes a red lacquered cup that slowly floats away. The ocean is blue wine, and the sky . . ."

She turned the white palm of her hand so it was facing upward.

"The sky is like a green oil. Viscous. No clouds, but still murky and full of dreams. The mountains are stuffed like velvet pillows. Here and there, the heat waves shimmer like thick coils of smoke rising fragrantly into the sleeves of a kimono. The larks are singing. In some faraway vale, the nightingale is calling, 'Isn't life a pleasure?' It has all it needs, and not a complaint to make. On a bright sunny afternoon like this, you close your eyes and right away you're drowsily dreaming. What do you think?"

"I don't know what I think." He looked away from the brightness of the spring day that her words had conjured. He focused on her.

"What are you feeling?"

He didn't answer.

"Are you having fun?"

"Fun?"

"Are you filled with joy?"

"Joy?"

"Do you feel alive?"

"Do you?" he countered.

"No, I feel sick, just the way I did when I saw you for the first time."

The wanderer sighed and took back his walking stick. Grabbing it with both hands, he held it near his knees, as if punting in the sea of love. Then he folded his arms and found himself staring at her.

28

"It's almost impossible to tell you how this sunny spring day makes me feel. It's like talking about a dream. This quiet sadness. Can't you feel it? It's like seeing the most vivid part of a dream, don't you think? It reminds me of when I was two or three, riding on my nurse's back, looking at a festival swirling around me.

"I feel more vulnerable in the spring than in the fall. That's why I'm so damp. This isn't sweat. It's something the sun has wrung from my heart. Not pain, not distress. More like blood being squeezed from the tips of a tree's tender leaves, as though my bones are being extracted and my skin is being melted. Yes, that's the perfect expression for times like this. I feel like I've turned into water, as though what's been melted of me will soon disappear, and that there will be tears—though neither of sadness nor of joy.

"Sometimes you cry when someone scolds you. Other times you cry when someone comforts you. But on a spring day like today, your tears are of this latter kind. I suppose they're sad. Yet there are different types of sadness. If fall is the sorrow of nature, then spring is the anguish of human life.

"Those people you see out there working in their fields—when fall comes they brace themselves, each doing his best not to be overwhelmed by melancholy. There's still strength in those dispirited legs. But in spring the strength is stolen away. They float up, as if they've been turned into butterflies or birds. They seem anxious, don't they?

"Invited by a warm, gentle wind, the soul becomes a dandelion blossom that suddenly turns into cotton and blows away. It's the feeling of fading into death after seeing paradise with your own eyes. Knowing its pleasure, you also understand that heaven is heartless, vulnerable, unreliable, sad.

"And when you cry out, is it because of sadness? Or is it just another indulgence?

"I feel as though I'm being sliced into pieces, as if my chest is being torn to shreds. It's neither painful nor prickling, more like a peach blossom in the sunlight, scattered to pieces, placid, serene, beautiful, and at the same time sad, as unreliable as a sky with no clouds or a green field turned into a sandy plain, like a previous existence, like what's before your eyes, like wanting to say what's in your heart but not being able to, something frustrating, regrettable, disturbing, irritating, more like being pulled into the earth than being lifted into the air. And that's why I had to lie down."

A serene look suddenly came to her face, like the sun shining brightly after a rainstorm.

"It bothers you when I talk this way, doesn't it? You still hold it against me because I said I felt ill after I saw you. Oh! Is something wrong?"

Staring vacantly into the air, listening without moving an inch of his body, the wanderer saw a violent rush of red and white swirling in the dazzling light of spring.

"I'm not feeling so well myself." He put one of his palms to his eyes.

"Why don't you lie down?"

"Maybe I will."

"Were you dreaming about something?" She spoke without thinking, then wondered if she had been too forward.

"If you took a nap feeling like this," he said. "I wonder what kind of a dream you'd have?"

"I'd see you."

"You'd what?"

"Like this. I'd see us just as we are."

"No. You'd dream of that man you love, the one you wanted to meet but couldn't."

"Yes, the one who looks like you."

"No, no."

They looked at each other, then threw down the freshly plucked grass they discovered in their hands.

"It's very quiet here. I suppose you're fond of this tranquility."

They could hear small birds constantly chirping in the pines on the mountainside.

29

"You know this place, Kashiwabara," the wanderer said. "It reminds me of a monster looking toward the sea. These foothills stretching down toward the water are like a mouth trying to gulp down heaven and earth, with rice paddies and wheat fields stuck in its molars. Look, out there in the valley, there's not a shadow anywhere. Those cloudlike shapes are nothing but wisps of mist. A serene landscape, all in all, but I think there's something disagreeable about it."

The woman trembled and said happily, "So you're feeling ill, too. I guess you didn't mind my story."

"Why should I?" He laughed.

Seeming a bit more relaxed, he looked back at the two-story house and the road that ran in front of it. The thatched roofs of the village and the leaves of the trees mixed with the crimson camellia blossoms. The rape field barely showed. It was cut off on one edge where it abutted the rice-seedling paddies. It stretched along the green of the foothills, turned a turgid ashen color, and continued until suddenly clipped on both sides by the mountain. Toward the far end of Kashiwabara, at a place where a low bank of mist seemed to be welling from the ground, was the station with its eerie echoes of flutes and drums. The wanderer stared vacantly in that direction.

"Over there," she said. "I heard the voice coming from that direction."

"What voice?"

"I was lying in bed, tossing and turning. I was feeling impatient, irritated, vexed, wretched. My whole body was tingling, and my bones were melting. And then the rain began to fall. It seemed to start over there, pounding on the eaves as it passed. I heard it in my sleep.

"I was listening to the festival music coming from the station, and maybe that's why. Look, even now it's still raining on the crowd over there. That's the only spot, where that mist is.

"The storyteller's voice came from that direction, with the rain, falling through the air. 'Yes, yes, yes. Listen up, everyone. Once again, your favorite "Life in Tokyo, Scenes of the City Vendors." The place is Kanda. Yes. In front of a wealthy merchant's shop. At the first light of dawn, the shop clerk is sweeping the street as a vendor passes by. *"Nattō! Nattō!"* he calls.'

"He had a thick, low, rattly voice. It was awful.

" 'Someone gave me a drink, and my voice is no good today,' he said. 'Please, help me out.'

"It was a disgusting sound, lingering like the tail of a falling star.

"I shuddered as I lay in bed, drawing my knees to my chest. And then I heard it again. 'Yes, yes.' This time a little closer.

"Eventually the man came right to our neighborhood, flitting like a plover from house to house, always saying the same thing, always begging for money. The warm, sticky rain seemed to be following him, going over there, coming over here, gradually walking this way.

"Tokyo, *nattō,* the merchant's shop, the clerk sweeping in front of the gate, all those things made me think of my past, of my parents and the place where I grew up. My body started to boil. Unable to bear any more, I bit the collar of my gown. I held myself in my own arms and fell into a trance. Finally, just as the rain started, the voice stopped in front of our house.

" 'Yes, yes, yes,' he repeated. 'Listen up, everyone. Once again, your favorite "Life in Tokyo, Scenes of the City Vendors." The place is Kanda. Yes. In front of a wealthy merchant's shop. At the first light of dawn, the shop clerk is sweeping the street as a vendor passes by. *"Nattō! Nattō!"* Yes. Someone gave me a drink, and my voice is no good today. Please, help me out.'

"He said exactly the same thing, in exactly the same way. By the time he reached my gate, I had heard him say his lines thirteen times, no more and no less."

30

"The maid didn't go out right away.

" 'Yes. Someone gave me a drink, and my voice is no good today. Please, help me out.'

"He coughed. It was disgusting.

" 'Help me. Someone gave me too much to drink, and I can't get my wind back. Help me. Please.'

"It was as though he were talking directly to me.

"When he said 'Please help me out,' he sounded so shameless. I could imagine him spitting all over everything.

"I heard the jingling of coins and the maid getting ready to go out.

" 'Mitsu? Mitsu?' I called to her. I had her come upstairs, where I was still in bed. 'What are you doing?' I asked. Even to me my voice sounded sharp.

" 'It's a minstrel.'

" 'A traveling performer?'

" 'Yes.'

"I could tell she was surprised. 'Don't give him any money. If he's a performer, let him perform. Tell him that. If he can't tell his stories, then he should call himself the beggar that he really is. Why should he drink until he can't do his job? He has no right provoking us with such arrogance.'

"I was filled with anger. My blood was boiling.

"I heard Mitsu's feet quietly descending the stairs.

"It turned out that he heard every word I said. I have a high voice, and he was standing right outside.

" 'What?' I heard him say in a challenging tone.

"I sat up in bed. I could hear the maid explaining to him that I was sick. And then I heard him ridiculing me. 'If she's sick, why doesn't she just drop dead? If she wants to get better, why doesn't she get better? What's all this whining?'

"I could just see his red face. I could see him snarling. Yes, that's just how it made me feel. 'All right, then. I will die. I'm not afraid of dying.' I stood up and walked feebly away from my bed. I fell to the floor and crawled toward the stairs. Just as I grabbed the balustrade, the rain started falling dark and heavy. I cried. The voice disappeared.

Did he go off somewhere? The rain stopped, and the bright sunlight showed again. Then I saw him standing barefooted, with a child strapped to his back. He was about forty, stoutly built, reminding me of the red ogres you see in paintings. That's the image that came to me just now as I was telling you about him.

"I thought of falling back into bed. But then I thought that if I went to sleep I might lose my mind, and so I came wandering out into the sunshine. Maybe I'm crazy, telling all these things to a stranger." She stared at the wanderer as if she had feelings for him. She had lovely eyes.

"Tell me. Do you really think there's such a thing as life after death?"

He didn't answer.

"It wouldn't matter if it were heaven or hell. If the person you love is there, you'd go as quickly as you could." She plucked at the horse-tail grass, one section at a time, entranced. "There's no way to know for sure. But it's too horrible to think that everything just ends when you die. If that's the way it is, it's probably better to live in agony, to be troubled and to waste away, never forgetting until the very end." She bit on the horsetails in her hand.

Amid the green of the embankment, both her skirt, thrown over the man's knees, and her sash became darker in hue. She spoke suddenly, now in a brash, flirtatious tone. "Stop that! What are you doing?"

She caught the wanderer, unable to answer her question about the afterlife, in the act of retrieving her notebook. It had an olive cover and a pink-ribbon binding, and was lying where it had fallen on the grass.

31

"Don't look at that! Give it back!"

She grabbed the edge of the notebook, but then drew her hand back. She turned straight ahead and faced the wheat field.

Sitting beneath the blue sky, he assumed a defiant posture, determined to change the subject. "You write poetry?"

She only laughed.

"You draw?"

She laughed again.

"I'd really like to take a look."

She had let go of the notebook, but her shoulder was still pressed against his. "Should I show you?"

He laughed innocently as the notebook fluttered open in his lap. The pages were like butterfly wings in his fingers. And there, written in pencil, was—

His face suddenly went pale.

They were written large and small, dark and light, all in confusion. Some were half-drawn, others misshapen, others trembling, some abandoned. He saw nothing but triangles, squares, and circles.

"What do you think? The people around here think I'm quite an artist. I come out to this embankment and this is what I do. Better than just sitting here, pretending I'm guarding the valley. My sketches are well regarded, you know. I was even thinking of bringing some brushes and art supplies out and setting up shop right here in the grass. Don't you think they're good?

"This triangle is a mountain, this square a rice paddy, and this circle the ocean. You can think of them that way. Or maybe the triangle is a doll of a young woman or a samurai dressed in a kimono, the square a body, and the circle a face.

"Or maybe it's something beneath the surface of the waves. If you ask the artist what she thinks these figures are, she'll say she doesn't know. And then you can make an arrogant face. Or else you can worship them as the posthumous name of the deceased."

The wanderer finally spoke up. "Posthumous name? What is it? Tell me the name!"

"Master Triangle, Round Round, Lord of the Square."

As she said this, she turned over and pressed her chest to the embankment, spreading her dyed sleeves over the grass, the skirts of her silk kimono trailing down to her calves. One leg was smoothly swimming as she raked the notebook toward her and started writing the three shapes one after another, as if jotting down a secret.

But then came the sound of drums to let them know they were no longer alone. Showing here and there in rich flashes of color, like a camellia blossom ablaze as it falls, spilling from behind the thatched roofs, hiding within the leaves along the rape field road, emerging lightning-quick above the pure yellow of blossoms, two dancers appeared like cocks flying and dancing about the eaves of a thatched hut—two red heads, two dragon heads, one high and another low, one leading, another following, entangled, mad, scraping the flowers, brushing the trees, there by the rape field, then gradually coming to the edge of the green wheat that stretched out from where Tamawaki Mio and the wanderer sat, finally passing in front of the gate of the two-story house. Dragon dancers!

They wore dirty yellow-green knickers. The dust kicked up by their muddy straw sandals seemed to float over the wheat field as they proceeded toward their destination. The drumming stopped as they quickly approached. They were itinerant dancers, the youngest about eight and the oldest about thirteen or fourteen. They cut across to the road leading to Kunoya, the red and white of peony blossoms showing brightly before the wanderer's eyes as the two quickly ran past.

"Wait. Just a minute." The woman called out and pushed herself up. The lion dancers kicked her clogs and sent them flying as she sat over on her side in the grass.

Both lions stopped and turned their heads toward her, their red hoods parted.

"You boys. Wait there, just a minute."

Ten, ten, ten. Again the small drum sounded. And then the big drum, *ton.* Coming alive to the sound, the lions began to shiver and dance. The small lion arched and bridged backward over the road. When he looked skyward, they could see his pale face—a round jaw, a well-shaped mouth, his double eyelids splashed with red.

32

"Oh, how marvelous! But don't get so twisted up on my account." She tried to settle them down, and eventually they came to a stop, their lions' heads towering in a heap. From beneath the red headpiece, a boy stood staring at her with round, pleasant eyes.

The other lion trembled until the drums fell silent.

The woman slid her knees over and pulled up her sash. She looked for her purse but found nothing.

"Wait. I want to give you a little something."

She quickly wrote a note in her book, ripped out the page, then handed it to the older boy. "Here. Take this over to that house on the corner. The one with two stories."

It looked as though she were writing a check.

The wanderer reached into the bosom of his kimono. "I have some change here," he said, but he was much too late.

"No. That's all right. Young man, go on. Go and get your money."

He held the stick for his drum in one hand. With the other he slowly reached out, then quickly grabbed the piece of paper. He gave her a bow and started off.

"And you. Come here."

The smaller of the two boys stepped forward.

He had a blank expression on his face, like a doll that had swallowed a stick. He only stared at her.

"How old are you?"

"Eight."

"Don't you have a mother?"

"Lion dancers don't have mothers."

"Even if you don't know about her, she may know about you."

Her white hand pulled him toward her. He fell back into her arms, his sandals rising toward the sky.

"See." She seemed calm as she looked back at the wanderer. "This boy could be my own child."

Suddenly the lion slipped out of her arms, twisting upside down, shaking its body, and then standing tall as if nothing had happened.

"Look at this!" The bigger lion rushed back. "Look! We're rich!" He bowed twice, hit his partner on the back, and struck his drum again. *Ten.*

"You don't have to do that."

The tail of the smaller lion settled to the ground as the boy inside the costume stared face to face with the other, who was still clutching the large piece of silver in his hand. Both of them were dumbfounded, their mouths agape like red lacquered trays, their eyes flashing.

"But I do have a message I want you to take for me. Wait just a second."

She immediately took up her pencil and wrote something in the margin of one of the pages of the triangles, squares, and circles. Her writing was like undulating water in the springtime. The wanderer saw what she wrote.

Should I have the chance
to see you again,
I'd search the four seas—
diving deep as the sea tangle.

He stared out at the ocean and its calm waves. Rising above the horizon, layered above the green wheat and the deep blue of the sea, was a mountain of snow. The reflection of Mount Fuji broke apart in the waves that lapped and thinly covered the sandy beach. The gables of a Western-style villa towered high in the sky. Two or three doves spread their wings and took to the air, loosely fluttering like a handkerchief.

She folded the message tightly and handed it to the younger dancer who, nodding his round face, seemed to understand. But suddenly he started off toward the two-story house, seeming to think he was supposed to deliver the message there.

"No. Not that way." She called to him. She smiled. "I just want you to take it with you. I'm not really sending it anywhere. If you drop it, that's fine. And if you lose it, that's all right too. It's a matter of emotion."

"You mean you just want him to take it?" the older lion asked. Receiving her nod, he showed a knowing face and plucked off the lion's mask from the younger boy, who looked up warily with surprise. "Put it in there so you don't lose it."

The two lions lined up together and bowed. Then they started away, fleeing for the ocean, their red hoods fluttering like mist upon the roots of the greening wheat.

33

Thirty minutes later, the wanderer appeared atop a sandy knoll that rose beside the indigo-colored Western villa, where he had seen the doves dancing in the sky.

Rather than continuing to the beach, he fell to the sand, looking exhausted, his legs stretched out before him. Wanting to see where Tamawaki Mio's message would go, he followed the dancing lions, using the occasion as an excuse to leave this woman who still seemed to have much more to say to him. Although his own legs were no match for those of the fleeing lions, he did manage to get away.

His first thought was to return to his room to take a nap. But on the road back from Kunoya, he saw a crowd of people gathered around the station. Among them were local talents—young men impersonating kabuki actors and married women stripping off their yellowish-green undergarments. They were performing some awful play, looking like goblins from Ōe Mountain. At any rate, he wasn't drawn to what was happening in the village at all.

So he chose to avoid the crowd and had come wandering through the rice paddies. Directly before him was the misty shawl of the mountain queen, perfectly shaped, white as snow. And as far as he could see the blue of the ocean stretched in every direction. On the beach were boats, creels, and strands of seaweed scattered about like horse fodder, none of the items trying to stand out from the others but all of them looking rather like old friends.

There were no other people around. It seemed like a moonlit night at midday, even quieter here than in the fields or in the mountains, every figure upon the white sand resembling the warmth of fog. In the blue sky, one dove danced while another, resisting the temptations of the gently lapping waves and the pressing breeze, remained steadfast upon its roost, cooing to the other. If a landscape as peaceful as this can't clear away the clouds in your heart, then it becomes like a bed that gives no rest.

When he thrust his hands into the sand, it formed neither depression nor mound. It simply crumbled into drops, building up around the edges. It was like grabbing water. And as he combed through the dune, he found only shells.

They were everywhere, even in places where there didn't seem to be any. He had only to part the sand to find more shells. Perhaps something else was living there, somewhere nearby. If he searched beneath the waves, he might find the very man who had been staying at the hut. Perhaps the gentleman was still alive and well. Isn't that why she had sent that message?

Should I have the chance
to see you again,
I'd search the four seas—
diving deep as the sea tangle.

The poem had originally been written by a beautiful woman who, in her own day, had dominated the world of Heian nobility. She was a person who once borrowed a straw raincoat from a peasant. He later composed a poem for her, and she was so moved by it that she invited him into her palace.

Needless to say, the one who copied this poem in her notebook was the same woman who scribbled the poem about dreaming at midday that he had seen earlier in the main hall of the temple—Tamawaki Mio.

Without having to give it much thought, he sensed a strange sort of resonance between Tamawaki's wife and the man who had been living in the temple hut. Their coming together was a promise they had made to each other in their dreams. The man, knowing the ways of both this world and the one beyond, had allowed himself to entertain a fantasy and then to make that fantasy his reality. As it turned out, it was an act that led him promptly to hell. Unlike him, the woman, half believing and half doubting, had felt compelled to express the turmoil in her heart, as if to say by her words that she would go to him as soon as she knew the truth of the afterlife, and as soon as she could ascertain where his spirit had gone.

Because of her hesitation, she could neither follow him nor keep on living. In spite of herself, she had been terrified of the street minstrel. Thinking he was a messenger from hell, she had started to lose her mind. Her determination to die was obvious proof of how demented she had become. From one point of view, the things the minstrel had talked about—the shop in Kanda, the purple dawn of Tokyo, the young shopkeeper sweeping the streets, and even the vendor's call—were perhaps the dawn of her life. And now, finally, the storm had come.

Be that as it may, he still wondered about the "message" and what had become of it. It seemed that Tamawaki's wife was trying to use it to divine the existence of the afterlife, and it bothered him that the dancers, rather than putting the poem away in a pouch, or sticking it into a sash, or placing it in a sleeve, had simply tucked it away somewhere inside the lion's head and run off. Doing whatever they could for their divine benefactor, for this woman who didn't expect them to dance yet showered them with silver, they accepted the poem as a matter of course and had put it in the most important part of their costume.

If a bird snatched the poem away, would the woman, believing she would meet her lover in the sky, grow wings and fly away? Hardly. And if a sheep devoured the piece of paper, would the lion dancers ever bother to come back and tell her what had happened?

The wanderer continued to work his hands through the sand. He looked down at the various shells that sifted out and mumbled the lines of the poem once again.

Should I have the chance
to see you again,
I'd search the four seas—
diving deep as the sea tangle.

He still heard no answer from the shells.

If they were able to speak for the great waters, then this colorful blizzard of blossoms strewn over the beach would never cease its whispering. Still, whether scooped from the sand or gathered by small children, the tiny shells were mute.

He threw them away and flopped over onto his side. The sand beneath his hips started to slide away, but there was no danger of being buried. With half-closed eyes, he looked toward the Nakitsuru Cape and, at a place about halfway there, saw the brilliant flickering of sea fire. It was the lion dancers' red costumes.

The two emerged from their clothes. From the cape all the way over to the small cliffs, no one else could be seen. With the play being performed at the station, drawing crowds from town and from the surrounding villages, who was going to be interested in watching a lion dance? Their job was to writhe through the crowds like mosquito larvae, but today would be a day of rest.

Still wearing their gaiters, they walked along the beach, one leading, one following, one moving ahead then falling behind, each carrying his lion's head along the edge of the surf's white line. Finally, the older boy walked away from the water and plopped down on the sand to rest, his straw sandals pointing toward the scattered strands of seaweed glistening like rays of sunlight.

But the smaller lion sprang to life, now charging the waves, now fleeing from them. To the wanderer, it felt more like observing an orphan than watching his own child play. Such a pitiful sight, to be taunted by the waves of the floating world. The lion's head had become enraged and was ferociously fighting back.

Win! This is a battle you must win!

The older one made a pillow of his cape and lay down, propping his knees up like small mountains, while the younger boy took off his sandals and started walking barefoot, playing in the water, skipping sideways along the beach. He stopped to take off his gaiters. He entered the water until he was knee-deep and stood quietly for a moment. Then he went back to the beach and took off his skirt. With his shirt rolled up, he walked in up to his waist and jumped the waves two or three times. Then he hurriedly returned to the beach again, took off all his clothes, and, now completely naked, dove straight into the water. Such admirable courage! Yet it didn't seem as though he knew how to swim. He struggled vigorously, fighting back at the water, which wrapped the child up like lightning, flying right and left as he struck at the waves with his hands and kicked with his feet. The wanderer could see splashes but heard no sound. The lion had become an infant, the white light patting his head and the green waves embracing his chest as if he were some blessed child and heaven and earth were giving him his postpartum bath.

The wanderer suddenly got to his feet and whispered a prayer for the child's safety.

Afterward he heard that the boy's youthful heart had been so overjoyed because of the money they received that he wanted to repay the kindness of that particular stretch of ocean. After playing for a while, he came out of the water and onto the beach. He leaned over the sleeping lion's shoulders, and when his partner awoke and turned over, he grabbed his lion's head and put it on his wet body.

He jumped back into the water and kept swimming until he had gone out much too far, his wake trailing back in two lines that spread in a V over the water. Heading toward Izu Cape, the lion's head became a small dot on the horizon.

Just as the wanderer glanced over at the other boy sitting cross-legged on the beach, he heard the sound of his drum—*ten, ten, ten!*—marking the rhythm of the waves. A pattern spread on the oil-like surface of the ocean; and, as the drum sounded, the boy rose up in the water and the lion's head flipped upside down.

The dancing had probably made the boy dizzy. How terrible that Tamawaki Mio's message to her lover in the other world was still inside the lion's head! Suddenly the wanderer lost sight of the young boy. He waited, but the boy didn't come back to the surface.

The drumming stopped, and the older boy on the beach stood up straight. Then he started sprinting toward the sandy hillock, straight toward the wanderer. He carried all traces of his having been on the beach with him—his skirts, his kimono, his leggings, his drum, his sandals. Kicking up the sand as he ran, he continued his escape from the water.

The waves pounded loosely.

Two or three others from the village came running up, all of them shouting and laughing loudly.

"The fool."

"The stupid idiot."

And when a policeman finally showed up, the wanderer went over to him. "A lion dancer—"

"Yes, I know. . . ."

They didn't find the body. It wasn't until the next day, with the low tide at dawn, that they discovered two people on the rocks at Cape Nakitsuru, the exact spot where the man who had stayed at the temple last summer was found. The boy's head was like a jewel pressed against the woman's breast, the red lion's cape still wet and tangled around her white arm. Beautiful and alluring, Tamawaki Mio had finally discovered the destination of the dead.

The wanderer would never forget how they had parted at the embankment, how he had looked back and seen her, holding her purple parasol to the side, her black hair weighing down upon her as she watched him walk away. As the sand on the beach spread and drew back soundlessly, hollowing out and filling back in, he thought of how the waves must have ravished her. From the sand there appeared only beautiful bones and the color of shells—red of the sun, white of the beach, green of the waves.

Osen and Sōkichi

(*Baishoku kamonanban,* 1920)

I'm embarrassed to say that the first thing that caught his eye was the scarlet of her crepe undergarment, bright as flame and dappled with cinnabar. Her skirts weren't folded back but hiked up high and held between her knees, allowing the crepe slip to flow softly down, hugging her white ankles, which were apparently being spared the kimono's unpleasant wetness. On her bare feet, so white they brightened the crimson around them, the woman wore thick, lacquered clogs, fastened with wisteria-colored thongs and splashed with mud. With one thigh twisted inward and feet slightly pigeon-toed, she sat in a corner of the waiting room as the rain continued to fall.

It was late in the afternoon, already past five, but the sky of that spring day was still bright above the platform at Mansei Bridge Station. Willows faintly glowing, cherry trees in bud, yesterday, today . . . just as Tokyo turned so intently toward the height of spring, coming alive with greens and crimsons and pale mists of lavender, the city was suddenly engulfed in a rain too heavy for the season. The land, the people, even the boats on Kanda River were darkened and drenched with the downpour. It wasn't the crimson plum nor the scarlet peach but the flowering quince that suddenly bloomed, as if dripping with blood, startling those who saw it.

Among the surprised was Hata Sōkichi, noted surgeon and scholar who, having recently returned to Japan after studying abroad, was working at the University Hospital's department of internal medicine. Noticing the color, he became the protagonist of this story.

He was a man of simple tastes, indifferent to matters of appearance. On his regular commute from Shiba-no-Takanawa to the hospital, it was his custom to take the train as far as Ochanomizu, then to walk the rest of the way. But after five or six days of steady rain, the roads had become seas of mud; and the commuters, dressed in dark suits and wearing leather shoes, looked like badgers sailing mud boats, as "The Legend of Kachikachi" puts it.

Although his fair skin and straight nose made him look more like the rabbit who tricked the badger, Hata Sōkichi was no exception. Intimidated by the muddy streets, he had taken the Hongō Street trolley as far as Mansei Bridge, where he skirted the bronze statue, passed beneath the red-brick overpass, then climbed the stone steps. With a minimum of walking, he planned to connect with the Kōbu Line, which would take him through the center of the city to his destination.

But a plan is merely a plan. It was a bad time of day to be traveling, and the rain had only made matters worse. Certainly, he had been prepared for a crowd at Mansei Bridge Station, but not for this black mountain of bodies that boiled and shoved around the tracks, pressing ahead as if to witness a fire or a flood. On the right stood the people bound for Nakano, and on the left those for Shinagawa, each side forming walls of two or more deep, even spilling onto the tracks here and there.

The train would soon come. But Sōkichi, knowing it would be impossible for everyone to board, shook the rain from his umbrella and, lightly holding it beneath his arm, quickly pulled his leather gloves over his wrists. His eye spotted the less crowded, greenhouse-like area on the platform, and he soon found himself stepping into a waiting room that smelled of rain and warm bodies. His muddy shoes were tiptoeing across the wet floor when he happened to see the startling color. He immediately remembered the large brazier in the middle of the main platform; and, looking away from the undergarment's crimson flame, he began side-stepping his way out.

But there by the doorway, suddenly, red once again.

1

This time it was only the cap of a station attendant. He stood with his arms folded, leaning back against a pillar, the black mountain of people surrounding him. When Sōkichi stuck his head out the door, the sparsely bearded redcap glanced over sullenly and said, "No power on the inbound. Breakdown on the outbound." He spoke mechanically, as if that were all he needed to say. Pressing the back of his neck against the pillar, he had placed himself above the fray.

"You say the power's out?"

"On the inbound. Breakdown on the outbound."

At once a chorus of response: "Oh, no!"

"Damn it all!"

"Just what we needed—"

A young schoolgirl, catching the crowd's frustration, hunched her shoulders and mumbled, "What'll we do now?" Judging from the redcap's repetitious delivery, none of the passengers was hearing the bad news for the first time, however.

Lying below this restless crowd were the railroad tracks, shaded from the daylight, curved like an inlet in this urban sea of mud. "Take your time," they seemed to say. "You might catch a mudfish here." The steel rails were restful and still, yet they laughed coldly and bared their dimly shining teeth against the background of the embankment.

Perhaps we can forgive the redcap for the indifference of his words; but surely we would require the derby-wearing professor, recently returned from abroad and looking quite at home in his three-piece suit, to maintain his composure, though jostled by the crowd.

Sōkichi was not a smoker, but he made an about-face to get to the brazier. Looking down at his shoes, he caught another glimpse of the crimson slip that flowed above the drenched earthen floor like a carp leaping into the air. Just then, the woman sitting next to the crimson lady rose from her seat. They were probably traveling together. The one standing was tall, dressed in a Shimada half-coat, her hair done up on her head. She had a long face and distinct features. First they astonished Sōkichi, then left him puzzled.

She reminded him of his cousin's wife. Although he was close to his cousin, his schedule of late had prevented them from staying in touch with each other. But he had attended his wedding, and the resemblance of the woman to his cousin's bride was so striking that he couldn't help gasping aloud. Actually, it wasn't the resemblance that startled him, nor that he should meet her in a place like this. It was more the impertinence with which she treated him, letting their eyes meet but then, as if he were a perfect stranger, looking away and out the window at the rainy sky.

She must be someone else. But her height, the unevenness of her hairline, her pale complexion, her light-blue hair ribbons, the comely shape of her hairdo, even the expression of her eyes when she looked up, all reminded him of his cousin's wife. When most women would knit their eyebrows, his cousin's wife had a habit of crinkling her nose, just as the woman was doing now. She was obviously tired from waiting for the train and putting up with the storm; her misery showed in the wrinkles around her mouth. Yes, she was a stranger. Yet Sōkichi still had to stop himself from automatically stepping forward and doffing his hat in greeting. Turning away in embarrassment, he found himself looking at the trees around the Kanda Myōjin temple, clustered among the misty, cloud-touched roofs of Shitaya and Kanda. The woman with the crimson slip was staring in the same direction.

2

She turned her proud face to the side, until the white makeup on her chin was about to touch her chest.

Startled, Sōkichi looked at her again and was reminded of someone else. The crimson woman had her hair pulled back on one side and fastened with a comb. She wore a black, formal jacket that rode low on her sloping shoulders. One delicate hand was concealed beneath the loosely flowing collar, while the other guarded a yellowish-green opera bag that rested on her knees. As she was clearly over thirty years old, the simple handbag looked as though it was meant to be a gift for a child. Taken together, her crimson undergarment, her unstockinged feet, the suggestive hairdo, and the formal jacket gave an impression of discord. She had painted her face with a thick, white paste and had enlarged her lips with a red ring of lipstick. As she looked toward the distant temple, her back straight and her chin held high, she seemed like a puppet come to life, her large eyes intently focused and the narrow collar of her kimono trailing down the pure white of her throat. She was more awesome than beautiful. Her eyebrows were incomparably lovely, gentle, and well-shaped. Those eyebrows, he knew, could only mean that she was the one.

In truth, the resemblance wasn't as perfect as that between his cousin and the woman traveling with her. Maybe he had been so struck by the match that the image so deeply implanted in his mind now forced itself upon the crimson woman. But those eyebrows. Sōkichi felt as if he had suddenly swallowed the crescent moon, and that it was sparkling in his heart with a joyous light.

Osen was her name, and she was the woman who once saved Sōkichi's life. It happened at the very spot where the crimson lady was now staring, the Myōjin Shrine.

"Almost too late! A razor!"

Even now, the sight of the temple filled him with terror. The rain clouds hovering over the wood seemed like a horrifying mask painted with lines of dreary gray. The roofs of the houses around the temple looked like rows of black teeth biting down on each other. Here and there, two or three red-brick buildings stood with their tin roofs torn up and sticking into the sky like the bright-red gums of a man-eating goblin. To those who see only the misty showers of spring, that wood, that grove of trees, must seem like three or four eyebrow brushes standing in a row. But to Sōkichi, recalling the time he nearly killed himself, the same trees resembled an untrimmed beard growing wildly into the sky.

Yes, rising like wild geese into that sky were the eyebrows of the crimson lady! Sōkichi glanced at the woman again. Her eyes were fixed, unblinking, staring at the same place.

Was it Osen?

His heart pounded like the sea; and the train station turned like the deck of a great ship until its bow pointed straight toward the Myōjin wood, which now seemed close enough to touch.

"Sloping down in that direction. That's Myōjin Hill."

In the house to the right and all the way to the end of the alley—

On the morning of that fateful day, Sōkichi had had one of his friends shave the boyish beard from his face. And that evening in the Myōjin temple grounds, he put the same razor to his throat!

But wait. I'm losing control of the story.

Sōkichi had come up to Tokyo without any definite plans and without a penny to spend on an education. As he had nowhere to call his own, he joined a gang of vagabond day laborers who helped him stay alive. These were people who, through indolence and dissipation, had been forgotten by the world. They were failed medical students, some of them well along in years—some even with wives, shabby politicians, businessmen of the lowest order, charlatans, and a few who were working toward their goal of becoming policemen someday.

He lived in a row house on Myōjin Hill with a half-starved ex-medical student named Matsuda, who was staying there with his wife. At the end of their street, fronted by a willow tree and a lantern, was a room overlooking the city, the perfect place for someone's kept mistress. Her name was Osen, a woman as lovely as a dewdrop. She was the one the crimson lady resembled.

3

Osen made her way through the world secretly. She was mistress to the leader of their group, an enormous statue of a man named Kumazawa, who, people said, was destined to become a successful businessman someday. Ostensibly, he had ransomed her from a brothel, but actually he had persuaded her to run away with him to Myōjin Hill, where he kept her secretly as his own. She was, of course, a prostitute. But Sōkichi was ignorant, then and now, of what exactly her status had been. At the time, she was simply a beautiful young woman, three or four years older than he, maybe more? To him she was the charming Osen.

It had been raining until the night before, just as it was now. But on that morning in March, the clouds had cleared like a flower in bloom. Although it was already ten, breakfast was yet to come. (I have to ask those of you who have never experienced real hunger to try to imagine what it must have been like for the boy.) No matter how long Sōkichi waited, there was nothing to eat.

Shortly after sunset the evening before, an order had been placed at the mistress' quarters for tempura-on-rice; and then again at one in the morning came a delivery of noodles that wafted their aroma all the way to Sōkichi's pillow. Knowing food had been brought in, he went to see if there might be a left-over morsel . . . and because the weather was good today he was even hungrier than usual! Holding his growling stomach, he opened the lattice door to the narrow street, lined on both sides with houses fronted with gutters, just as three men appeared from the shadows of the willow tree at the end of the alley. The broad-shouldered one, wearing a soiled cotton jacket, was Matsuda, owner of the row house. He glanced over at Sōkichi, who drew back into the entrance. Matsuda lifted his little finger. "What's she doing?" he asked in a quiet voice.

"She's still asleep."

With no real reason to join the waking world, Matsuda's wife was still wrapped in her blanket, sound asleep. Hearing Sōkichi's report, Matsuda stuck his tongue out at his wife and passed by in silence.

The next one to appear was a handsome priest, slender-faced and pale, his freshly shaven head tinged with a shadow of stubble. He wore a formal, black half-coat over his gray kimono. Actually, the jacket was Osen's, its crepe sleeves lined with red. Though he had come to their street just the night before, holding his crystal-beaded rosary and wearing a purple surplice draped like a precious cloud over his shoulders, now he was wearing a kept woman's clothes. And right behind him followed a dark-skinned, sunken-eyed, large-mouthed politician-turned-businessman. As he walked past, he pretended to strike the priest's round head with his fist, grinning and looking out the corner of his eye toward Sōkichi. Having forsaken the world of politics, he had shed his formal attire and now wore a short cotton jacket and knit pants. He was called Small Plate because of his saucer-sized bald spot.

All three men had spent the night playing cards and were now on their way to the public bathhouse. Headed the opposite direction, Sōkichi wandered over to where Matsuda's woman lived with Kumazawa's mistress, Osen. Not only did he find nothing to eat, but he was immediately put to work, cleaning up after the men.

"Sorry to make you do housework." Osen, holding the skirts of her many-layered kimono, picked up her black velvet cushion and retreated from her place before the brazier. Beneath the kimono was the enticing undergarment, tied up with a narrow under-sash.

"Why be sorry?" laughed a short, rotund man named Amaya. "The boy's ours, isn't he?" Amaya's hair was long and uneven. He had a pot belly, around which he wore a stiff merchant's sash and an apron tied neatly with a plaited cord. He, too, was a failed medical student, now preparing for a career in business. Amaya and Osen went into the next room, which they shared with Matsuda's mistress, who was already well along in years. Sōkichi, weak with hunger, his stomach growling wretchedly, managed to get the sweeping done.

"Good job! Nice work!" Amaya said happily. "Please, madame." He turned to Osen, picking up some cushions and returning them to the brazier. For such a stocky man he was surprisingly quick. Until a few days before, he had been living across the alley in the same row house as Sōkichi, lounging around on a rented quilt as if he were a potato worm. But Kumazawa was often away on business and brought Amaya over to the second house to keep an eye on Osen and take care of things generally. Because she was Kumazawa's lover, Osen was considered Amaya's better, and his attentiveness toward her was only to be expected.

"There," he fluffed up a matching cushion for her, turned it over, then backed away. "If it pleases your highness." In word and spirit he was witty and light, but the movements of his body were jerky, as if his body were a huge stone. And no wonder: he had been stricken with beriberi. Though he had been able to stay up playing cards with everyone else, he didn't have the strength to walk with the others to the bathhouse.

"Please don't bother." Osen entered from the next room, holding her skirts of printed silk off the floor. A comb held her hair on top of her head.

4

It was still too early in the year for cherry blossoms. As Osen took her place by the brazier, a branch of flowering quince, or some other flower, accompanied by the faint scent of sunshine, threw its silhouette upon the paper-covered windows. Sōkichi expected Kumazawa to take his place across from her, dressed in his matching Ōshima kimono and jacket, a gold watch chain trailing into one pocket, but—

"Is the master out?" he asked Amaya.

Kumazawa was nowhere to be seen, nor had he been among those who went to the bathhouse.

From the end of the hall echoed a roof-raising cough of someone loudly clearing his throat. Apparently Kumazawa was in the privy.

"In here."

"My goodness." Matsuda's woman laughed as she passed from the next room to the kitchen.

Osen looked down at her lap and smiled. "Not very charming, is he?"

"But that's what got you." Amaya drummed on his apron. "That's how you fell into his hands."

"Really. Now you've gone too far."

Even young Sōkichi knew that Amaya had said something wrong, probably something obscene.

"Sorry." Amaya bowed many times. "And to show my sincerity, allow me to touch up your face a bit for you. As I said last night, I'm not that good. But I can still pass for a pretty fair valet. Trust me." He turned to Sōkichi. "You, go get the razor."

Sōkichi understood why he had to fetch it. Even if Osen could sneak away to the bathhouse, she couldn't very well visit a barber. Neither would her situation allow someone to be called in to do her hair for her. Sōkichi did as he was told. He borrowed a razor from the landlord's mistress and brought it to Amaya.

"But where's the washbasin! Use your head, boy!"

Sōkichi could tell that Amaya and Osen had something to talk over.

"I suppose you'd like me to display my skills on someone else first?" Amaya asked her.

"I doubt that's necessary."

"There's nothing to worry about. If I make a mistake, it's only the boy. Look. He needs a little work around that mouth anyway."

Sōkichi was helpless.

"Look up, way up. How's that? Good work, don't you think?"

Osen anxiously watched Amaya's hand. Her face, moving like a veil of fine silk behind a plume of steam, flickered in the corner of Sōkichi's eye.

"Look, just like this. A little here, a little there."

"Stop!" Osen couldn't help getting up to her knees now. The movement of her sleeves blew their fragrance to Sōkichi's nose.

"What's wrong?"

"You'll shave them off!"

"What? The eyebrows?" The razor stopped for a moment, then continued. "Who cares?"

"No. Not above the eyes!"

"Look, I'll be shaving your neck. Why are you worried about the boy's eyebrows?"

From inside the toilet came the sound of yawning, clear as a bell.

"Now don't start laughing!"

"Why not?" said Amaya. "Why not laugh? Why not cry? Who cares about the boy's eyebrows?"

"No!" Osen rose to one knee and came forward. The rustling of her clothes swished in Sōkichi's heart like the far-off sound of an angelic bird making its way toward him. Osen became a mermaid emerging from the waves of the tatami mats.

"But don't you wonder about this boy's mother?"

Her arm, whiter than snow, reached up and stopped the razor in Amaya's hand. She took it away from him and brought the blade to her chest. She held it, stared at it. "You have such nice eyebrows," she said, looking up at Sōkichi. "Your parents must really love you."

Sōkichi could see the whiteness of Osen's bosom. He knew the purity of her gentleness and yearning. But then the pattern and color of her clothes and the blackness of her hair threw shadows in his eyes. With her sleeve upon his shoulder, he pressed his face to her collar and began to weep uncontrollably.

"Is that razor sharp enough?" Matsuda's woman asked from the other room. "I was going to send it out—"

Later that day, after night had come to their street, Sōkichi told everyone he was going to take the razor to the barber's shop for sharpening. But actually he had plans to kill himself with it.

As for the details—

5

The three members of the gang came back from their morning bath, and everyone sat down to a game of cards, including Kumazawa, who had finally emerged from the toilet. Breakfast turned out to be sushi, stewed tofu, and a little *sake.* Amaya suggested that with tea they have some of the Sōma crackers that were made and sold in an alley in Miyamoto-chō, just at the bottom of the steep flight of steps running down Myōjin Hill. They would be his treat to Osen—salted and crisp, flecked with soy sauce, and marked with horse-bit patterns. It was Sōkichi's misfortune to be the one sent to buy them.

Ah, the appetite of a seventeen-year-old! He could barely manage to get three meals a day; and though this was by no means a difficult errand, his hunger pangs became even sharper than they had been earlier that morning. The pain spread to the bottom of his stomach, as deep as a tumble down a steep flight of steps. Tempura, noodles, baked sweet potatoes—the smell of any one of these would have tested anyone's ability to endure. But a whiff of the golden-brown Sōma crackers made Sōkichi's hands tremble with desire. He was nearly starved, and the beads of cold sweat that began running down his body were impossible to ignore.

Seven *sen* still bought a lot of crackers in those days. From a large bagful, Sōkichi stole just two, two crackers as round as silver coins. He paused at a landing where the path up the hill was so steep he could reach out and touch the steps before him. Shielded only by a thin covering of ginkgo leaves and the branches of the firs and Chinese nettles towering far above, Sōkichi faced the drainage ditch that ran along the cliff and partook of forbidden fruit for the first time in his life. He chomped down on the hard crackers like a horse champing down on a bit. How wonderfully delicious!

But he was immediately overwhelmed with guilt and embarrassment, as if he had thrown himself into a ditch and fallen to pieces like the crackers that seemed to break apart inside his stomach rather than in his mouth. It was as if he had bumped his head on an overhanging eave and poked his eye on a spike, his entire body warm with the spurting blood as he crawled like a snake up the serpentine stairway. He felt like the love-tortured Oshichi, dashing up the steps to watch the city burn, the sunlight glaring in his eyes, turning blood-red, flowing down the steps toward him. He washed himself at the Myōjin Temple's holy laver and felt a horrifying chill run through his entire body.

"Heh, heh, heh!"

The men had sat down to play a game of cards, laughing among themselves. Sōkichi immediately sensed the danger when he entered the room, feeling his face flush with guilt as he handed the bag of crackers to Amaya.

Turning over a card and aligning it with another, Amaya passed the bag to Osen. She looked tired and hadn't joined the game. "Here. See what you think."

Osen received the bag from where she was sitting on the opposite side of the brazier. She put it down by her knees, peered in, and innocently said, "I'll check for poison." How those words pained Sōkichi! Had his guilt been all he had to bear, the story would have ended here. But there was more.

"Heh, heh, heh!"

The sound of muffled laughter had entered Sōkichi's ear from the very moment he returned. Looking away from the cracker that Osen picked from the bag, he was struck from the side by the snickering of Small Plate Heishirō. With his fat cheeks, diamond-shaped face, and narrow, deeply set eyes, he laughed and crinkled his stubby nose. *"Heh, heh!"*

Small Plate seemed to have drawn a bad hand and was out of the game. Holding his silver-plated pipe, he propped up one knee, placed his cheek on top of it, and laughed uncontrollably.

6

"Take that." The landlord turned over a card, and the priest flashed his red sleeves.

"Damn you!" The priest threw his card down.

Small Plate's snickering was louder now.

Kumazawa reached for his *sake* cup with one hand as he stared down at the contest of bush clover, iris, cherry, and peony as the cards fell one by one onto the velvet cushion. "What's wrong with you?" He glanced over at Small Plate, who laughed again, as if he were a bug that had just eaten a mouthful of pepper.

"Idiot!" Kumazawa licked the corner of his mouth and held out his cup. Osen took the heated *sake* flask from its copper boiler and paused. "Something wrong?"

"Sorry." Small Plate laughed again. "Can't help it."

"He's been possessed," Amaya mumbled in disgust.

Everyone fell silent, but with the silence came only more laughter. Small Plate fell over on his side, beating his ribs with the gooseneck of his pipe as he writhed on the tatami. "Help! *Ho, heh, heh!* I can't stand it!"

The red-faced Small Plate, eyes watering, squirming in agony, found a cup of cold tea, gulped it down, and immediately started to choke. He reached for an ash pot, but it was too late. He coughed and sent up a cloud of ashes.

The priest pointed toward the wall. "Sōkichi. Open the window!"

As if leaping from a mattress of needles, Sōkichi jumped up and slid the paper-covered shutter to the side. Quickly, the blizzard of ash was sucked out the bay window and into the blue sky, disappearing over the ocean of Shinagawa. Standing at the window, Sōkichi could see the chimneys of the Kuramae district and Asakusa's twelve-story Ryōun Pavilion to the north. Directly below was the avalanche of a cliff, and slightly beyond the clutter of rooftops were the oiled paper doors of the place where he had bought the crackers. The small shop was clearly visible in a patch of sunlight.

He could also see, running off into a deep, dark hollow, the flight of stone steps he had taken. It twisted sharply up Myōjin Hill like a huge centipede. It gnashed its teeth at the dead end, crawled out of the gutter, ran along the black spike-topped fence, and squirmed in an ugly, filthy line, its tongue licking a morsel of bread. Sōkichi felt the blood drain from his face. He knew at that moment that he had been seen eating the crackers! Small Plate, who was wiping drool from his knee, had seen him from the window! Small Plate let out a loud sigh, and the last rumblings of his laughter echoed in Sōkichi's ear.

"Sōkichi," Osen asked, "aren't you going to have a cracker?"

Had the cliff been more jagged, Sōkichi would have jumped out the window at that very moment, with the sound of Osen's voice still ringing in his ears. It was because of her that his shame was so unbearable, and he wanted to dash himself into pieces. Wasn't she the one who had protected his eyebrows? Wasn't she the one who had made him yearn for the woman who had given him life?

"I've got something to do at home," he managed to say.

By "home" he meant the row house in the alley. But Sōkichi walked right past it and on to the Myōjin Shrine, where he wandered the grounds and hid from the stares of others, forgetting even his hunger, crying until the stars appeared in the cloudy sky.

That night he said to Matsuda's woman, "I'll take the razor to the barbershop if you like. I'm going that way anyway."

Sōkichi purposely avoided the front door. He sneaked into the mistress' quarters by way of the kitchen and got the razor from Matsuda. He felt Osen's presence in the next room and even smelled the fragrance of her perfume. But she made no attempt to come to him.

Out in the alley he could see the silhouettes of Kumazawa, the priest, even Small Plate, outlined beneath the row house's red lights. He could hear their voices, too. Luckily, no one heard or saw him leave.

7

"What are you doing? What do you think you're doing?"

She seemed like a wondrous bird with a beautiful woman's face, sweeping down from the trees to grab his sleeve. He was leaning back against the trunk of a ginkgo tree that was being used as a corner post for one of the empty stalls behind the main temple. Just as he was about to slash his throat, Osen came. She wrested the razor from his hand. Everything seemed like a dream.

"Thank goodness I got here in time!" Osen turned and prayed to the shrine while still holding Sōkichi in one arm. "I had a premonition about this. I heard you . . . say in the kitchen that . . . you were going to take the razor. My heart nearly stopped! 'Hata-san! Hata-san!' I called for you. But you had already gone. I couldn't help thinking you might try something like this, so I came looking. I didn't know where to look. I stopped at the barbershop near the main gate, but they said they hadn't seen you. 'Too late,' I thought. I was in a daze, but thank the gods who led me here. Hata-san, it wasn't me who saved you. Your parents are looking after you. Do you understand?"

Like a child, Sōkichi buried himself in the softness of her bosom. He wrapped his arms tightly around her sash and girdle.

"Look, the moon," she said. "The Buddha."

He never forgot that moment. The half-moon seemed to be descending from a black cloud, its light shining upon the treetops of the ginkgo towering above, like the gentle contour of his dead mother's breast.

"The future's yours," said Osen. "Even if you were a woman, this would be the springtime of your life. So why would you want to kill yourself? Unless it's . . . because of me." Sōkichi could feel her chest tremble against his. "Why end your life just because they say you ate those crackers? It doesn't matter. You know that I'll always . . ." She paused, then continued. "Anyway, come to my house. No one's there tonight."

Urging him on, she searched for her wooden sandals, the crimson of her undergarment showing against her white legs. Osen seemed beside herself. Without thinking to get Sōkichi's shoes, she grabbed his hand and breathlessly hurried him away, escaping from the horror.

When they passed the temple, she scooped water from the holy laver and sprinkled a few drops on Sōkichi's head. Was she trying to ward off evil spirits? Was it the god of death she feared?

"Health. Longevity. Learning. May our wish be granted." Her eyes were filled with tears as she pressed her wet hands together and bowed toward the shrine. The white of her neck showed in the moonlight.

"Now drink. Calm yourself. I'll drink, too." She slowly lifted the dipper to his mouth. "Look how I'm shaking."

Sōkichi had already noticed.

"Hata-san, we're not going back to that place. You'll never have to go back there again. I'll risk my life to save you. Anyway, I just asked the shrine to forgive us. You know why? That water on your head, I sprinkled it on you so when we got home . . . I could give you a priest's haircut with this razor and then we could sleep together. That priest from Kishū was going to make love to me tonight anyway. It was all Kumazawa's and Amaya's idea. They were going to walk in on us so they could blackmail the priest. They made me go along with their plan.

"You see, the priest had brought some treasures from Mount Kōya and was going to sell them here in Tokyo. But Kumazawa duped him. He said he'd sell them to some rich businessman for him. But what he really did was to pawn everything then spend all the money. When he was asked to pay it back, he thought of this scheme because he had noticed the priest looking at me.

"Sōkichi, I'm not a strong person. I got mixed up with those people because I depended on Kumazawa's strength. But after hearing their plans . . . and seeing your eyebrows." Osen gently patted Sōkichi's shoulder. "I hate Kumazawa. Imagine him barging in on me and the priest! I decided I was going to sleep with you instead. Then when he came in, I'd sit up and tell him exactly what I thought. We'd give him the satisfaction of seeing us run off together in the middle of the night. But I thought those men might do something to hurt you, and then it would be too late. So I'm not going through with my plan. No. Come on, Sōkichi. Let's run away now. Leave everything to me. You can't go back there."

As they descended the stone steps that led down the far slope of the hill, Sōkichi felt as if he had passed over a wolf-haunted pass and could now see a valley of promise before him.

"This is the place, isn't it?" Osen smiled. She pulled a purse from her sash. The sash was a cheap-looking thing, but her purse was the color of spring.

"Let's walk while we eat," she said. "You're such a weakling."

In the dark alley leading to the main street, she fed him the rice crackers from her mouth—sweet, fragrant, broken up by her teeth.

8

Returning home from night school, Sōkichi walked the back streets of Okachimachi to a cheap tenement building that stood between a used-bottle store on one side and a rag shop on the other. He nearly collided with a man emerging from the front door.

Osen suddenly slid open the door and welcomed him into their one-room apartment. Her futon was already spread on the floor. Osen added charcoal to the brazier that was placed next to her pillow and fanned the coals with tissue paper. She grilled rice cakes for Sōkichi on a battered wire rack lowered at an angle over the heat. When the cakes were done, she cooled them off by blowing on them while she told Sōkichi the story of the lovely Urazato. Osen was even more beautiful than her heroine. And even though the snow wasn't falling as in the story, the cherry blossoms accumulating on the damp cinders of their small back garden were even more heartrending.

And there, behind the back fence! Was it Tokijirō, Urazato's lover, coming to rescue her with a bandanna tied over his head? Osen jumped to her feet and tried to close the back doors. But the man hurdled the fence and rushed to the veranda. The end of a snakelike tether was showing at his sleeve. "You're under arrest."

Osen fell back on her knees, pushing Sōkichi behind her. "What about him?"

"The boy's none of my business."

"Sō-chan, for your breakfast tomorrow . . . I bought some beans. They're in the covered bowl. You can eat them with pickled ginger."

Carrying his sandals in one hand, the policeman opened the door to the front entry. Osen searched for her sandals while he unlocked the front door. As soon as they were out in the street he quickly tied her hands. Her slender waist suddenly disappeared beneath his rope, and her drooping shoulders floated before the dark willow trees. Osen had long since pawned her jacket and undergarments, and her skin showed whitely beneath a single layer of silk.

Walking barefoot, Sōkichi followed. Through his tears he saw only darkness, a piercing gust of wind scattering cherry blossoms through the dim light of a street lamp.

"Please, sir." Osen suddenly stopped. "Sō-chan." Osen hung her head without looking back. But then she turned, and Sōkichi, looking into her face, saw her eyebrows.

The young man was speechless.

"Sō-chan. I'll give you my spirit."

She folded it as the policeman pulled her along. Soon it was there, nestled in the palm of her hand, a crane of white tissue paper.

"Follow this to wherever it takes you." She blew her warm breath into the bird and it came to life. With the marks of her lips showing faintly red against the crane's bluish-white body, the bird flew among the floating blossoms, dancing in the air as it led Sōkichi to the gate where he was taken in.

The inbound and outbound trains came at almost the same moment.

Sōkichi remained, transfixed.

As he looked on, the woman who resembled his cousin's wife quickly approached the crimson lady and began straightening the coat that had fallen from her shoulders.

"It's here."

"My taxi?" asked the crimson lady, still staring off in the distance.

9

Three or four trains, all of them washed clean of mud, came and left in quick succession, making the young platform attendant wonder why Sōkichi and the others had still not left the waiting room. "Are you getting on or not?"

"This woman's not well," said Sōkichi, offering his arm to the crimson woman, who looked up at him blankly.

After the station attendant left, Sōkichi looked tenderly at the woman's face and exchanged glances with the two who were accompanying her. "Let me call a cab. But could we not go to Sugamo? I'd like to take care of her myself. My name is Hata."

When the third woman saw the name "Hata Sōkichi, M.D." written on his name card, she straightened like the letter *P* then bowed like the letter *Z*. She had come along to help. Sōkichi, seeing that he could trust the one who looked so much like his cousin, learned that the crimson lady had been a prostitute at a brothel in Shinagawa. She had lost her mind and was now being taken to Sugamo. She insisted on going by taxi and refused to cooperate when the trains came. The woman with the *marumage* hairdo was apparently the brothel owner's daughter. Her helper, the one with shorter hair, glared sourly at the madwoman, whose name was Osen.

Surprised by his unexpected visit, the attendants and white-clad nurses gathered quickly and quietly. Dr. Hata Sōkichi calmly declined their offers of assistance. "This is a personal visit. Please, everyone go back to what you were doing."

Alone, he entered the special room where Osen was lying with her clothes in disarray. Kneeling beside the bed, he placed a razor in her hands and buried his forehead in her bosom. He embraced her, oblivious to the world around them, and drenched his beard with his tears.

Afterword

A DISCUSSION OF THE TALES

The Surgery Room

Kyōka's first published work was *Crowned Yazaemon (Kanmuri Yazaemon),* which appeared serially in the literary column of the *Kyoto Morning News (Kyōtō hinode shinbun).* Beginning its run on October 1, 1892, it turned out to be far from the great success for which Kyōka had hoped. In fact, so poorly was the novella received that Iwaya Sazanami (1870–1933), a Ken'yūsha writer who had become the literary editor of the newspaper, immediately received over twenty letters from disappointed readers, all asking that the story be discontinued. Sazanami implored Ozaki Kōyō (1868–1903), who was Kyōka's mentor and the one who had recommended him for the job, to "change to another writer if possible, and to come up with some way to release the present one." Kōyō refused to comply on the ground that such an action would be a crushing blow to his student.[1] Protected from any knowledge of just how poorly his work was being received in Kyoto (Sazanami claimed to be losing readers by the day), Kyōka had the satisfaction of seeing his manuscript printed in full. The final installment appeared on November 18, with two afterwords following in December.

It is not hard to imagine the difficulties that the *Kyoto Morning News* readers had with Kyōka's first publication. *Yazaemon* offers little new in the way of theme, its plot is difficult to follow, its characters are numerous and weakly developed, and, even for a Japanese story of this period and type, its scenes are strangely disconnected. No doubt, these shortcomings are in part due to Kyōka's choice to rework an already existing story and to his assumption that his readers would already be familiar enough with its general outline. *Kanmuri Yazaemon* had been preceded by Takeda Kōrai's (1819–1882) *The Pine of Kanmuri, the Storm at Mado Village (Kanmuri no matsu mado no arashi),* a *kusazōshi,* or illustrated fiction, in two bound volumes of three books apiece, which first appeared in the fall of 1885. This parent work is a straightforward report of a peasant uprising that took place in Kanagawa Prefecture in 1883. It illuminates the avarice of Matsugi Chōemon, who deceitfully acquired land from the peasants of his village. The peasants' appeal to a higher authority succeeds, only to be overturned by Matsugi's legal advisers. Driven to a point of desperation, the villagers plan and successfully carry out a vendetta. Kanmuri Yazaemon, whose character is developed only through an aside that shows his son's reaction to a reporting of the rebellion, is their leader.

Kōrai's commitment to the facts is unwavering. A representative example of the newly emergent Meiji reportage, his account also includes mention of how the newspapers of the time eagerly took up the story and how the public's sympathy for the rebels influenced the Kanagawa peasants' eventual exoneration. From other documents we know that, in fact, the Kanagawa uprising was indeed a newsworthy event, and that it became the material not only for Kōrai's *kusazōshi* but also for the raconteur Matsubayashi Hakuchi's oral account, which was taken down and published as *A Fire and Sword Showdown at Mado Village (Mado-mura yakiuchi sōdō)* by Imamura Jirō in October of 1898, six years after the initial publication of Kyōka's story. From the existence of this and other versions, we can assume that interest in the event was sustained. At the time of Kyōka's writing, the rebellion was probably already part of the common imagination, though he seems to have overestimated his reader's ability and willingness to fill in the gaps in his own version.

Kyōka was attracted to the dramatic potential of Kōrai's account, as well as to its strong indictment of class oppression. But to this rather straightforward incident of class struggle he added various human entanglements that remind us of the bizarre, rococo patterns of Bunka-Bunsei–period drama (1804–1830). Tangled à la Nanboku, the threads connecting the principal characters in Kyōka's story tie themselves into a melodramatic knot. Kanmuri Yazaemon's sister Onami is the wife of Shinjurō, whose daughter Kohagi is forced to marry Ishimura Jirozō, the son of Ishimura Gohei. Gohei is the main villain of the story and is finally killed by Yazaemon, but only after Kohagi's failed attempt to assassinate Iwanaga, the lecherous lord of the province who colludes with Gohei in his oppression of the peasants. Kohagi's marriage to Gohei is actually part of Iwanaga's long-term plan to acquire her for himself. Knowing this, Kohagi takes a sword to her bridal bed. Her murderous intentions are discovered, however, with the result that her father, Okino Shinjurō, is incarcerated and her mother, Onami, is tortured to death.

Onami's death is the turning point of the story. It persuades her brother, the reluctant Yazaemon, to fight. Ishimura and Iwanaga must be killed. As the new leader of the rebellion, Yazaemon replaces Unosuke, who (in an additional complication of the original story) is Kohagi's real beloved and also the illegitimate son of the evil Lord Iwanaga, who raped Unosuke's mother. Unosuke's adoptive father, Togama Rihei, is no less unfortunate, for he is falsely accused by Gohei of bribing Iwanaga. A scapegoat for Gohei's own crimes, Rihei is thrown into jail and executed. Knowing this past misdeed, Yazaemon delivers Iwanaga to Unosuke, who at the story's climax has the pleasure of killing Iwanaga, his biological father.

After his debut with the complicated *Crowned Yazaemon,* Kyōka did not attract considerable critical attention until three years later, with the publication of two short and comparably simple stories, "The Night Patrol" (*Yakō junsa,* 1895) and "The Surgery Room," (*Gekashitsu,* 1895). From the perspective of one reviewer writing for the influential coterie journal *Imperial Literature (Teikoku bungaku),* "The Surgery Room" established Kyōka as "an author of promise . . . clearly one of Japan's best new writers." The story was admirable for possessing "a certain progressive spirit . . . enriched with the latest thought from modern Europe."[2] This "latest thought" was, in a word, Victor Hugo's, made available to Kyōka through the translations of Morita Shiken (1861–1897), who produced free and readable translations of a number of Hugo's stories. As a young and aspiring novelist, Kyōka devoured these, learning from them both a sense of narrative style and a critical point of view.[3]

The "Shiken style" was famous. Japanese rhetorical parlance otherwise categorized it as the "detailed style" *(shūmitsu buntai),* a colloquial form of Chinese read according to the rules of Japanese pronunciation and syntax (as in *kanbun kuzushi*). As up-to-date as this translatorese seemed to the Meiji-period reader, Shiken's prose, with its generous use of Chinese compounds, was in reality not far removed from the language of Takizawa Bakin (1767–1848), or even from that of translated Chinese novels such as *The Water Margin (Shui-hu chuan).* Like these traditional styles—whether Bakin's mixing of the elegant with the colloquial *(gazoku setchū),* or *The Water Margin*'s melding of Japanese and Chinese *(wakan konkō)*—Shiken's was yet another hybridized idiom, a linguistic compromise both troubled and enriched by the intense cultural borrowing that characterized literary Japan at the turn of the century. It is not surprising that Kyōka, being well acquainted with all three of these styles, produced something resembling them in this story.

The most distinguishing feature of "The Surgery Room" was not style, though, but its sense of social justice. As for the matter of Victor Hugo's influence, Kyōka's perspective was so spiritually new that the critic and theorist Shimamura Hōgetsu (1871–1918) had to coin a term to name the achievement. Like the equally brief "Night Patrol," which immediately preceded it, "The Surgery Room" was labeled a "conceptual novel" *(kannen shōsetsu):* a fictional work written to express an explicit social message or "concept."[4] These works were considered new because Kyōka chose to indict the social context of aberrant behavior rather than simply to condemn the criminal. Following Hugo's example, he saw the goodness of bad people—in this case the adulterously minded Doctor Takamine and the Countess Kifune, who were, at the same time, people of beauty and pure feeling. The author suggests that in another social context they would not have been forced to destroy themselves. By locating their desire within the inherently evil setting of marriage-as-usual, Kyōka boldly chose to point a critical finger at Meiji society at large.

Of course, we can easily think of other possible sources of this critical attitude. One was the traditional identity of the Edo-period fictionist, the "playful scribbler" or *gesakusha,* who saw himself as marginal and therefore critically disposed toward the high tradition as established by the sinocentric man of letters (who sometimes put on the *gesaku* hat). Even if Kyōka's version of the *gesakusha*'s well-worn formula of "praising virtue and chastising evil" is utterly, even melodramatically, sincere in comparison, he undoubtedly absorbed some of this cynical posturing from his extensive reading of Edo-period fiction. In a similar way, Kyōka's roots in the artisan class—his father was a crafter of precious metals and lived in the provincial castle town of Kanazawa—separated him from the upper (samurai) class, affording yet another critical perspective on the rulers and the rules. Finally, and perhaps most significant of all, was the role played by aesthetics. As I have already mentioned in the introductory essay, Kyōka's sense of social responsibility was, as Akutagawa Ryūnosuke (1892–1927) aptly put it, a "morality grounded in poetic justice."[5]

As it was for the romantic poet Kitamura Tōkoku (1868–1894), Kyōka's standing up for the downtrodden was poetically right. It was beautiful to criticize the Meiji upper crust and, more specifically, to decry the institution of marriage that oppressed the true emotions of people such as Countess Kifune and Doctor Takamine. The Meiji patriarchy was ugly and brutish, and beautiful women such as the countess were its most obvious victims. Like Poe, Kyōka was similarly addicted to the gothic possibilities of love as a substitute for social and economic power. So for both writers there could scarcely be anything so powerfully affecting as the death of a beautiful woman. "Did you see how those men were moved by true beauty?" Takamine makes the point. "Now that's a subject for your art. That's what you ought to study!" The dialogue on feminine beauty, as shared by the two young men to whom Takamine refers, forms the central portion of Part Two. Aware of Countess Kifune's beauty, they are nevertheless unaware that she, being "noble, elegant, and beautiful," must die because of her loveliness. Being more able than they to appreciate her full beauty, Takamine is also fated to perish.

The critical tendencies of the time dictated that this melodramatic story be seen more as a treatise on moral and religious principles than as a romantic exploration. From our perspective today, we can see how contemporary critics were not ready to perceive the real thrust of Kyōka's early career. But, then again, this was a period of profound social and literary change, making the mapping of any writer's career a difficult proposition. By 1895, when "The Surgery Room" appeared, the Meiji government's conservative reaction to two decades of enthusiastic learning from the West was well under way. The year also marks a juncture in the development of Japanese letters when most everyone, Kyōka included, was searching for a new narrative language and experimenting with fresh narrative forms. Given the growing dominance of a new notion of "literature" *(bungaku)* as advanced by antitraditionalists such as Taoka Reiun (1870–1912) and Hōgetsu, it was no wonder that the critics chose to see Kyōka's work as ideologically rigorous.[6] However we might feel about the ideology, one point all can agree upon is this story's dearth of explanation. Takamine and the countess fall in love after a single glance and stay enamored until what amounts to their double suicide nine years later. Again, progressive-minded reviewers chose to understand this melodrama as the work of a protonaturalist, penetrating the observable surface to grasp the deeply hidden principles by which modern society worked. In fact, young Kyōka had no such objectives in mind. Despite the final *kannen*—"Religious thinkers of the world, I pose this question to you. Should these two lovers be found guilty and denied entrance into heaven?"—we should not exaggerate the critical rigor of this story. This "concept" is better understood as a pole of the writer's personal, aesthetically constructed mythology rather than an axiom of some nascent social science.[7]

Already in "The Surgery Room," four main elements of Kyōka's mythology were being developed in ways that continued to exert influence upon him throughout his career. First of all, there is the ubiquitous encoding of red and white, as seen in the description of the operation itself: "A red winter plum fallen to the snow, the smooth trickle of blood flowed down her chest and soaked into her white gown." The combination of these colors appears as early as *Crowned Yazaemon* and continues throughout Kyōka's career. Prior to "The Surgery Room," its most graphic appearance is in *The Living Doll* (*Iki ningyō,* 1893), the author's first and only attempt at writing a detective novel in the style of Kuroiwa Ruikō (1862–1920).

> How cruel! Fuji gasps for breath. Her face, once flushed, now becomes pale as she succumbs to the agony of torture. "Please! Kill me!" Hers is the death wish of a virgin. Knowing that his plan will be foiled if he kills her now, Tokuzō, as if losing heart in the midst of battle, rubs his arms and rests his whip . . . without the strength to stand, she collapses and faints. (1:188)

This passage represents the first time Kyōka put into words the image of the young beauty, tied and beaten, that so captivated him as a boy. Kyōka's father, Izumi Seiji, wanted his son to follow him in his trade as a metal craftsman and did what he could to guide Kyōka's course. As an important first step, he brought home sheets of tracing paper that Kyōka was to use to copy sketchbook pictures—bamboo, orchids, and sparrows—traditional images that would provide a template for his future work as a metal carver. Kyōka, who had already demonstrated a fascination with pictures, took to the tracing exercises with uncommon passion. But it was discovered that what he was replicating with such enthusiasm was not his father's well-ordered cosmos of bamboo leaves but certain pictures he had discovered in his mother's personal library. According to his younger brother, Toyoharu, Kyōka's favorite image, one that he "reproduced again and again with the greatest fidelity," was "of a pitiful young woman, tied to a tree and beaten."[8]

White legs flashing against crimson undergarments, white skin marked with red wounds, a rag of white silk bearing a message written in blood—these presentations of white and red in *The Living Doll* are echoed in "The Surgery Room" as Kyōka entangles the beautiful with the erotic and plays the whiteness of death against the flush of life. This color scheme enables a second aspect of the developing mythology: the archetypal heroine. Red marks on pale skin are an emblem both of taboo and of transcendence, expressing the bipolarity inherent in Kyōka's depictions of women. Reflecting his yearning for his dead mother, they are not only simultaneously alluring and maternal, but they must also be subjected to violence and death in order to qualify for the honor of providing salvation for Kyōka's heroes. Their complexity results from a structural imbalance. Whereas Kyōka generally wrote about two types of men, he was essentially interested in only one type of woman. As is intimated in the figure of Countess Kifune, Kyōka's heroines are doubly complicated, a color-encoded site of confrontation between the loving and the lustful, the weak and the strong, the sensitive and the brutish.

Her beauty is grounded upon Kyōka's resentment of the Meiji patriarchy and upon a paradigmatic appreciation of women that owes less than is at first apparent to his publically stated position as an early advocate of women's rights. Although in an essay like "Love and Matrimony" (Ai to kon'i, 1895) he takes up a subject of social importance, here in this "conceptual novel" Kyōka is not describing women as they exist in society so much as he is giving us an idea of femininity grounded in the structure of *amae*, or the interplay of female spoiling and male dependence. Given the place of this story within the context of his life's work, the pretense of social relevance is less important than the story's affirmation of what can never be real. Like the countess, the author's other women are objects of sacrifice, reflective of a personal need for them to be of the dead but never unavailable to the consciousness of the living. Unfortunate in their beauty, tempting yet nurturing, they are pitifully oppressed while being divinely powerful. Kyōka's sympathy is with them, certainly. But it is also undeniable that, as in Christian aesthetics, the possibility of inner peace is predicated on the intense, nearly unimaginable suffering of another.

A third familiar element of the emerging archetype is the portrayal of the count and other noblemen of Meiji society as early manifestations of the brute, that locus of worldly success with all its crassness. Kyōka's feelings toward authority were complex. Although he was sorely dependent upon the power of women, he resented most masculine manifestations of authority. He was against militarism and spoke out against war. He decried the inequities of marriage, which favored men and made life miserable for women: "Marriage is a cruel and vindictive law that has been designed to restrict and oppress love and to steal away one's freedom. From old it has been said that beautiful women are unhappy. But this is only because society makes them unhappy. If it weren't for marriage, how many women would become miserable? All the terrible aspects of love—conflict, deceit, despair, suicide, illness, and so on—result from marriage" (28:243).

Kyōka reserved his greatest contempt for men of the business world who had wealth but no taste and refinement. Though his appreciation of high culture tempered his resentment of the aristocracy, he still criticized their pretentiousness and their hypocrisy with regard to the poor. As for the imperial family, as a rarified sign of Japanese culture it remained beyond criticism. The tale is told that Kyōka would always remove his eyeglasses, take off his hat, close his eyes, and utter a silent prayer whenever he passed by the Imperial Palace, whether in a train or bus.[9] His respectful regard for the emperor was comparable to his admiration of physicians. They both deserved honor because they stood close to the sources of life, one spiritual and the other physical.

Finally, in "The Surgery Room" we see Kyōka's early efforts to offset the insensitivity of patriarchy by his creation of a fourth vector of the archetype: the highly sensitive, sexually hesitant male protagonist. The birth of the weak male was the most important accomplishment of this story. It marks the beginning of a process of masculine regression in which Kyōka's male protagonists, such as Ren'ya in "A Bird of Many Colors" (*Kechō,* 1897), become much younger than the women of their interest. Ennobled, tempted, even crazed by an inextinguishable yet rarely tested desire, characters such as Doctor Takamine continue to dance with taboo in the many works that follow because they are required to be both seduced and mothered by the women of their interest. In the world but not necessarily of its spirit, they make beauty but not love. So doing, they maintain a steady erotic tension that enables Kyōka's vision of human salvation to repeat itself with the obsessive regularity of unrequited love. For reasons that will become clearer to us, this salvation was not free of incestuous overtones. Nor was it long-lived.

The Holy Man of Mount Kōya

Kyōka must have sensed that his newly won status as a writer of conceptual novels came largely through a misreading of his work, and that he had been temporarily caught by a spotlight while on the way to another position on stage. Rather than dwell in this light, and despite critical expectations for more of the same "stories about ideas," he departed from the formula established by "The Surgery Room" and set out to pursue more pressing issues of personal salvation. Having gained recognition as a social critic, Kyōka increasingly tailored his work to fit private needs, in effect, ignoring the advice of those readers who came to have more and more influence over the course of modern Japanese letters.

He developed his own eccentric vision by connecting the traumatic events of his life—the deaths of his mother and father, and an attempted suicide—with a constellation of images that he had gleaned from his boyhood perusal of his mother's library of *kusazōshi,* from his exposure to the theater, and from the legends and folktales that he heard from "the beautiful young women of the neighborhood" (1:iii). Of his earliest memories of his mother, Nakata Suzu, Kyōka wrote:

> When my mother moved to Kanazawa, she brought a number of *kusazōshi* with her from Tokyo and kept them in a special box normally used for storing dolls. Of the longer works, she owned *The Tale of Shiranui* [*Shiranui monogatari*], *The Eight Lives of Siddharta, A Japanese Library* [*Shaka hassō Yamato bunko*], *A Mirror of Our Times* [*Jidai kagami*], and also incomplete collections—five or eight volumes each—of other *kusazōshi.* She took special care of these books, but whenever she was looking the other way I'd be into them. Not to read, though. I was only three or four at the time, so all I did was lay the beautiful pictures out on the floor as if setting them out for a summer airing. This dashing samurai, that sad young woman. . . . As I kept looking at those pictures, I gradually became curious to know the story behind them. I went to my mother, who was too busy with her sewing to answer my questions, and persisted until I finally got my way. Now that I look back on it, I must have been a nuisance. My poor mother. (28:653–654)[10]

These works of illustrated fiction played an especially important role in the development of Kyōka's imagination. Not only did he associate them with his mother, but through their graphic wealth he gained access to a rich legacy of orally and textually transmitted folklore and legend. This is one reason why even ancient sources of the Japanese narrative tradition inform the iconography of Kyōka's work, giving depth to his visual style by tying the author's modern, highly personal use of imagery to an existing, well-developed tradition. By studying the works of *kusazōshi* that Kyōka read as a child and later purchased and read as an adult, we can see, for instance, that the water imagery which contributes so importantly to the tension and mystery of his work carries traditional associations traceable to the earliest chronicles and songs. In both the *kusazōshi* and in Kyōka's work, water connotes danger, metamorphosis, violence, and death.[11]

In "The Holy Man of Mount Kōya" (*Kōya hijiri,* 1900), Kyōka set this and other images into a narrative structure that established the central myth of his fictive world. In this privileged narrative or metastory, a young (or otherwise sexually hesitant) man encounters a dangerously alluring yet nurturing woman in a watery and therefore threatening environment. The hero becomes a trespasser in the world of the sacred and the dead. He experiences both horror and fascination, and returns from his encounter having learned something important about his own nature and the deeper meaning of love.

When we compare this myth with the general contours of "The Holy Man of Mount Kōya," we see how closely they coincide. The young priest crosses a flooded road and enters a mountain wilderness. He encounters an older woman who is alluring yet also nurturing. While with her, he is horrified during his night on the mountain and also fascinated by the woman's powers. Because his sexual desire is bridled by the commitment he has made to a religious order, he overcomes temptation long enough to learn the truth about the woman. Affording both horror and comfort, his close encounter with her teaches him something about his own sexual nature and the meaning of love.

This basic pattern is usually much less straightforward in other works, and perhaps this is one reason why "The Holy Man of Mount Kōya" has become Kyōka's best-known work. It is not Kyōka's best writing; but it is Kyōka at his most understandable, because here he took the time to establish the principal images of his personal mythology within the narrative itself. As a consequence, this tale of the wandering monk is an important key to the vast and often maddeningly difficult expanse of writing that follows: the early stories build up to it, and the later ones are significantly informed by it. To be sure, there are many variations and exceptions to the rule. Kyōka departed from the archetype temporarily, during his late fifties and early sixties. Yet when we consider the entire sweep of his career, it is obvious that he was working toward something like this pattern in the earliest stories and that, once established, he returned to it with religious regularity.

After 1900, Kyōka made less of an effort to develop the images of the metastory in a narrative manner. That is to say, he did not employ the elucidating powers of narrative to give meaning to the images that appear in a story. Rather, he used the well-defined images of the archetype to lend their already established meaning to new stories. This largely explains why the later works, such as "Osen and Sōkichi," are more difficult to follow. Unless we know the metastory and the relationships among the various images that appear, we are often unable to understand why one scene follows another, or why characters act in the manner they do. In other words, the fragmented structure and oblique expression of later works follow from their paratactic formation from visual tropes established by the archetype.

Although Kyōka is justly reputed to be a difficult writer, the overall form and import of the stories and plays is highly predictable because the act of writing itself came to have ritualistic import. Kyōka was an artist whose obsessive intensity and fineness of focus doomed him to repeat himself. Driven by the profundity of his fear, he discovered some possibilities while missing others. Because he required the drama of the metastory, for instance, Kyōka freed himself from the need to discover late-modern techniques, such as psychologically complicated characters, fixed third-person narration, and persuasive linear emplotment. His passions placed him, not within the widening world of discursive realism, but rather in the realm of a formalistic pictocentrism that expressed itself not in finely honed lines of analytical thought and description but through the more impressionistic and lyrical points and planes of concentrated visual matter.[12] Kyōka's formalistic approach to writing allowed him to concentrate on style, because the continuing presence of an archetype meant he could turn his attention to the act of writing at the level of word and image. Largely indifferent to the representational concerns of the literary mainstream, he was able to discover the suppressed figurative wealth of the early-modern narrative tradition, a graphic mode of visuality made unpopular by the antifigural reformation of Japanese letters *(genbun itchi)* in the body of the Japanese language itself. What

Kyōka discovered as a modern writer was that words themselves are *bakemono*—deformed and deforming locations of sight and sound. Routed by the phonocentric biases of modern realism, the banned visuality of nineteenth-century Japan had fled into the very body of language. In the word-as-image, the forgotten "imagistic splendor," to recall Mishima's idiom, waited to be rediscovered and emancipated.

Of this process of revival, Mishima was right in saying that Kyōka's visual language was not "an intellectually contrived anachronism." If anything, it was, as I have already said, a consequence of emotional need. As his regard for language anticipates the neoperceptionalists, such as Yokomitsu Riichi (1898–1947) and Kawabata Yasunari (1899–1972), and the concerns of modernism, Kyōka might be considered to have been ahead of his time. We must remember, however, that he was in a sense consciously retrograde in his enthusiasm for folklore, superstition, and legend—the stuff of which a story like "The Holy Man of Mount Kōya" is so obviously made. His relevance to the poststructuralist era flows from his heightened awareness of the artificiality of language. But we must remember that he arrives at this point not by way of the inquiries of linguistics but because he never stopped believing in the power of words.

We now know that while the positivistic and pragmatic emphases of Meiji institutions attempted to clear the air of feudal ghosts, they also had an effect of stimulating interest in the traditional Other, whether that be Kyōka's attempts to reinstitute the archetypes of legend, Orikuchi Shinobu's (1887–1953) study of myth and ancient song, Yanagita Kunio's (1875–1962) explorations of folklore, or Lafcadio Hearn's (1850–1904) exotic preservations of a vanishing Japanese culture. To the extent that critics continue to discuss Kyōka's work as fantasy *(gensō)*, however, we can also see how the tenets of realism have come to influence the critical writing on the author's work.[13] To call this story a fantasy is to risk misunderstanding Kyōka's relationship to the metastory and to the spirits that move about within it as "characters." As Kyōka himself once stated, "Monsters are the concretization of my emotion" (28:697). The same could be said of his words. They, too, are concretizations of his emotion. They are *bakemono*, or beings of transformation.

We can find the beginnings of the author's regard for monsters in the exaggerated characters of the early stories, people such as Hatta

Yoshinobu in "The Night Patrol" and Otei in "The Maidenhair" (*Bakeitchō,* 1896). More specifically, we find precedents for the woman wizard tucked away in the mountains in works such as "Mino Valley" (*Minodani,* 1896), "Of a Dragon in the Deep" (*Ryūtandan,* 1896), and "Seishin's Nunnery" (*Seishin no an,* 1897). The grotesquerie of stories such as these is grounded in legend and folklore and reflects an early-modern episteme as refracted by a late-modern point of view. In the case of "The Holy Man of Mount Kōya," the debt to legend is clarified by a preliminary draft written several years previous to 1900, which would indicate that many works of Kyōka's earlier career, including the conceptual novels, were conceived either after or while the author was first struggling to write what has become his most famous story.[14]

Muramatsu Sadataka discovered the draft manuscript in 1956. It is approximately twenty-three regular manuscript pages in length (four hundred characters per page), and was being kept in the childhood home of Meboso Kite, Kyōka's paternal grandmother. It bears no inscription, but there is little doubt that Kyōka wrote it. Entitled "The White Witch's Tale" *(Shirakijo monogatari)* and inspired by local legend, it is a first-person account of a young man's encounter with the uncanny. The narrator travels through the mountains, in this case from Tsuruga to Takefu, over the Kasuga Pass. Though warned of the dangers ahead, he feels compelled to wander where few dare, eventually encountering, as in "The Holy Man of Mount Kōya," both a horse and an old woman. She has "a face like jewels and skin like snow" and is fair, as her name suggests. But her eyelids are painted crimson, thus establishing the erotic color scheme introduced to us in "The Surgery Room." She snuggles seductively against the young man's knees. But the story ends just as the carefully prepared seduction is about to begin.

We are left to speculate as to why the story was never finished. Perhaps Kyōka, though committed to the journey, was not yet sure of the destination. Certainly, the truncated eroticism suggests both a technical and a spiritual deficiency, a facility in building interest without the ability to fulfill the possibilities. When we consider Kyōka's early solutions to this impasse, as demonstrated in "The Surgery Room," we note how romance tends toward melodrama, even torture and worship. What he could not do in 1895 but learned to do in the waterfall scene of "The Holy Man of Mount Kōya" was to aestheticize the violent aspect of the erotic, as generated by both his sense of fear and his need for female comfort, by exploiting the ambiguity of visual signs. The mendicant, thoroughly tempted and ready to give up his ascetic life, does not take her into his arms but *sees* the woman in the turbulent water, being pulled apart like a blossom.

> The smaller stream was trying to leap over the rock and cling to the larger one, but the jutting stone separated them cleanly, preventing even a single drop from making it to the other side. The waterfall, thrown about and tormented, was weary and gaunt, its sound like sobbing or someone's anguished cries. This was the sad yet gentle wife.
>
> The husband, by contrast, fell powerfully, pulverizing the rocks below and penetrating the earth. It pained me to see the two fall separately, divided by that rock. The brokenhearted wife was like a beautiful woman clinging to someone, sobbing and trembling. As I watched from the safety of the bank, I started to shake and my flesh began to dance. When I remembered how I had bathed with the woman in the headwaters of this stream, my imagination pictured her inside the falling water, now being swept under, now rising again, her skin disintegrating and scattering like flower petals amid a thousand unruly streams of water. I gasped at the sight, and immediately she was whole again—the same face, body, breasts, arms and legs, rising and sinking, suddenly dismembered, then appearing again. Unable to bear the sight, I felt myself plunging headlong into the fall and taking the water into my embrace. Returning to my senses, I heard the earthshaking roar of the husband, calling to the mountain spirits and roaring on its way. With such strength, why wasn't he trying to rescue her? I would save her! No matter what the cost. (5:639)

This scene provided Kyōka with a solution. Written at least five years later than the unfinished "White Witch's Tale," it opened the way for his further development as an artist. Standing out from the rest of the story in its lyrical force, this imagistic description of woman and water indicates the limitations of narration, that point at which the desire for being overwhelms the seductions of becoming.

This passage taught him the appropriate relationship between himself and language, and, at the same time, the necessary link between language and the metastory. It pointed the way to what became the hallmark of Kyōka's style, an intensely visual idiom that employs the connotative powers of language to invoke a state of presence that allows him to gain ritual access to what he most wanted and needed to write. In short, "The Holy Man of Mount Kōya" facilitated what Kyōka thereafter stated as his principal desire to "pass through reality to reach a still greater power" (28:696).

As we might anticipate, Kyōka's rejection of the representational thrust of modern letters was not something that most critics of the day either understood or appreciated.

> Previously concerned with the serious and tragic, Kyōka used to seek out and bring to life the dark tides of fate within his short, poetic pieces. His thought was simple. His rhetoric was clear. Consequently, he was able to place himself one step ahead of the competition. A young writer should aim for maturity in the pursuit of his various interests, but Kyōka has not done this. He should try to sharpen his skills of observation, to read, and to gain more experience. So why then has Kyōka, who is still a young writer, gone backwards to learn such foolishness? Why has he thrown away his simple, refreshing perspective? What compels him to give up concise, straightforward writing?[15]

In a word, it was a discovery of the metastory and the forging of ritual language that made "foolishness" possible. It was an indulgence that would sustain Kyōka for the next twenty-five years.

One Day in Spring

Kyōka's dedication to such an antirepresentational mode of vision came at a price. By 1905, the unrealistic quality of his work had begun to restrict his opportunities to publish. His clash with the proponents of naturalism—including Tokuda Shūsei (1871–1943), who was also one of Ozaki Kōyō's (1868–1903) students—has been considered by many scholars to be the principal reason for his leaving

Tokyo to live in the coastal town of Zushi near Kamakura.[16] Kyōka was openly disdainful of the naturalists and of their belief in the possibility of creating a transparent language that would allow the writer to depict reality as is, *ari no mama.* Despite his differences with what was quickly becoming the naturalist mainstream of the *bundan,* however, I am inclined to agree with Yoshida Masashi, who has recently argued that it was the death of his grandmother Kite that contributed most to the physical and mental deterioration of which Kyōka wrote in his chronology.[17]

MEIJI 39 (1906), 2ND MONTH.
I lose my grandmother.

MEIJI 39, 7TH MONTH.
My health continues to deteriorate. We rent a house in Tagoe, Zushi, and go there to recuperate. What begins as a summer's stay eventually stretches to four years. I eat practically nothing but gruel and potatoes.

10TH MONTH.
I publish "Shunchū" in New Fiction *(Shin shōsetsu).*

In a nap at midday
I met my beloved,
Then did I begin to believe
In the things we call dreams.

Rain leaks into the room, owls call from the trees. The wind snaps the branches of the Zelkova. It pierces the roofing and stabs at us through our ragged bedding.

The reeds are scattered about our frost-cold pillows. The crab spiders gather and scamper over the tatami.

I complete the sequel to "One Day in Spring." A butterfly? A dream? I am practically in a trance. Reading and enjoying the poetry of Li Ch'ang-chi. (1:viii)

Kyōka, who wrote this chronology well after the events indicated, incorrectly records the dates. We know from other sources that his stay in Zushi actually lasted from July 1905 until February 1909, and that his grandmother died on February 20, 1905, also one year earlier than indicated above. These adjustments retain the possibility of his grandmother's influence as argued by Yoshida, however.

We have other reasons to suspect that Meboso Kite's death was a factor in Kyōka's removal to Zushi. Yoshimura Hirotō suggests that the periods of greatest mental instability during the author's life were always tied to the death of someone close to him, usually a family member. His father's passing away in 1894 and the financial burden it caused drove him to consider suicide. Looking back to 1906, we see that the very course of his life was determined by the death of his mother. Though it is easy to exaggerate Kyōka's longing for her, it is undeniable that his literary career developed largely from a need to fill the spiritual emptiness her absence created. Meboso Kite was her replacement, the woman who most cared for him while she was alive. And so, as Yoshimura argues, it is reasonable to think that when she died, Kyōka was shaken.[18] "I couldn't tell day from night," he elsewhere described his state of mind at this time. "I never slept well, nor did I ever feel that I was wide awake. I had only the vaguest notion of who I was."[19]

Without going into the details of Yoshimura's extended studies of the relationship between mental disease and art, we can say that it was during this period of severe mental instability that Kyōka wrote some of his finest stories, including "One Day in Spring" (*Shunchū* and *Shunchū gokoku,* 1906) and "The Grass Labyrinth" (*Kusa meikyū,* 1908). Both works are powerfully suggestive, flooding the reader with streams of engaging rhythms and striking images that lead us to the border of transgression and, finally, to an aesthetic epiphany that is more a state of limbo than an increased clarity. Never sure of our bearings, we are nevertheless made aware both of the minute, idiosyncratic world we have entered and of its relevance to the world we have left behind.

We might read "One Day in Spring" as we would mull over our dreams, though this is not to say that the troubled Kyōka did not have a clearly conceived purpose in mind as he wrote. Even his espoused method of "letting go" *(mukō makase)*—first harboring some creative notion, then giving free reign to the imagination during the writing process—clearly admits to artistic intent. In this case, his borrowing from the ninth-century poet Ono no Komachi gives an unmistakable direction to this dreamlike narrative.

In a nap at midday
I met my beloved,
Then did I begin to rely
On those things called dreams.

By displaying this poem on the pillar at the Cliff Palace Temple, Tamawaki Mio restates the issue that Komachi made famous centuries earlier: at what point does reality end and the world of dreams begin?

Placed in the context of "One Day in Spring," the poem's focus is made relevant by the possibility of romantic love and, for Kyōka, the inseparable issue of death. In his confused, trancelike state, in this reiteration of red and white, he finds the truth of the human situation: that unencumbered love and peaceful death are not unimaginable as we can dream of both, although the former is impossible to attain and the latter is otherwise unknown. This being the case, the conclusion is obvious: "if it is in our dreams that we meet the people we love, why wouldn't we dream as much as we could?"

In "The Surgery Room" and "The Holy Man of Mount Kōya," there are great dangers for anyone who chooses to dream of either possibility. The same holds true for "One Day in Spring." Although it might have been enough for the Heian-period poet to turn her kimono inside out and anxiously await her lover's return, here both Tamawaki Mio and her lover must die in order to be together. Their place of reunion is not the sacred Kannon temple but the sepulcher-like *yagura,* one of a number of squarish tombs that can still be found today, carved in the mountains behind the Gandenji in Zushi.[20] The "gentleman" joins her there, back-to-back in a physically impossible yet poetically unambiguous pose. Trying to make sense of this imperfect embrace, the gentleman says to the priest, "If that had really been me on that stage, I should have died there."

Ultimately, their place of lasting union is not this sacred mountain space but the ocean, an image that, in Kyōka's iconography, usually connotes danger and death. The sea is a passageway to love's fulfillment, yet the exacted toll is nothing less than the life of the traveler. Reflecting the radical physicality of Kyōka's sense of cause and effect, the ocean is actually connected with the mountain through the mysterious Snake Cavern, "an ancient cave, filled with water" that stretches for twenty-five miles "into the heart of the range." The connection is proven when, crazed with passion, the gentleman throws himself into the cave and is later found dead on the rocks at Nakitsuru Cape, in the exact spot where the bodies of Mio and the young lion dancer are later discovered.[21]

Of all the characters in "One Day in Spring," this young boy is the most pathetic. Having neither home nor parents, he and his companion must earn their living by dancing like "mosquito larvae." Mio regards him as a child, perhaps her own; but her kindness toward him is complicated by the message she asks him to deliver.[22] For the purposes of the metastory, the young lion dancer's death represents a sacrifice that must be made so that the always precarious balance between survival and extinction can be brought into equilibrium, if only for a moment. In fact, Mio and the love-crazed gentleman are also assigned the same role. All three are sacrificed to the greater project of romance. That they must die is a given. As was the case in "The Surgery Room," their desire for love is stifled and ultimately destroyed by a society that mocks the dream.

Kyōka's inclusion of Li Ch'ang-chi's (791–817) poem "Song of a Palace Beauty" underscores the impossibility of such love. Like "The Surgery Room," the poem is also about a trapped woman.[23] Gazing over the fence, the wanderer is filled with a desire to rescue Tamawaki Mio. She is valued for her beauty. But she is too lovely to be fully appreciated by a man like Tamawaki, a member of the Meiji nouveau riche. She is his toy, a pearl before swine. Too good for the men around her, she is typical of Kyōka's many downtrodden heroines.

> Did Tamawaki acquire her as security for a loan? Did he buy her? Some said she was the daughter of an aristocrat who had run onto hard times. Others said she came from a wealthy household that had fallen apart. Some were convinced she was a high-ranking geisha, or that she had once been a high-class prostitute. There was no end to

> the rumors flying about, including one theory that she was the guardian spirit of some bottomless lake. Nobody knew who she really was. (10:262–263)

Mio is a mystery, a combination of great weakness and strength. She is the city cousin of the witch of "The Holy Man of Mount Kōya" and even reminiscent of Countess Kifune in "The Surgery Room." Alluring and strikingly beautiful, she is at the same time ill and oppressed. A gentle maternal figure, she is also a temptress, a "demon" who is truly intimidating to the wanderer when he comes down from the mountain.[24] However we choose to label these poles of her character, we already understand that she is not at all unusual among Kyōka's heroines. To reiterate, female figures such as Mio are both extremely weak and strong because of their role as saviors of men. They suffer degradation so that they may have the opportunity to save creatures who are less able than they. Because they are better than the world around them, they are unappreciated and tormented by men like Mio's husband. This, at least, is the gentleman's perspective. And it is also Kyōka's.

As I have already suggested, analysis of Kyōka's heroines has long been an important key to understanding his work. The author conflated his mother's image with those of many other strong female figures, literary and real: Maya Bunin, the mother of Shakyamuni; Kishibo, the cannibal-turned-guardian-of-children; the spirited daughters of Edo; the young girls who lived in his neighborhood in Kanazawa, including his cousin Teru; the exotic Milliard, based on a Christian missionary who came to Kanazawa from Tennessee; and even the novelist Higuchi Ichiyō (1872–1896), whom Kyōka viewed as a rival and, possibly, a romantic interest. Motherliness and allure are the threads that tie these many women together; and if these qualities seem incompatible, Kyōka deftly manipulates the relationship between hero and heroine in ways that will narrowly circumvent violation of the incest taboo. Consequently, as already suggested by the intense eroticism of this and other works, sexual desire remains fervently *un*fulfilled: the man is often hesistant because of age or out of principle, or else the union of man and woman is blanketed by death, as it is here.

Thus we understand the manner in which Mio dies.

> They didn't find the body. It wasn't until the next day, with the low tide at dawn, that they discovered two people on the rocks at Cape Nakitsuru, the exact spot where the man who had stayed at the temple last summer was found. The boy's head was like a jewel pressed against the woman's breast, the red lion's cape still wet and tangled around her white arm. Beautiful and alluring, Tamawaki Mio had finally discovered the destination of the dead. (10:333–334)

Mio's beauty is fatal to both the gentleman and the young boy. Yet her death makes possible the simultaneous fulfillment of her love for a man and her love for a boy. This is Kyōka's ideal sense of culmination. The metastory insists on having it both ways at the same time: mother as nurturer and mother as lover. The frequency with which the author returned to this ideal seems to suggest, however, that the saving effect of such a story was fleeting even if powerfully created. In reality, boys are not men, and mothers are not lovers. Even in the literary dream, taboos still exert an inescapable power.

The sexual tension between hero and heroine is a point often taken up by Kyōka scholars, but there is a yet unmentioned parameter of desire that needs to be discussed, for it is crucial to the narrative success of Part 1. I am talking about the subtle erotic force that engulfs the wanderer and the priest who tells him the story of Tamawaki Mio and the unfortunate "gentleman" who became obsessed with her. The priest is supposedly a disinterested teller of the tale, but his obvious absorption in this story of lust and madness generates in the hearer both a heightened curiosity about what he is saying and an uneasiness about the reliability of the priest's narrative.

We receive the story through the wanderer. He is portrayed as a listener who wants both to believe and to doubt.

> He had no particular thoughts about the priest's story, neither judgments to make nor opinions to give. He had simply taken in all that had been said, filling his mind until his heart, too, had become full. Walking quietly alone, he felt the need to run the story through his mind again in an attempt to understand it. There was probably nothing to be suspicious about, as the story came from a priest; and he had no reason to doubt the man, even though the priest's parting words had seemed a bit abrupt: "See you." (10:288)

The priest's manner of reporting works well for the reader because the priest knows how to use the story to ensnare his listener and keep him for as long as he possibly can. Certainly, the priest's keen sense of timing and his provocative innuendo—"He was a man like you"—go well beyond the Buddhist tradition of *hōben,* or the use of narrative expedients in order to convey the serious import of religious teachings.

Like the Kōya mendicant, this priest, too, is ambivalent about his life of worship. Caretaker of an institution in decline, he cannot take a perfectly enlightened view of his solitude. "It's lonely living alone, you know. You saw how I came hurrying out when I noticed you. By the way, do you mind if I ask where you're staying?" His interest in this second visitor seems to be aroused by motivations other than religious zeal. He admits to loneliness, trapped within the decaying buildings that surround him. If Tamawaki Mio is a kept woman, the priest is a kept man, uncomfortably faithful to the image of Kannon. In a puzzling reversal of roles, the wanderer explains to the priest that Buddhism *is* to be taken seriously, and that Buddhist icons compare favorably with human beings: "You could say a carved figure is nothing but wood or metal or earth, decorated with gold, silver, and gems to add color. But what about people? Skin, blood, muscle, the five organs, the six organs, join them together, add some clothes, and there you have it. Never forget, sir, that even the most beautiful woman is nothing more than this" (10:237).

The wanderer's misogyny can be subsumed within a Buddhist disregard for matters of the flesh, a notion we might expect the priest to share. But the more relevant and knowable point here is how his and the priest's distancing attitudes toward women combine to generate the story that follows. In relaying the narrative of the gentleman's folly to the wanderer, the priest feels compelled to protect the gentleman who once lived in the temple hut, although he feels no compunction about telling *her* story. His detailed knowledge of what happened follows from his keen interest in this gentleman, just as his motive for narrating is to replace the dead man with the wanderer, the hearer of the tale.

There is something slightly self-interested about the priest's motivations, and so his gestures are vaguely sinister. "The priest pointed down the mountain toward the two-story house, his sleeves forming a veil of blackness." Ultimately, the visitor declines the priest's offer to accommodate him in the hut. He decides to walk away from the cool solitude of the temple grounds, down the steep flight of stairs, and into the valley of the mundane. Following the example of the warrior in the ancient tale "How the Goblin at Agi Bridge in Ōmi Captured People," he attempts to do battle with the demon woman even though his first impulse is to avoid her altogether.[25] Waiting for him to come to her, Tamawaki Mio is as eager for his company as the priest had been.

Although the wanderer first hears of the secret code of triangle, square, and circle from the priest in Part 1, he must learn their meaning from this woman in Part 2. Entitled *Shunchū gokoku,* the second half of this story is essentially an unraveling of this code, another presentation of the images established earlier and a second experience of doppelganger for the wanderer. Having gone through the frightening episode of seeing himself in the gentleman's tale of passion and death, the wanderer is next forced to see himself through the eyes of this woman who, like the priest, immediately notices his resemblance to her drowned lover. Upon reading Part 1, we expect but cannot be sure that the wanderer will die too.

He is caught within many circles of desire—the priest's, the gentleman's, Tamawaki Mio's—all of them implicating his own personal sense of estrangement. Similarly, all these desires are engulfed by the wider cycle of the seasons, the mysterious power of spring as it links winter's death with the life of summer. The sadness of spring, this season of purgatory, is Tamawaki Mio's theme.

> "It's almost impossible to tell you how this sunny spring day makes me feel. It's like talking about a dream. This quiet sadness. Can't you feel it? It's like seeing the most vivid part of a dream, don't you think? It reminds me of when I was two or three, riding on my nurse's back, looking at a festival swirling around me.
>
> "I feel more vulnerable in the spring than in the fall. That's why I'm so damp. This isn't sweat. It's something the sun has wrung from my heart. Not pain, not distress. More like blood being squeezed from the tips of a tree's tender leaves, as though my bones are being extracted and my skin is being melted. Yes, that's the perfect expression for times like this. I feel like I've turned into water, as though

> what's been melted of me will soon disappear, and that there will be tears—though neither of sadness nor of joy." (10:308)

With her troubled though eloquent discourse, she prepares the wanderer to discover the triangles, squares, and circles in her notebook. This is his moment of truth. Kyōka succeeds in making it more astonishing than the gentleman's discovery of himself in Part 1.

> He laughed innocently as the notebook fluttered open in his lap. The pages were like butterfly wings in his fingers. And there, written in pencil, was—
>
> His face suddenly went pale.
>
> They were written large and small, dark and light, all in confusion. Some were half-drawn, others misshapen, others trembling, some abandoned. He saw nothing but triangles, squares, and circles. (10:319–320)

When he asks the meaning of these images, Mio gives both a very general and a very specific answer. The play between the two is crucial.

> "This triangle is a mountain, this square a rice paddy, and this circle the ocean. You can think of them that way. Or maybe the triangle is a doll of a young woman or a samurai dressed in a kimono, the square a body, and the circle a face.
>
> "Or maybe it's something beneath the surface of the waves. If you ask the artist what she thinks these figures are, she'll say she doesn't know. And then you can make an arrogant face. Or else you can worship them as the posthumous name of the deceased."
>
> The wanderer finally spoke up. "Posthumous name? What is it? Tell me the name!"
>
> "Master Triangle, Round Round, Lord of the Square." (10: 320–321)

Like stones in a Zen rock garden, the figures may signify widely: an ocean, a face, and so on. Or they may be tied specifically to the beloved of her dreams: his ocean, his face. As pronominals, they are both common and proper in their signifying force.

No wonder, then, that attempts to interpret this passage have run the gamut from Jungian breadth to geographic particularity. In one far-ranging exploration, Yoshimura Hirotō considers the figures' similarity to the geometrically configured mandala of esoteric Buddhism. Examining them on this cosmological level, Yoshimura invites comparisons with medieval European alchemic drawings, the famous Zen calligraphy of Sengai Gibon, and so on.[26] Less far-reaching but more helpful, I believe, is Matsumura Tomomi's suggestion that Kyōka employed these images in "One Day in Spring" because he saw these shapes in the many *gorintō,* or Kamakura-period grave monuments that he saw during his almost daily trips to the Ganden Temple.

These vertical markers still stand in great numbers around the main hall. Built of five stone shapes stacked one upon another, they are composed (from the ground up) of a cube that represents the earth, a sphere that represents water, a cone that represents fire, a half-moon that represents the wind, and a gem that represents the emptiness of the sky. Kyōka no doubt recognized in these monuments, covered with moss and standing in the *yagura* tombs behind the main hall, an anthropomorphic resemblance to the "five hundred to one thousand small stone statues" that are mentioned in the story but are not to be found in the immediate area. Most likely, he also saw in them the figures for the many tortured women that suddenly appear around the stage on which the gentleman sees himself draw a triangle, a square, and a circle (the two-dimensional forms of these *gorintō* shapes) on Mio's back.

The triangles, squares, and circles are signs of an undifferentiated reality, symbols of dreams and madness and death, unreserved in their proliferation of possible meanings and identities. Despite this lack of coherence, however, their emotional force is all too clear to the wanderer, who desires one thing and one thing only. "What is it? Tell me the name." When he hears "Master Triangle, Round Round, Lord of the Square," he knows he is spared because he does not recognize the name as his own. This knowledge establishes the beginning of difference and makes meaning, at least for him, possible. He knows that his fate is not Tamawaki Mio's. In fact, by writing the figures on Mio's body, the gentleman of the priest's story has distinguished himself from the wanderer by naming his passion for her. The gentleman signed a death pact, which he has honored though she has not. Triangle, square, and circle are his will, a final statement of his earthly passion, a promise he leaves with her. His writing of the name is a step he dares to take because of Komachi's poem and the promise it suggests. Dreams are real. Lovers will meet again. Death is not final.

For Mio, the triangles, squares, and circles are similarly expressions of love; but her incessant scribbling of them expresses, quite in contrast, her lack of faith in the promise of Komachi's poem. Tormented by voices and by the dark, pounding, yet strangely dry showers of this mysterious spring day, she is far more skeptical than her lover. It is doubt, not passion, that has driven her mad. Thus, she uses the figures differently, not to commit herself to love (and death) but to divine the truth of the afterlife, employing them as a poem of pure imagery—△ □ ○—which provides a purely associational link with the first poem.

To progress beyond Komachi's poem, the one she displayed in the temple shortly before her lover killed himself, she must borrow the strength of yet a third poem.

Should I have the chance
to see you again,
I would comb the four seas—
diving deep as the sea tangle.
(10:325)

This verse by Izumi Shikibu is Tamawaki Mio's answer of commitment to the many triangles, squares, and circles she has scribbled in her notebook. She gives it to a young boy, one of two lion dancers who happen to pass by on their way to the ocean. And he, by unknowingly sacrificing himself in her service, delivers the message to the land of the dead.

The wanderer is witness to the boy's death. After bidding farewell to Tamawaki Mio, he follows the trail of the two lion dancers, wondering what will become of both the message and the messengers. From atop a sand dune strewn with seashells, the wanderer observes the boys on the beach and looks for an answer to his question about how this dream in which he has been engulfed will finally end.

The wanderer continued to work his hands through the sand. He looked down at the various shells that sifted out and mumbled the lines of the poem once again. . . .

He still heard no answer from the shells.

If they were able to speak for the great waters, then this colorful blizzard of blossoms strewn over the beach would never cease its whispering. Still, whether scooped from the sand or gathered by small children, the tiny shells were mute.

He threw them away and flopped over onto his side. The sand beneath his hips started to slide away, but there was no danger of being buried. With half-closed eyes, he looked toward the Nakitsuru Cape and, at a place about halfway there, saw the brilliant flickering of sea fire. It was the lion dancers' red costumes. (10:330)

As he watches, the young dancer swims out to sea with the poem still tucked into his lion's mask. Suddenly, Tamawaki Mio's unfortunate messenger disappears under water.

They didn't find the body. It wasn't until the next day, with the low tide at dawn, that they discovered two people on the rocks at Cape Nakitsuru, the exact spot where the man who was staying at the temple last summer had been found earlier. The boy's head was like a jewel pressed against the woman's breast, the red lion's cape still wet and tangled around her white arm. Beautiful and alluring, Tamawaki Mio had finally discovered the destination of the dead.

The wanderer would never forget how they had parted at the embankment, how he had looked back and seen her, holding her purple parasol to the side, her black hair weighing down upon her as she watched him walk away. As the sand on the beach spread and drew back soundlessly, hollowing out and filling back in, he thought of how the waves must have ravished her. From the sand there appeared only beautiful bones and the color of shells—red of the sun, white of the beach, green of the waves. (10:333–334)

Like the triangle, square, and circle, these shells, too, are language. They form the fourth and last poem in the sequence. Belief, as expressed by Ono no Komachi's poem, leads to promise, as represented by the triangle, square, and circle. Promise leads to conviction, as stated in Izumi Shikibu's poem. And, finally, conviction leads to death—the final verse of shells in the sand, these beautiful bones that speak silently of the dead. They are a lonely and condemning skeleton, a trace of life and passion that can, and must, be read in whatever way possible.

We know from a letter that Kyōka wrote to his brother Toyoharu on October 30, 1906, that the death of the young lion dancer was central to his conception of this story. To understand the meaning of this death, we have only to consider the metastory. The watery fate of the boy, the gentleman, and Tamawaki Mio express the author's will to meld maternal and erotic love as they are both heightened by the presence of death. The expression of this desire is hardly a new accomplishment for Kyōka. What *is* new is that in writing "One Day in Spring" Kyōka overstepped the usual limits of the Japanese language to establish an idiom of geometric shapes in an attempt to express the beautifully haunting truth of love. Could this radical assertion of the grapheme be the "highest potential" of which Mishima spoke? Could this lyricism be the truth of *monogatari,* haunted things speaking for and of themselves: bones, shells, red sun, white beach, green waves? These "beautiful bones" are the intermingling of *iro,* as color and eros, with the steady mystery of nature and the irrepressible swell of spring as it leads us beautifully toward death.

Osen and Sōkichi

"Osen and Sōkichi" (*Baishoku kamonanban,* 1920) is a work from Kyōka's maturity. It demonstrates a seasoned, if indulgent, writer at work. The story's prose flows easily and is perfectly cadenced; its theme is familiar yet still allows for accident and discovery. As for structure, the shape of this narrative is less than clearly successful if we insist on reading for plot and plausibility. Although the story is little more than an assortment of established pieces fit together with transitions that are often confusing to the reader, this fractured sort of narrative is, nevertheless, Kyōka at his practiced best, anticipated by the other three stories in this collection: the melodrama of "The Surgery Room," the formulaic clarity of "The Holy Man of Mount Kōya," and the dreamlike rambling of "One Day in Spring."

"Osen and Sōkichi" begins with a glance and a rapid laying out of the necessary bits of code. Knowing exactly what he wants to write, Kyōka wastes no time.

> I'm embarrassed to say that the first thing that caught his eye was the scarlet of her crepe undergarment, bright as flame and dappled with cinnabar. Her skirts weren't folded back but hiked up high and held between her knees, allowing the crepe slip to flow softly down, hugging her white ankles, which were apparently being spared the kimono's unpleasant wetness. On her bare feet, so white they brightened the crimson around them, the woman wore thick, lacquered clogs, fastened with wisteria-colored thongs and splashed with mud. With one thigh twisted inward and feet slightly pigeon-toed, she sat in a corner of the waiting room as the rain continued to fall. (20:238)

The familiar combination of red and white reminds us, again, of "The Surgery Room," the crimson and white associated with the witch of "The Holy Man of Mount Kōya," and of that crucial though largely unexplained scene in "One Day in Spring" where the wanderer identifies with the gentleman who killed himself for love: "In the vacantly staring eyes of the wanderer, who had been listening intently and not moving an inch of his body, a violent rush of red and white swirled in the dazzling light of day." Why red and white? As we have seen, Kyōka's work requires the two colors to appear together: red blood flowing over white skin; red lips setting off a pale complexion; a woman's red undergarments and the whiteness of her legs; and the implied but never stated colors of the sexual act—a man's semen or the whiteness of tissue against the inner lining of a woman's kimono. Here again, eroticism and violence are intertwined and ever present.

These colors indict him for exulting in and, in this sense, exploiting the female image for his own narrowly conceived purposes. Yet it is hardly surprising that in his day most of his readers were women.

> I believe that of all the writers now working today, the strongest feminist [*feminisuto*] among them is Izumi Kyōka. No other writer writes about women so frequently. The warm sympathy he extends to them, his gentle praise, his sense of appreciation, and the strength

> of his passionate love for them is infinitely greater than the concern of politicians who champion women's rights to govern. Many of his works are praises of beautiful, noble women who shine in both body and spirit; and his understanding and observation of them is utterly thorough. . . . I know of no other writer who is as inspired in his depiction of women.[27]

This is the opinion of one female novelist, Yoshiya Nobuko (1896–1973), writing in 1925. She was able to appreciate Kyōka's understanding of women's suffering, but there were many, of course, who could not. Even Kyōka's closest friends were left to wonder about the author's true feelings about women. Satomi Ton (1888–1983) was left utterly confused by his mentor's brand of philogyny. "Someone tell me. Did our teacher like women or not?"[28]

In the case of "Osen and Sōkichi," Osen is introduced in a way that piques both erotic interest and pity. If we eventually come to a deeper appreciation of her derangement, Kyōka initially shows us only the wildness of brilliant clothes and exposed legs—expressions (judging by Sōkichi's wanting to get away) of a disturbing though inherently mesmerizing sexuality. Waiting at the crowded train station, Hata Sōkichi begins reconnecting himself to Osen through these signs. "Noticing the color, he became the protagonist of this story."

Hata is a famous physician on his way across town. He is trapped because of the untimely rain that has turned Tokyo into a sea of mud and by the failure of his train to arrive on time. He tries to distance himself from the crimson lady, but there is something familiar about her. It is her eyebrows, "incomparably lovely, gentle, and well-shaped." Eyebrows are a familiar metonym for both feminine and masculine beauty. Not only does Osen have lovely eyebrows but, at a later point in the story, she rescues Sōkichi's from being shaved off. The importance of eyebrows to the author is clear, for from this moment Sōkichi begins to associate Osen with his mother, "the woman who gave him life." Later, the image will suggest the moon, similarly beautiful and curved. "Sōkichi felt as if he had suddenly swallowed the crescent moon, and that it was sparkling in his heart with a precious, joyous light." As the moon, it also forms an additional link, through the name *nono-sama,* which can refer to either the cresent moon or to the Buddha.

"Look, the moon," she said. "The Buddha."

He never forgot that moment. The half-moon seemed to be descending from a black cloud, its light shining upon the treetops of the ginkgo towering above, like the gentle contour of his dead mother's breast. (20:262)

To Kyōka's imagination, eyebrow, beautiful woman, mother, moon, Buddha, and breast belong together in the same family of images. They supply a counterbalance to the color red by adding an element of motherliness to the erotic, thereby making the character of Osen far too inclusive and complicated to be easily identifiable as either madonna or whore.

Image engenders image. The rain continues to fall. As I have already pointed out, the water imagery in Kyōka's stories follows traditional patterns as found in the nineteenth-century *kusazōshi* of his enthusiastic reading. While enabling and associated with cleansing and life, water also connotes danger, violence, death, and metamorphosis. Having confronted such an encoding in his mother's illustrated books, and having at one point in his life nearly thrown himself into the Kanazawa Castle moat, Kyōka was doubly haunted by water. It was a constant reminder of death and of the need to reestablish emotional balance through the process of narration. Although associated with danger, it is also enabling and therefore expressive of the risk one must take in seeking reprieve from the pain of separation. In fact, without water, the story does not progress. Not until "Osen and Sōkichi" becomes sufficiently water-logged by the spring rains does the outer narrative frame fracture and slough away. Like a sprout swelling out of its seed covering, the story within the story emerges.

This explains why the Mansei Bridge Station suddenly becomes a water-going vessel. It is a strange passage, one that is difficult to understand if we do not understand the function of water in Kyōka's metastory. "His heart pounded like the sea; and the train station turned like the deck of a great ship until its bow pointed straight toward the Myōjin wood, which now seemed close enough to touch" (20:245). Now the story of Sōkichi's involvement with Osen can develop. As was made clear by "The Holy Man of Mount Kōya" and "One Day in Spring," only by passing through water are we allowed access to the world beyond.

The difficulty of this fragmented style is trying. But the logic that guides these images is not hard to understand. To reiterate, the images come directly from the archetype—woman, young man, water. They are locked into place by Kyōka's need to save himself through narrative repetition. Rather than articulated by the text in which they figure, the images are used for their considerable burden of already established associations. As a consequence, the narrative develops in preconstructed pieces, which are held together by the associative forces that link image with image.

The power of this highly visual process of creation is demonstrated most clearly in those instances where the story's fragments actually overwhelm Kyōka's ability to place them in narrative order. Once the image of the ship appears, for instance, the narrative begins to progress too quickly for Kyōka to manage.

> *"Sloping down in that direction. That's Myōjin Hill."*
>
> In the house to the right and all the way to the end of the alley—
>
> On the morning of that fateful day, Sōkichi had had one of his friends shave the boyish beard from his face. And that evening in the Myōjin temple grounds, he put the same razor to his throat!
>
> *But wait. I'm losing control of the story.* (20:245)

Within the space of a few sentences, the outline of the entire story pours forth: we progress from water to hill, to the house at the end of the alley, to beard, to temple ground, to razor. Overwhelmed by this too-rapid progression of associations, Kyōka chooses to make his passive position with respect to these images perfectly clear. *"But wait. I'm losing control. . . ."* Of course, his admission is also a challenge. For those readers who cannot find a similar appreciation for this flood of imagery, the text escapes as a collection of pieces.

The body of this story, anticipated in this manner by the watery prelude, is autobiographical. Inspired to become a writer upon reading Kōyō's *Confessions of Love (Iro zange)* and "Summer Decline" *(Natsu yase),* Kyōka set out for Tokyo on November 28, 1890. His ambition was to study with Kōyō, but when he descended to the front portico of the Shinbashi station, his courage was stolen away by the size of the buildings before him, the width of the street, and the bustle of the crowds. It was not until October 19, 1891, almost a year later, that he finally met Kōyō and was accepted as the famous writer's first live-in student. During the interim, he was penniless and changed residences numerous times, drifting between Tokyo and Kamakura. The hardships of those days are remembered in "Osen and Sōkichi." They appear as a flashback, a structural device that Kyōka often used to accommodate the associational, paratactic nature of his narrative imagination. Rather than providing a single, external, omniscient narrator, Kyōka gives us numerous internal narrators who recall the story into being.

Suddenly Sōkichi is only seventeen years old, living with a group of vagabonds, "people who, through indolence and dissipation, had been forgotten by the world." On his way back to the tenement, carrying a bag of rice crackers from a neighborhood shop, he gives in to his hunger and makes the mistake that will nearly cost him his life.

> He paused at a landing where the path up the hill was so steep he could reach out and touch the steps before him. Shielded only by a thin covering of ginkgo leaves and the branches of the firs and Chinese nettles towering far above, Sōkichi faced the drainage ditch that ran along the cliff and partook of forbidden fruit for the first time in his life. He chomped down on the hard crackers like a horse champing down on a bit. How wonderfully delicious! (20:255)

Sōkichi thinks he is out of sight, but his deception fails. He soon discovers that he was in full view of at least one of the people in his group, Small Plate Heishirō, whose laughter fills pages in the original text but is greatly abbreviated in my translation. Humiliated before Osen, to whom Sōkichi is secretly attracted, he tries to kill himself that evening. The place is the Myōjin Temple. Osen, mistress of the leader of the group, is the one who saves his life.

> "What are you doing? What do you think you're doing?"
>
> She seemed like a wondrous bird with a beautiful woman's face, sweeping down from the trees to grab his sleeve. He was leaning back against the trunk of a ginkgo tree that was being used as a corner post for one of the empty stalls behind the main temple. Just as he was about to slash his throat, Osen came. She wrested the razor from his hand. Everything seemed like a dream. (20:261)

Kyōka probably found inspiration for this bird/woman image in Mantei Ōga's *The Eight Lives of Siddharta, A Japanese Library (Shaka hassō Yamato bunko),* one of the main illustrated texts in his mother's library. The image first appeared in the early story "A Bird of Many Colors" (*Kechō,* 1897) and found further amplification here.[29] As in his mother's *kusazōshi,* the transforming creation of new beings from old continued to be a principal mode of expression in Kyōka's work made possible by the plastic nature of the visual images he was aggregating. To the extent that his characters were constructed in this iconographic manner, they lack delineation and interiority. The semantic border between one image and another is vague and ill-defined—bird blending with woman, one connotation linking and melding with another. If the more transparent language of realism sought to exclude semantic possibilities as it attempted to locate and contextualize the observably particular, Kyōka's visual tropes work through a grossly opaque and generic process of inclusion. They invite ambiguity, allowing Osen, like Tamawaki Mio, to be mother and lover at the same time. She is savior and temptress, a complicated figure who is nevertheless too two-dimensional to be considered a psychologically differentiated character.

The story jumps ahead. No obvious transitions are provided. Sōkichi and Osen are living together in a cheap tenement building. Returning home from school, he brushes shoulders with a man, a client, who is hurrying to get away. The door opens. Osen's bedding laid out on the floor tells us that she has been prostituting herself in order to keep Sōkichi fed and clothed. Thus we sense a possible interpretation of the enigmatic title, *Baishoku kamonanban.* Echoing the tension of red and white, Kyōka simply juxtaposes *baishoku,* or prostitution, and *kamonanban,* a bowl of noodles in broth, topped with strips of duck meat and scallions. In the figure of Osen, the distinction between the erotic and the nurturing is blurred, as Kyōka insists that she must be providential in *every* way while still remaining above reproach.[30] This, of course, is impossible, and so Osen must suffer. She must bear not only the public stigma of prostitution (which Kyōka, who married a geisha, did not necessarily accept), but also the private burden of being a nurturing woman who must be available to the needs of the less-than-resourceful men in her life. In the fullness of her sexuality, Osen is both oppressed and exalted. Her insanity and the double suicide that is suggested by the story's conclusion indicates the difficulty of this role as recognized by both Osen and Sōkichi.

In a scene reminiscent of the erotic tenderness of Tamenaga Shunsui's (1790–1843) *Plum Calendar* (*Shunshoku umegoyomi,* 1832), Osen grills rice cakes for Sōkichi while telling him the story of the lovely but ill-fated Urazato. The allusion foreshadows her own tragic fate, as the numerous connections between "Osen and Sōkichi" and Urazato's story, Tsuruga Wakasanojō's "The Crow at Dawn, A Dream of Light Snow" (*Akegarasu yume no awa yuki,* ca. 1772), are played out.[31] Like Countess Kifune, Tamawaki Mio, and Osen, Urazato is also a kept woman. As punishment for attempting to escape from the brothel, she is bound and tied to a pine tree that stands in her compound's snowy garden. While her life slowly drains away, she dreams of her lover, Tokijirō, sneaking over the rooftops, coming to rescue her.

In both written and staged versions of *Akegarasu,* Tokijirō's head is covered with a bandanna. Without offering much in the way of explanation to the reader, Kyōka retains the image but employs it differently. Rather than send her lover to rescue Osen, he dispatches an officer of the law, who jumps over the back fence and arrests her for moral indiscretion. The officer represents the Meiji patriarchal order that also provided a sinister backdrop for "The Surgery Room" and "One Day in Spring." He tethers Osen, then leads her off to jail. Heartbroken and vulnerable, the sobbing Sōkichi follows after.

> Osen hung her head without looking back. But then she turned, and Sōkichi, looking into her face, saw her eyebrows.
>
> The young man was speechless.
>
> "Sō-chan. I'll give you my spirit."
>
> She folded it as the policeman pulled her along. Soon it was there, nestled in the palm of her hand, a crane of white tissue paper.
>
> "Follow this to wherever it takes you." She blew her warm breath into the bird and it came to life. With the marks of her lips showing faintly red against the crane's bluish-white body, the bird flew among the floating blossoms, dancing in the air as it led Sōkichi to the gate where he was taken in. (20:267–268)

Again, we encounter the bird image, magically providential. Again, we find the colors red and white. And once again we notice Kyōka's radically literalistic sense of cause and effect: having blown her spirit into the crane, Osen literally loses her mind. She and Sōkichi become separated by the events of her arrest. But, inspired with her breath, the paper bird takes to the air and leads Sōkichi to the people who take him in and help him become Doctor Hata, the famous surgeon whom we have already met in the story's opening paragraphs, and a type of gentleman familiar to us in the figure of Doctor Takamine (literally, Towering Peak).

Once again, the story leaps forward, returning us to the original time frame of the narrative. Sōkichi, convinced that the woman in the station's waiting room is Osen, persuades her attendants to let him take her to his hospital. Another leap, and the story ends with his visit to her private room. He kneels beside her bed and places a razor in her hands.

The ending is vague. Kyōka does not tell us what happens. But if we recall the metastory that grounds Kyōka's work, the conclusion is clear. In a final demonstration of red and white, and in the spirit of Miyoshino and her lover Inosuke, who (as the models for "The Crow at Dawn") also killed themselves with a razor, Osen and Sōkichi will end their lives together. In doing so, they join Countess Kifune and Takamine, Tamawaki Mio and her lover.

Closing the Circle

Kyōka continued to write until his death in 1939, producing over the many years of his career some three hundred stories, plays, essays, and travelogues. He departed from the fundamental structure of the metastory only during the last ten years or so of his life, as his male protagonists finally began to display a more mature sexuality, in works such as "Of the Mountains and the Sea" (*Sankai hyōbanki,* 1929) and "The Snow Willow" (*Yuki yanagi,* 1937). For Kyōka, this development represented nothing less than a crisis of identity, reflected in the strangely amorphous and autobiographical turn of his latest works. His final story, however, returns to the metastory in dramatic fashion. "The Heartvine" (*Rukōshinsō,* 1939) is a compelling remembrance of that moment which made it possible for him to survive: when a young woman supposedly threw herself into the dark waters of the Kanazawa Castle moat just as Kyōka himself was about to do. The event first appeared in the early story "The Night Bell Tolls" (*Shōsei yahanroku,* 1895), which he wrote in Kanazawa after his father's death on January 9, 1894, had left him grieving and struggling beneath the burden of his family's financial situation. "The Heartvine" returns to the same scene of sacrifice, as if the dying Kyōka needed to affirm one last time the principal vectors of the archetype that had guided his career and had allowed him to extend his life into the quiet obscurity noted by Tanizaki Jun'ichirō.

Intensely personal and often perversely elliptical, his work has nevertheless drawn and held the attention of a small but devoted readership. I have already mentioned that there were many women among his readers and that they appreciated Kyōka for his depictions of female suffering. Also among his supporters were a number of younger writers who came to dominate the world of letters in a way that Kyōka himself never did. Akutagawa Ryūnosuke, for instance, had a volume of Kyōka's work open near his bed when he committed suicide in July 1927. The Nobel laureate Kawabata Yasunari (1899–1972) was another steadfast admirer. Tanizaki, who came to know the author by way of the cinema, for which he wrote screenplays of Kyōka's works, can also be counted among his most ardent supporters. During the decades following the Second World War, Mishima Yukio stands out as one of Kyōka's most admiring readers. He correctly predicted that Kyōka's resurrection would begin with the staging of his more experimental plays. Today, his work is well regarded by a number of contemporary writers, including Kōno Taeko, Tsushima Yūko, and Murakami Haruki.

The impetus for the present critical interest in Kyōka's work comes from many places: a critique of the Eurocentric foundations of "modern Japanese literature," a heightened awareness of literature as a system of signs, the increasingly visual nature of communication in technologically advanced societies, and the economic success and social stability that have given the Japanese more confidence in their own cultural traditions. These issues deserve more attention that I can begin to give them here. For our purposes, it is probably enough to say that Kyōka's indebtedness to the theater, to the oral tradition, and to the highly figural *gesaku* texts of the nineteenth century, coupled with his ability to create new forms of visuality within the imposed limitations of the word-centered *kindai shōsetsu,* make his work particularly relevant to any attempt to read modern Japanese literature in the context of its own narrative traditions.

In North America, Kyōka has always been highly regarded by a handful of scholars. Donald Keene and Juliet Carpenter have written introductions to his work, and a number of doctoral dissertations have dealt in a more particular way with various aspects of his writings.[32] It is also true, however, that because of modernity's presumption of progress, which has defined the late-modern era in terms of its distance from rather than closeness to Edo-period culture, Kyōka has not been given the amount of attention that authors such as Natsume Sōseki (1867–1916) or Mori Ōgai (1862–1922) have received. As serious an impediment as this bias may be, perhaps a more telling factor working against Kyōka's reception is the sheer difficulty of his prose. The complexity of his writing is a considerable deterrent to a full examination of his work outside Japan. But now that Kyōka is in fact being actively studied and translated, we can expect that his stories and plays will provide—as Tanizaki suggested—a counterpoint to those writers who found themselves more securely located within the mainstream of literary production.

Having said this, I should also mention that the difficulty of Kyōka's writings similarly works against their reception in Japan today. Changes in orthography, usage, and material culture have rendered Meiji-period texts largely unreadable to any but the most determined readers. Few of his texts have been annotated, though the need is now beyond question. Given the vast changes in the Japanese language that have taken place over the past hundred years, it is more likely that significant increases in his readership will come about as the result of the translation of his work outside of Japan. In an unintended way, Tanizaki's prediction of Kyōka's work becoming "classical" has come true. The work of specialists continues, but on a more popular level Kyōka's reputation still depends on visual productions of his work, whether for the screen or stage.

For those familiar with the general contours of the Japanese narrative tradition, the contemporary rediscovery of Izumi Kyōka establishes a satisfying irony. This writer who was viewed in his own time as old-fashioned now finds a place on the cutting edge. Although, as I have mentioned, the works themselves are not widely read, the sentiment expressed by them has aged far better than that expressed by most of his contemporaries, especially those who were so intently focused upon distancing themselves from their own culture in order to become more acceptable to a Western point of view. As proposed by Tanizaki, we might attribute Kyōka's longevity to an accruing of "classical luster." But, then again, the vicissitudes of his reception over the years demonstrates why the very notion of classics is worth questioning. If nothing else, Kyōka's reemergence should highlight the changing nature of literary attitudes and methods while turning our attention to much larger cultural patterns. His critical reception today suggests a geometry of cycles both obscured and heightened by Japan's involvement with the logocentric West, just as Japan once was influenced by China and Korea. Now, as the cycle completes itself, the Western postmodern and the Japanese early-modern engage each other at the late-modern though stubbornly pictocentric point of Izumi Kyōka.

NOTES

1. Kyōka later wrote about the incident in his autochronology: "Not wanting to snip the bud at first bloom, Kōyō-sensei valiantly negotiated for its continuation. I didn't find out about it until afterward. My first publication was made possible only by Sensei's great charity" (1:v).

2. *Teikoku bungaku* (August 1895). Quoted in Muramatsu Sadataka, *Izumi Kyōka jiten* (Tokyo: Yūseidō, 1982), p. 34.

3. Tezuka Masayuki, "Izumi Kyōka to Morita Shiken," *Izumi Kyōka*, Nihon bungaku kenkyū shiryō sōsho (Tokyo: Yūseido, 1980), pp. 226–237.

4. For Hōgetsu's review, see "Shōsetsukai no shinchō o ronzu," *Waseda bungaku* (January 1896).

5. " 'Kyōka zenshū' ni tsuite," *Kyōka ron shūsei*, Tanizawa Eiichi and Watanabe Ikkō, eds. (Tokyo: Rippū shobō, 1983), p. 199.

6. In a memoir entitled "About My First Work" (*Shojosaku dan*, 1907), Kyōka thanks Taoka Reiun for his favorable review of "The Night Patrol." The review to which Kyōka is most likely referring appeared in *Literature for Today's Youth (Seinenbun)* on May 10, 1895. Its enthusiastic praise—"we can

infer about Kyōka that he will advance without hesitation to the realm of the masters"—certainly did much to establish Kyōka's reputation. There is good reason to believe, however, that Reiun did not write this particular review. The one he did put forward was equally fervent, if less detailed. It appeared somewhat later, on July 1, in the same journal: "The truth is that Kyōka has gotten where he is today through Kōyō's effective guidance and protection. Kyōka is truly gifted. . . . He has flown from the nest of outmoded thought, and has broken new ground for the *shōsetsu*. . . . If Kyōka continues in his efforts, he may very well surpass Kōyō and Rohan."

7. Here I am following Noguchi Takehiko, *Kanshō Nihon gendai bungaku: Izumi Kyōka* (Tokyo: Kadokawa Shoten, 1982), pp. 8–10.

8. Muramatsu Sadataka, *Izumi Kyōka* (Tokyo: Bunsendō, 1966), p. 37.

9. Teraki Teihō, *Hito Izumi Kyōka* (Tokyo: Nihon tosho sentā, 1983), pp. 218–219.

10. The first appearance of this essay was in *Shin shōsetsu* (January 1901). In this brief listing of books that influenced him most, Kyōka, in addition to his mother's *kusazōshi*, also mentions a few "difficult" books, such as *The Nanba War Chronicle (Nanba senki), The Water Margin (Suikōden),* and *The Romance of the Three Kingdoms (Sankoku-shi).* As for modern literature, Kyōka notes newspaper novels, Morita Shiken's translations of "The Blind Messenger" *(Ko shisha),* Ozaki Kōyō's *Confessions of Love (Iro zange),* and Rohan's *The Buddha of Art (Fūryū Butsu).* Noteworthy Edo-period writers included Bakin, of whom Kyōka eventually grew tired, Shikitei Sanba, Santō Kyōden, Jippensha Ikku, and Ryūtei Tanehiko, who remained very much in favor.

11. For a discussion of these points, see my "Water Imagery in the Works of Izumi Kyōka," *Monumenta Nipponica* 46, no. 1 (Spring 1991): 43–68.

12. The changing nature of the visual culture in which Kyōka wrote is discussed in my "Pictocentrism," *Yearbook of Comparative and General Literature* 40 (1992): 23–39.

13. If one were to use, for example, Tsvetan Todorov's structural typology, then Kyōka's work, which wants to accept as true the bizarre or improbable, is more marvelous than fantastic, because the level of uncertainty is insufficient for fantasy. Yet Todorov's casting of the marvelous, from the beginning, is based on an essentially modern episteme, which, for the sake of argument, heightens the difference. Kyōka's fiction is corrosive to such clarity since the author believes in the improbable *as* improbable—that is, through his awareness of the imagination and its willfulness. For Todorov's analysis, see *The Fantastic: A Structural Approach to a Literary Genre* (Ithaca, N.Y.: Cornell University Press, 1975).

In the critical literature on Kyōka, some of the more illuminating criticism of his work approaches the issue of the fantastic from a structural point of view. Pieces such as Waki Akiko's *Gensō no ronri,* Kōdansha gendai shinsho, vol. 348 (Tokyo: Kōdansha, 1974), and Noguchi Takehiko's "Gensō no bunpōgaku," *Kokubungaku: kaishaku to kyōzai no kenkyū* 30, no. 7: 26–34, succeed by leaving the question of belief open for consideration.

14. The dating of this manuscript varies widely. Muramatsu Sadataka places it as early as 1889 or 1890, in his "Shoki shūsaku 'Shirakijo monogatari' to 'Kōya hijiri' no seiritsu," *Izumi Kyōka* (Tokyo: Bunsendō, 1966), pp. 263–269. However, in an earlier essay, "Shirakijo monogatari ni kansuru nōto," he tentatively placed it much later, at 1893 or 1894. Mita Hideaki places it at 1893 in " 'Shirakijo monogatari' seiritsu kō," *Izumi Kyōka no bungaku* (Tokyo: Ōbunsha, 1976), pp. 279–284. Oka Yasuo sets the date at 1893, in his " 'Kōya hijiri' seiritsu no kiban," *Izumi Kyōka,* Nihon bungaku kenkyū shiryō sōsho (Tokyo: Yūseidō, 1980), p. 157. Matsumura Tomomi considers June–November 1895, in his "Kyōka shoki sakuhin no shippitsu jiki ni tsuite—'Shirakijo monogatari o chūshin ni' " *Mita kokubun* (November 1985). Kasahara Nobuo, in *Izumi Kyōka: Erosu no mayu* (Tokyo: Kokubunsha, 1988), p. 33, now follows Matsumura.

15. Togawa Shūkotsu, "Saikin no sōsakkai," *Taiyō* (December 1896); quoted in Nakatani Katsumi, *Izumi Kyōka: shinzō e no shiten* (Tokyo: Meiji Shoin, 1987), p. 49.

16. As Richard Torrance argues, Shūsei himself was not totally sympathetic to the most forceful proponents of naturalism. See *The Fiction of Tokuda Shūsei and the Emergence of Japan's New Middle Class* (Seattle: University of Washington Press, 1994).

17. Yoshida Masashi, "Izumi Kyōka, sobo no shi to 'Onna kyaku,' " *Gakuen* (January 1989): 120–129.

18. *Izumi Kyōka: geijutsu to byōri* (Tokyo: Kongo Shuppan Shinsha, 1970), p. 35.

19. Quoted in Yoshimura Hirotō, "Kyōka mandara," *Kyōka kenkyū* 4 (1979): 53.

20. These tombs were mostly carved out of the mountains of Zushi when the nearby city of Kamakura was a center of governance in Japan (1185–1333). They housed the graves of the wealthy and politically powerful. Though once lavishly decorated, they are now dilapidated. I thank Matsumura Tomomi and Yoshida Masashi for taking me to see them.

21. As is the case with the tombs, the Snake Cavern also exists. This water-filled cave is situated no more than fifty yards from the main temple, not in the mountains behind it, as described in the story. The local understanding was that the Snake Cavern connected with the Benten Cave at Enoshima. A huge snake supposedly lives in the cave.

22. The poem Kyōka uses is a slightly altered version of the original by Izumi Shikibu (b. ca. 976) as contained in the *Izumi Shikibu zokushū.*

23. Kyōka first learned of Li Ho's (style, Ch'ang-chi) poetry through Sasakawa Rinpū, who presented him with a copy of Li's work. Throughout his life, Kyōka remained an enthusiastic reader. In many ways, the two were kindred spirits: both were obsessed with death and the fragility of life, both spent their careers as writers depicting countless scenes of female suffering, and both did this by utilizing very private systems of imagery. Like Kyōka, Li Ho was criticized for his overly elaborate style and lack of what J. D. Frodsham called "inner unity." For more on Kyōka's regard for Li Ho, see "Izumi Kyōka sensei to To Ri Chūkichi," *Kyōka zenshu geppō,* no. 2 (Tokyo: Iwanami Shoten, 1940). I have depended on Frodsham's translation as contained in *The Poems of Li Ho (791–817),* (Oxford: Clarendon Press, 1970), pp. 93–94.

24. For two analyses of this ambivalence, see Matsumura Tomomi, " 'Shunchū' no sekai," and Takakuwa Noriko, " 'Shunchū,' 'Shunchū gokoku' ron," both in *Ronshū Izumi Kyōka* (Tokyo: Yūseidō, 1987), pp. 111–125 and 126–146.

25. For the original story, see *Konjaku monogatari-shū* 27:13. Hearing of a goblin who haunts a certain bridge, one brave warrior outwits him by applying a thick coat of oil to his horse's tail. The goblin tries to stop him as he passes by, but his hands cannot get a grip on the horse. Kyōka also alludes here to a story in the "Tsurugi no maki" of the *Taiheiki,* where a certain Watanabe Tsuna lops off the arm of a goblin that turns itself into a beautiful woman. For a discussion of these and other allusions, see Suda Chisato, " 'Shunchū' no kōsō," *Ronshū Izumi Kyōka,* vol. 2 (Tokyo: Yūseidō, 1991), pp. 108–127.

26. Yoshimura Hirotō, "Kyōka mandara," *Kyōka kenkyū* 4 (1979): 53–71.

27. "Izumi-sensei no kakareru josei," *Shin shōsetsu* (May 1925), pp. 11–14. In Kyōka's day, the term *feminist* would often have meant something akin to "a ladies' man." Its usage here, though, is closer to the one familiar to us today.

28. "Sensei no kōaku kan," *Satomi Ton zenshū,* vol. 10 (Tokyo: Chikuma Shobō, 1977–1979), pp. 322–323.

29. For a study of this connection, see Yoshida Masashi, "Izumi Kyōka to kusazōshi," *Bungaku* 55, no. 3 (March 1987): 37–52.

30. Muramatsu Sadataka believes that this is an overinterpretation of the images. His thinking is simply that, because Kyōka was fond of this dish, *kamonanban,* he used it in the title for emphasis, as if to say, "Now here's a

story for you!" It was an inside joke shared between him and his closest associates.

31. *Akegarasu* itself is based on the 1769 double suicide of Miyoshino, a prostitute of the Tsutaya house in the Shin Yoshiwara brothel, and Inosuke, the son of a wealthy merchant of Asakusa's Kuramae district. Their death forms a model for Osen and Sōkichi. For an English translation, see Thomas Blenman Hare, trans., "The Raven at First Light: A Shinnai Ballad," in *New Leaves,* Aileen Gatten and Anthony Chambers, eds. (Ann Arbor: University of Michigan, Center for Japanese Studies, 1993), pp. 115–125.

32. Donald Keene, *Dawn to the West: Japanese Literature in the Modern Era* (New York: Holt, Rinehart, and Winston, 1984), pp. 200–219. Juliet Carpenter, "Izumi Kyōka: Meiji-Era Gothic," *Japan Quarterly* 31, no. 2 (April–June 1984): 154–158. Dissertations written primarily about Kyōka's work include the following: Jean Funatsu, "Through the Colored Looking Glass of Izumi Kyōka: Reflections of the Kusazōshi" (Harvard University, 1972); Mark Jewel, "Aspects of Narrative Structure in the Work of Izumi Kyōka" (Stanford University, 1984); Charles Shirō Inouye, "Izumi Kyōka and the Visual Tradition" (Harvard University, 1988); Cody Poulton, "A Dissertation on the Fireflies, A Discourse on the Stars: The Major Plays of Izumi Kyōka" (University of Toronto, 1990).

ABOUT THE TRANSLATOR

CHARLES SHIRŌ INOUYE is associate professor of Japanese at Tufts University and a research associate at Harvard University's Reischauer Institute of Japanese Studies. He is director of the Japanese Program in Tufts' Department of German, Russian, and Asian Languages and Literatures, and has recently been elected to the executive committee of the Asian Literatures Division of the Modern Language Association. He began his research on Izumi Kyōka as a Monbushō Scholar at the Kobe National University, where he studied under Noguchi Takehiko. He completed his Ph.D. at Harvard, writing his dissertation "Izumi Kyōka and the Visual Tradition" under the direction of Howard Hibbett.

Lightning Source UK Ltd.
Milton Keynes UK
UKHW011250160120
357072UK00001B/71/P